By the Dimming Light

By the Dimming Light

Above the Rain Collective
2024

Above the Rain Collective
abovetheraincollective@gmail.com
North Georgia, USA

Contributing Editor: J.A. Sexton

Publisher's note:

ISBN: 978-1-7377970-9-8

First Printing February 2024

julietrose.author@gmail.com
authorjulietrose.com

Cover graphics and interior formatting by J.A. Sexton
Above the Rain logo artwork by Bee Freitag
Cover art: Eva Mout https://www.ursusart.studio/

For Kylan and Kyla

Table of Contents

1. Page 11 - 1981
2. Page 16 - Thirteen Years Later
3. Page 23 - Nothing Left
4. Page 30 - Sunup to Sundown
5. Page 39 - After the Fall
6. Page 47 - Up the Steep Hills
7. Page 54 - Down, Down in the Valley
8. Page 61 - From Afar
9. Page 68 - Up Close
10. Page 75 - The Door Opens
11. Page 83 - Father's Son
12. Page 90 - Beyond Words
13. Page 97 - To Rise Again
14. Page 105 - It Comes
15. Page 113 - In the Light of Day
16. Page 121 - The Weight of it All
17. Page 129 - Stay Still While Running

18. Page 137 - From One to Three

19. Page 145 - The Tender Journey

20. Page 152 - In Circles

21. Page 161 - Can Run

22. Page 170 - Can't Hide

23. Page 177 - Devil's in the Details

24. Page 184 - As Fast as They Can

25. Page 191 - Arise With the Sun

26. Page 199 - To Face the Truth

27. Page 208 - The Other Side

28. Page 215 - The Uncovering

29. Page 223 - Beyond the Stars

30. Page 231 - Home Again, Home Again

31. Page 239 - A New Day

32. Page 248 - Power of Belief

33. Page 255 - At Peace

34. Page 262 - Sweet Freedom

35. Page 271- It Runs Deep

36. Page 279 - What Home Means

37. Page 287 - 2002

As children, we're warned about the boogeyman, the creature under the bed, the beast in the closet. We don't understand most monsters walk among us. Monsters come in many forms. Could be behind the friendly face of the guy at the gas station, or the neighbor who offers to shovel the walk. People silently live with monsters in their midst, hidden behind closed doors, kept in the dark with secrets. The monsters depend on the discretion of those around them. So, we leave the closet light on, we check under beds, we avoid the recesses of the yard where the boogeyman lives. All the while letting the real monsters around what is most precious.

1981

She ran ahead, giggling as she waved her flashlight back at him. Caleb blocked the light from his eyes with his free hand, grasping his flashlight with his other. Man, he wanted to catch up to her and tackle her in the grass, press her to him. Kiss her mouth. They spent the evenings on each other's front porches but were never out of their parents' eyesight long enough to do more than kiss.

Well, except for the night after prom a couple of months back. Then, they'd booked a room and explored each other through cheap wine coolers and nerves. He thought he might be more nervous than her. It didn't stop them from coming together... awkward, sloppy. He finished quickly but pulled out in time. He thought so, anyway. It was both their first time. Since then, they'd done what they could with the limitations of always having family around.

They grew up together, two streets away, rode the same bus. Went trick-or-treating together. Vacation bible school, summer camps. Shannon was the girl down the street and he'd never paid her much mind. Until tenth grade. When she got on the bus on the first day of school that year, he felt something stir in him. He couldn't take his eyes off her. Her bashful side-eye, let him know she felt the same. From then, on they were a couple. She wore his letter jacket and his class ring on a chain around her neck. He carried her notes in his backpack. Prom night they took it to the next level.

It was a small town, Mountaintop, Kentucky. Everyone knew each other. Their neighborhood was only one way in, bordering the national forest. Each home was on a couple of acres and all the kids hung out together. In the summer, there were block potlucks. During the holidays, they went to each other's houses for cocoa and caroling. It was the epitome of American life.

Caleb knew there was a world outside of Mountaintop but had no interest in it. Like his parents, he wanted to settle down there. Raise a family. He took woodshop at school and apprenticed with a local carpenter until he surpassed his teacher. He was going to marry Shannon and they were going to make a life right there, maybe even in the same neighborhood as their parents. Nothing else mattered.

Caleb ran to catch up with Shannon and grabbed her around the waist as she squealed.

"Caleb! We are going to wake up the neighborhood," she chastised.

"Well, you sure are with all that caterwauling."

Shannon grinned at him, pushing her curly blond hair out of her face. "Sly boy. We're almost to my road, will you wait til I get to the top and flash my light?"

"I can walk you up if you want. Maybe cut off our lights and make out?" he suggested.

"I see what you're getting at. My mom will kill me if I'm late. I'll be fine. I'll call you once I get to my room. We can talk for a bit."

"Shan, I want to do more than talk. I want to be with you." He ran his finger down her arm, meeting her eyes.

She shook her head. "Not tonight. I'm already a few minutes late. I want to, Caleb. Let's maybe go camping. Now that we've both graduated, I don't think my parents will throw too much of a fit."

Caleb watched her, desire clouding his mind. "Yeah, okay. Next weekend?"

Shannon smiled and batted her eyes. "It's a date. I'd better go. I need to run now to get there before my dad sends out the dogs."

Caleb kissed Shannon hard and let her go, watching her retreating form head up the hill. Her flashlight bobbed up and down with her movement, making it easy to see where she was. He knew she'd made it to the top when she clicked the light a few times in a row. He clicked his in return and turned to walk back home. He was going to marry her. Then he could be with her as much as they wanted.

The lights were off when he got home, so he crept in silently to not stir his parents awake. His older sister, Tammy, was heading back to her room from the bathroom and tapped her wrist, letting him know he was coming in past curfew. He shrugged at her and ducked into his room, collapsing on his bed. He considered taking care of the pressure in his pants but sleep won out.

The phone ringing woke him a little bit later and he remembered Shannon said she'd call. He grabbed the phone off the receiver before it woke up his parents and cleared his throat. "Hello?"

"Caleb is that you?" Shannon's mother on the other end sounded frantic.

"Mrs. Post? Yes, this is Caleb." Why was Shannon's mother calling him so late?

"Is Shannon there with you?"

"No, ma'am. I walked her back, uh... sorry, what time is it?" Caleb looked at the alarm clock. "She went home almost an hour ago. I walked her to the street and she clicked the light to let me know she'd gotten to your driveway."

"Are you sure? Caleb, are you sure?" Her voice went up multiple octaves and she sounded like she was being strangled.

"Yes, ma'am. She said she'd call me when she got in but I must've dozed off. I thought you were her calling. What's going on, Mrs. Post?"

"She's not here. My husband is out looking for her, now. I need... I need to go. I have to call the police. Her bed is undisturbed and we didn't hear her come in. Can you come this way?"

Caleb jumped out of bed, his heart thumping in his chest. He saw Shannon click the light. She was home. He threw on clothes and banged on his parents' door. His mother came to the door, her brow furrowed.

"What's going on, Caleb?"

"Shannon is missing. I walked her to her street, but her parents said she never came in. I need to go over there. They are calling the police."

His father was up out of bed by then and half-dressed. "I'll go with you."

They bolted out of the house, being passed by police cars driving in the direction of Shannon's house. Caleb picked up his pace, his heart telling him what his brain was refusing to believe. As they crested the hill to the Post house, a deep, low wail broke through the darkness. Shannon's father was distraught somewhere in the woods. The police took off after the sound with Caleb and his father close on their heels.

They were stopped before they made it to Shannon's father, but Caleb could see it between the cops trying to block them. Shannon lying on the ground, her blond hair stained red from blood. He fell to his knees as he saw her glassy eyes staring past him to another world.

Thirteen Years Later

T he room smelled like sweat and vomit. Probably because it contained sweat and vomit. Caleb rolled over and groaned, fishing around the floor for the bowl he kept beside the bed. Feeling his fingers hit the plastic rim, he yanked it toward him just in time to lean over the edge of the bed and spew the rest of his stomach contents into the almost full bowl. He collapsed back on the bed, wiping fresh beads of perspiration off his forehead. He tried to sit up but the room spun chaotically, causing him to dry heave.

The phone began ringing on the bedside table, rattling his brain. He considered smashing it against the wall to stop the incessant trill.

He cracked an eye and grabbed the phone when he realized the time. "Yeah?"

"Caleb? Where the fuck are you? Ronald is pissed and threatening to fire you," his work buddy, Mick, said on the other end of the line.

"Damn, sorry. I had a little too much to drink last night," Caleb replied as he eased himself up and placed his feet on the floor.

Silence sat between them as they both knew Caleb had a little too much to drink every night... and most days. Caleb cleared his throat, catching a glimpse of himself in the mirror. He looked like shit. Dark circles permanently shrouded his eyes and his hair was matted and unkempt, having grown to his shoulders. He shook his head, forcing the room to spin again, and swallowed the bile which made its way up.

"Tell Ron I'm on my way. Car trouble. He ain't going to fire me. I'm the best carpenter he's got."

Mick sighed into the line. "While that's true, the best carpenter in the world doesn't do anyone any good if he doesn't show up for work, Caleb."

Caleb chuckled. "Point taken. Let me grab a quick shower and I'll be there."

"Fucking hurry, Ron's taking it out on the rest of us."

The line went dead and Caleb hung the phone on the receiver. He stood up, holding onto the wall for balance. A cup of coffee and a shower should make him functional. Enough. He eyed the vomit bowl, weighing if he should leave it, however, he knew his sister Tammy was coming over to help with their father and she'd reem him if it was there.

When he picked up the bowl, his thumb slipped into the still-warm, chunky liquid and he resisted the urge to puke again, holding it away from him and focusing his eyes dead ahead. Miraculously, he made it to the bathroom without a spill and dumped the contents into the toilet, flushing it before the stench filled the room.

In the shower, he did the best he could to work the mats out of his hair and braced himself with his elbow against the wall. He stood under the stream until the water ran cold and cut it off. At least the room stopped moving. After toweling off and brushing his teeth, Caleb felt more human and used his hand to wipe the steam off the mirror. Still looked like shit.

Downstairs, he heard his father calling for his mother, and quickly put on the clean work clothes he'd laid out. He made his way down the stairs and pushed open his father's bedroom door. His father was only sixty-two but looked eighty, now. The last ten years had taken their toll.

"Dad, did you need something?"

"Where's your mother? She was going to bring me my glasses," his father replied through hoarse whispers.

"Remember? Mom passed away eight years ago. Your glasses are beside you on the nightstand." Caleb pointed at the thick glasses not ten inches away from his father's hand.

His father fumbled for the glasses and slipped them on, staring at Caleb in confusion. "Yes, that's right. I miss her."

"I miss her, too, Dad. Come on, let's get you some breakfast. Tammy should be here any minute."

Helping his father down the hall, Caleb glanced at their family photos. His eyes rested on his mother's face in the last one. She died five years after Shannon. Throat cancer. He'd stayed to help his father after that. Or, at least, that's what he told himself. Sounded better than he stayed because it was easier to. To drink himself into oblivion. To try and blur the memories. Now, though, his father did need him. After his mother died, his father began to show signs of dementia.

Doctors said it was early onset but that grief may have helped speed it along.

He settled his father in the kitchen and rooted through the fridge for something easy to make when the phone began to ring again. He ignored it this time, knowing it was work calling back. Tammy came rushing in and set her bag on the table as she gave their father a peck on the cheek, pushing her wavy, red hair out of her face.

"Sorry, had to get the kids to school this morning. Missed the bus. You haven't made breakfast yet?" She eyed Caleb, her frown saying she disapproved of the state of him. "Rough night?"

"Don't give me shit, Tammy. I gotta go. I'll be back before your hospital shift. Dad needs to eat." Caleb grabbed his keys and headed for the door.

He and Tammy took turns caring for their dad with only small breaks from a home healthcare nurse. Tammy was a nurse at the hospital, so she worked mostly evening shifts and he worked days. It wasn't ideal, but was the best they could manage with their incomes. Eventually, they knew their father would need more care, but they wanted to keep him home as long as possible.

His mind drifted as he sped toward the job site. They were all just surviving. After Shannon's death... murder, everything changed. Their small town became a strange place. People eyed each other on the street. The murder was never solved, which didn't help matters.

No clue as to who committed the crime.

In the moments from when Caleb walked her almost home, to when her parents discovered her missing was around an hour. In that time, she'd been dragged into the woods, strangled, and stabbed over thirty times.

No motive, no suspects.

Well, that wasn't entirely true. At first, they suspected Caleb and put him through the wringer. He was technically an adult at eighteen, so his parents weren't allowed into the interrogation room. The investigators said horrible things to Caleb. Accused him of heinous acts. Broke him down until he was bawling with his head in his hands and doubting his own actions. A lawyer swooped in and stopped that, but not before the damage was done. Not only had Caleb lost the girl he loved, he was destroyed psychologically as a boy on the cusp of manhood. He began drinking heavily then and never stopped.

In the end, they determined either a transient passing through or a hunter had seen her ascend the hill to her home after she and Caleb split off, then waited until she was alone to grab her and take her into the woods. No one heard or saw anything. A crime of opportunity, they said. That made it sound like shoplifting to Caleb, not murder. He should've walked her all the way home, made sure she got in safely. He didn't and she was murdered.

Shannon's father killed himself a couple of months later. People said he couldn't take the horror of having seen his only child brutally stabbed to death in the woods. Of having let her down. Caleb could relate. Shannon's mother still lived by herself in their home, but hardly ever left. Caleb would drop her by groceries and put the mail by the door. A small penance for his failure to make sure Shannon was safe.

As he drove into the job site and cut the engine, he wiped the tears he realized were running down his cheeks. He coughed forcefully to clear his throat and checked himself in the mirror. He looked hungover but not like he'd been crying. He put his hand on the door and paused, one last memory surfacing. The one that drove him to the bottle every time. The memory, reminded him of what could've been if he'd simply walked her home that night. He was back in the interrogation room, the investigator leaning on the table, his eyes fixed on Caleb's face.

"Son, this will go easier if you just admit what you did to that girl."

"I didn't, I swear. I walked Shannon to her street, then watched as she got up to her house," Caleb insisted through tears. "I love Shannon, she's everything to me."

"That so? You weren't afraid she was going to mess up your life? Tie you down? Trap you?" the investigator asked, almost like he was sympathizing with Caleb.

"I don't understand. She's my girlfriend, I wanted to marry her. I would never hurt her."

"Sure, sure. High school fantasies, I get it. Get married in a few years, buy a house. But then she dropped a bombshell on you, didn't she? Something no young man about to go off into the world wants to hear. Scared you, right? You wanted out and there was only one way."

Caleb stared at the man, lost in confusion. What was he talking about? What bombshell? "She didn't tell me anything. About what?"

The investigator's eyes shifted away for a moment, then landed back on Caleb's face. "Acting ignorant won't save you here, boy. It's time to grow up and own your responsibilities. You and that girl slipped up and she got pregnant. You didn't want to be a father, so you took care of it the only way you knew how. You stabbed her and her unborn child to death, so you could be free."

The sounds Caleb made at that exact moment tore through the police station halls, causing others to run into the interrogation room to see what was happening to create such horrendous wailing. They found Caleb curled up in a ball on the floor, screaming in grief as he came to grips with the fact that everything he'd ever wanted in his life had been ripped from his soul.

Life as he knew it was over.

Nothing Left

A fter a hard day of work, Caleb drove to the river and stood on the bank, his work boots sinking into the thick mud. He did this almost every day, trying to convince himself to submerge his body in the murky depths and let go. Let it end once and for all. He never summoned the courage and let out a ragged breath of frustration. He knew his father needed him and it would be unfair to Tammy to leave her alone to care for it all. She had her own family now, as well. He scanned the surface of the dark water and considered his options. After all, there was more than one way to drown. Tonight, like the uncountable nights before, would have to be by the bottle.

Movement caught his eye and he squinted toward the motion on the other side of the river. A man was watching him from the trees and Caleb jolted. He peered back at the man and noticed something was off. Maybe the trees were casting shadows but the man looked to be at least fifteen feet tall.

Gangly. As Caleb watched, the man turned and moved deeper into the woods. Caleb felt his heart begin to race as he realized it wasn't a man. It couldn't be. The figure, now in motion, not only was extremely tall, but it also moved like a deer. Fluid and delicate, like it was part of the trees themselves. It didn't appear to be wearing clothes, though, in the denseness of the foliage it was hard for Caleb to be sure. As quick as it appeared, the creature slipped into the anonymity of the darkness and was gone from sight.

"What the fuck?" Caleb whispered, rooted in fascination and fear to the spot. Water was seeping into the soles of his boots, so he took a step back into the grass. He watched and waited to see if the being came back, then common sense took over and he realized he needed to move. If it did come back, he could be in danger.

In just a few moments, he went from considering how to kill himself to fearing for his life. He backed away, still keeping his eyes on the forest across the river. As he made his way to his truck, Caleb picked up the pace and yanked the door open so hard, the truck shook in response. He climbed in and slammed the door shut, his hands trembling from the encounter. If there'd even been anything there. Could've been the trees casting shadows or a deer. Or a person.

"I'm losing it," he muttered, knowing that ship had sailed. He'd been on the brink for a long time. He shifted the truck into gear and headed for the liquor store in town. His mind played over what he'd seen at the river and a knot formed in his stomach.

What if it was real? The creature. What if it lived in the woods around them and sought out easy prey? Shannon.

They'd never caught who murdered her. They chalked it up to a drifter or hunter who'd been in the area and saw her alone. Eventually, the case went cold and there were no subsequent murders in the area, so that logic seemed to make sense. In the years since, people stopped locking their doors again and forgot even in small towns, bad things happen.

Caleb still got weird stares and judging eyes from those in town who believed he'd murdered Shannon and gotten away with it. He didn't care. Nothing was worse than knowing he didn't protect her and she'd suffered when he was right down the road. He deserved whatever punishment came his way. Whether or not he wanted it to, his imagination played scenes of what he thought happened in the moments from when he turned to go home to when she was murdered. He tortured himself with the worst possible images. Shannon suffering and begging for help. Begging for him to save her.

Once at the liquor store, he parked and let the truck idle. What if there was a monster in the woods and it had come back out to kill again? He shook his head. He *was* losing it. He cut the engine and shoved the door open. In the years since Shannon was murdered, he'd tried to find answers. Make sense of any of it. This was another rabbit hole. There was no creature in the woods killing people. It was simply his brain trying to put the puzzle together.

"Caleb!" Mo, the liquor store owner shouted in greeting as Caleb came in. "Got our delivery today, I ordered extra of the vodka you like."

Caleb raised his hand and considered how bad off he must be if the liquor store was making sure they were stocked just for him. "Thanks, Mo. How's the baby?"

"Good, good. He's on the move. Debbie has to block off all the exits to keep him contained."

"Already? How old is he now?"

"Five months," Mo answered as he pulled out pictures from his wallet to show Caleb. The baby was the spitting image of Mo, olive skin and deep brown eyes.

"You have your hands full," Caleb remarked, looking at the dark-haired baby who had a twinkle of mischief in the curve of his smile. A pang went through Caleb's heart as he mentally figured out how old his and Shannon's child would be now. Twelve. Their child would've been twelve. He pictured a girl with golden, curly hair.

"Don't I know it?" Mo replied, laughing.

Caleb grabbed two bottles of vodka and set them on the counter. He eyed the selection of paraphernalia by the register, considering if he looked like less of an alcoholic if he bought some other things. He grabbed the paper and some peanuts to add to the pile. Mo rang it all up and didn't make Caleb feel like he was doing anything wrong. Caleb scooped up the bag and smiled half-heartedly at Mo.

"Tell Debbie I said hello. See ya, Mo."

"I will. You should come around for dinner sometime," Mo answered with a grin, the light shining off his silver-capped canine.

Caleb nodded and pushed open the door, holding his bag of treasure to his chest. How bad could it be if the liquor store owner was inviting him over for dinner? The bottles clanked together as he set them on the seat. He backed the truck out and headed for home. The home health nurse had been there a couple of hours and they couldn't afford to pay her for more than that. Tammy covered the mornings until after lunchtime but had to get home for the kids to get off the bus. It was never-ending.

After talking to the nurse and making his father dinner, Caleb settled into his nightly routine. He cut on the television and cracked the first bottle of vodka. To pretend like he wasn't drinking to escape, he put a splash of orange juice in the glass and took the first sips slowly. He was only fooling himself. Glass after glass was empty before he knew it and the cloak of blurriness came over him. The orange juice was abandoned and he committed to the clear liquid that went down like water.

His father dozed off in the recliner next to him and Caleb watched him. He was a good father. He loved his kids, he'd loved his wife. So much so, her death sent him over the edge. That was something he and his father had in common. Not being able to save the women they loved.

Sometimes, Caleb imagined a life where both Shannon and his mother were still alive. The children Shannon and Caleb would've had, the grandmother his mother would've been. Instead, they were all fractured. His father was barely in reality most of the time, Caleb and Tammy trading off on his care. Day in and day out. There were no family get-togethers, no holiday photos.

Caleb stood up and shook his father awake. "Hey, Dad, let's get you to bed."

His father stirred and peered at him, his eyes clouded with confusion. "Don't forget, Tammy has dance practice."

"I won't, Dad. Come on, let's get you up." Caleb put his hands under his father's arms and guided him up.

They made their way down the hall and Caleb helped his father change into pajamas. Once his father was situated on the side of the bed, Caleb sat next to him and made sure he took his nightly pills. It reminded him of when he was little and his father would come in when Caleb had nightmares. He always comforted Caleb and never made him feel like he was overreacting. It made Caleb think of what he saw in the woods.

"Hey, Dad, you ever hear of anything living in the forest around here?"

"A bear?" his father replied, almost like a child.

"Um, maybe. More like a creature, or a large man?" Caleb said, his words sounding stupid as soon as they left his mouth.

His father stared at him, his eyes suddenly clear. "Caleb, watch for the wildman."

"The wildman? Oh, like the Kentucky Wildman? Bigfoot?"

His father nodded, then his eyes went back to their disconnected state. "Watch out for bears."

"Got it. Love you, Dad," Caleb whispered and helped his father settle under the covers.

He paused at the door and smiled at his father tucked in with the covers up to his chin. His father reached out to the other side of the bed and stroked the empty space.

"Tell your mother to hurry up and come to bed. I can't sleep if she's not next to me." His old man's voice sounded lost.

"Dad..." Caleb began and knew it was better to let his father believe for a moment. "Okay, I will. I'll make sure Tammy makes it to dance practice, as well."

"Caleb?"

"Yeah, Dad?"

"You're a good boy. One day you'll be a good father. I'm glad you have Shannon."

Caleb froze and stared, his heart in his throat. Fuck, it was all too much. His father rolled over and went to sleep. Caleb cut the light and made his way back down the hall. His father meant well, but sometimes taking care of someone who didn't know the line between the past and present was a heavy burden. Especially, because in his father's mind, no one ever really died. They were always just in another room, or down the street. Caleb thought that reality might be comforting, then considered it would be a constant state of waiting, longing. The people never came into the room or knocked on the door. They were still just as gone as dead. The missing was all the same.

He settled himself into the chair and stared blankly at the television screen, the image of the creature popping into his mind. Kentucky Wildman. He'd grown up hearing the myth of the Bigfoot-like creature that lived in the woods of Kentucky. He tried to match that story with what he saw, then shook his head. Now, he was believing in Bigfoot? He poured another glass of straight vodka and took a large swallow, letting the burn find its way down into his soul.

There was more than one way to drown.

Sunup to Sundown

Tammy slammed her purse on the table and let out a long sigh. Caleb could tell she was losing her patience with him and his nightly boozing. He rubbed his face and watched her from across the kitchen, waiting for her to let him have it. She eyed him and shook her head.

They both knew it was pointless for her to try and get him on the right path. The harder she pushed him to stop drinking, the more he pulled away. Instead, she turned her back on him and began to wash the sink load of crusted and smelly dishes.

"Diane?"

Caleb heard his father call from the living room. Diane was his mother's name. His father was getting worse. Caleb glanced at Tammy for a moment, then headed to where his father was reading in the recliner, his glasses perched on the end of his nose.

"Hey, Dad. You need something?"

"No, was just going to let your mother know the Hanover house next door is up for sale. I guess they finally moved to Florida."

If by moved to Florida, he meant they both died a couple of years before, then he'd be right. Caleb thought about reminding his father of this fact but decided it really didn't matter. Dead or gone, the house had been empty for years. Caleb walked over and peered out the front door. Sure enough, a for sale sign had been jabbed into the front lawn. He liked having no neighbors, so was hoping whoever bought it kept to themselves. As he was about to shut the front door, he saw a red pickup truck pull into the driveway blasting Pink Floyd. His friend Stephan was gesturing from the front seat. Caleb waved him over and waited for Stephan to come in before shutting the door.

"Hey, man. Was going to see if you had some free time today to help me finish that deck. Maybe go play some pool after?" Stephan asked as he sauntered into the living room.

Caleb and Stephan had been friends since grade school when they tussled over something stupid neither could remember at recess. Stephan stood about an inch taller than Caleb but was more thin and wiry. Over the years, they'd been best friends and fought over girls more than once. Caleb always suspected Stephan had a crush on Tammy but was wise enough to not cross into that territory.

As if sensing his presence, Tammy came to the kitchen door, wiping her hands on a dish towel. She glared at Caleb, then gave a sweet smile to Stephan. "Hey there. You trying to get my worthless sop of a brother to do anything other than shove his face in a bottle?"

Silence filled the room and Caleb's cheeks burned. They almost never let anyone in on what went on behind closed doors, however, it was clear Tammy was at the end of her proverbial rope.

Stephan coughed lightly and glanced between them. "I come at a bad time?"

Neither of them spoke, now regretting dragging him into their family business. Caleb snatched his jacket off the coat rack and glowered at Tammy. He met Stephan's eyes and gestured toward the door.

"Nah, man. Sibling bullshit and all that. Let's talk outside." Caleb knew he was bailing on Tammy but needed to get out of the house. "Tammy, you alright if I go help Stephan with his deck?"

Tammy's mouth dropped open in disbelief and shook her head. "I guess it doesn't fucking matter, since you aren't any help here, anyway. Just go and I'll take care of things, like always."

"Tammy! Don't use such language. Your mother would turn in her grave," their father admonished. At least for the moment, he remembered his wife had died.

"Sorry, Dad," Tammy muttered and headed back into the kitchen where the sound of harshly washing dishes resumed.

Caleb met Stephan's eyes and shrugged. "No time like the present."

They went out to Stephan's truck and sat for a moment. Caleb stared at the for sale sign next door and wondered if things were about to change. Stephan let the truck idle, turned down the radio, and faced Caleb.

"None of my business, but your sister seems super pissed off."

"You're right, none of your business, and she is."

"Anything I can do to help?"

Caleb laughed bitterly, then sadness washed over him. "No. I suck. Can you fix that?"

Stephan shook his head. "I doubt it. Drinking too much?"

"I suppose. Man, it's just all weighing me down. Shannon, my mom, now my dad. I didn't think my life would end up this way. It's fucking barren."

They sat with that thought for a moment, then Stephan backed out of the driveway. He turned his coffee-brown eyes on the house near them. "Saw your neighbor's house is up for sale? It's been empty a while."

"Yeah, I prefer it empty," Caleb answered honestly.

"Who knows, maybe someone cool will move in. Maybe a pretty lady," Stephan joked, then realized his error.

Caleb gritted his teeth and stared out the window. That's the last thing he needed in his life. There'd been no one since Shannon and he intended to keep it that way. Life ended that day for both of them.

As they began to pull off, Tammy came to the door and watched them. Stephan gave her a quick wave, which she returned and Caleb swore he saw her blush. She was married with children, so like him, there was no moving forward. Only memories and missed opportunities.

"Your sister is something special," Stephan murmured, almost to himself. "Should've jumped on that when I had the chance. She's a fine-looking woman."

"Dude, you're talking about my sister. Besides, aren't you with..." Caleb forgot the name of Stephan's latest girlfriend.

"Nah, she got sick of my shit and left. Carrie. Probably for the better. She was wanting to get married and I don't see myself ever doing that."

"Wise. You're a train wreck," Caleb teased, feeling the tension from the morning draining.

"Ha! That's coming from you. You really want to go there?" Stephan asked, brushing his light, golden-brown hair out of his face as the wind whipped it around. He grabbed a bandana out of the glove box and fastened it around his forehead to keep the hair out of his eyes.

Caleb chuckled and shook his head. "Touche. Maybe get a haircut, you fucking hippie."

They both laughed and for a moment it was like they were back in high school without a care in the world. They pulled up in front of Stephan's trailer and got out, grabbing supplies from the back of his truck. After hauling everything around to the back, they got to setting posts and laying out the framework. By the end of the day, the deck was pretty much finished except for the railings and stain. They sat on it, each drinking a beer. Stephan rocked back in his chair, his face getting serious.

"You know, you're like a brother to me, right? I'd do anything for you. But, man, you've got to get your shit together before you end up dead."

Caleb peered into his beer bottle, gazing at the bubbles rising to the surface. He eyed Stephan with a frown. "Tammy put you up to this?"

Stephan nodded, then shrugged. "She mentioned it, but don't be mad at her, Caleb. I mean anyone can see you're spiraling. You look like a fucking ghost. Even now, I can see your hands shaking. You're in deep trouble, man. If you don't stop, this will kill you."

"There are things worse than death."

"Shut the fuck up. Seriously, imagine what your dying would do to your family. I get it, Shannon's death was terrible. I can't even imagine. However, you can't go back and life keeps moving on. You're my best friend, but I feel like I don't even know you anymore."

Caleb felt anger rise in him and imagined punching Stephan in the face. He clenched his fists and bit the inside of his lip to prevent himself from saying anything he might regret. He met Stephan's eyes in a harsh glare and swallowed back the peppery feeling in his throat. "How about the next time you and my sister decide to gang up on me, just don't, yeah? Neither of you have a clue what it is like to see someone you love murdered, then get blamed for it."

"No, we don't, but we can say what it is like to watch someone slowly kill themselves and not be able to stop it."

Caleb stood up, guzzled the rest of his beer, and chucked the empty beer bottle as hard as he could at a nearby tree, feeling some satisfaction as it hit its target and shattered into countless shards. "I'll walk home."

He stormed off the deck and snagged his jacket from one of the posts. Stephan rose to stop him, but Caleb was already moving at a fast pace down the road. He could hear Stephan saying something to him, but didn't care and kept walking. About halfway home, he heard a car slow near him and was about to turn and give Stephan a piece of his mind when he saw Tammy with her children in the car. She pulled up and rolled the window down.

"Hey, we're grabbing pizza to bring home. You want to come along? The nurse is at the house with Dad for the next hour or so."

Caleb wanted to tell her to take a flying leap but the eyes of his niece and nephew stopped him in his tracks. They were excited to see him, and even more excited at the prospect of him joining them for pizza. He climbed in and stared at Tammy.

"Can you just not try and fix me, right now?"

Tammy nodded, then glanced back at the children, not wanting to cause a scene in front of them. "I love you, Caleb. You're my baby brother and I can't stand the thought of losing you, okay?"

Caleb could see the reflection of the children in the back seat, reminding him of when he and Tammy were little. How they vacillated between fighting and being each other's confidant. He couldn't imagine life without her, either. "Okay. Where's Bob?"

"He had to work late. Or, so he says. I can't talk about it here, maybe later. The kids and I are going to stay over at Dad's place tonight. Get some Grandpa time in."

"Grandpa!" One of the children yelled in excitement from the back seat.

Caleb tried to read Tammy's face, to see what was really going on. She darted her eyes to him, then set her mouth. Sometimes he forgot he wasn't the only one with problems. It seemed like Tammy and her husband were spending less and less time together. She waved it off as part of responsibilities, however, Caleb could see it was more. He reached out and squeezed her hand.

"I'm sorry, Tam. I really am. Thanks for coming to get me. We can talk later."

After too much pizza and ice cream with the kids, Caleb's dad offered to tuck the children into bed and read to them. For some reason when they were around, he seemed more lucid. He corralled them upstairs as Tammy and Caleb made coffee, then sat at the kitchen table. Caleb hadn't wanted to ask her to stop by the liquor store, and the beer he'd had with Stephan had long since worn off. His hands shook terribly and he caught Tanmmy staring at them. He cleared his throat and she jerked her eyes up to meet his, her cheeks flaming.

"Caleb..."

"Tammy, don't. I know. But I'm here and not driving to the liquor store, so let's talk. What's going on?"

She stared at the cup of coffee in front of her, then looked up with tears in her eyes. "Bob left. Well, the house is in his name, so temporarily. He met someone else. We're getting a divorce and I need to move out. I already talked to Dad. The kids and I'll stay here until I can get a place of my own."

Caleb was speechless. Bob had pursued his sister for years, to the point of even stalking her. Said he couldn't live without her. Now, he was discarding his family? Rage filled Caleb and he pictured drowning Bob in the river. Holding him under until his thrashing stopped and no life was left in him. He slammed his hand on the table as he stood up and shoved his chair back.

"I'll kill him!"

"Kill who?" a tiny voice sounded from behind him.

Caleb spun around to see his niece, Sara, staring at him wide-eyed, clutching her teddy bear to her chest. She pushed her red, curly hair out of her face and stared at him. He shook his head, not sure how to undo what he said. Tammy jumped up and guided the small child out of the room, but not before Caleb heard her speak again.

"Who is Uncle Caleb going to kill, Mommy?"

After the Fall

The sound of car doors slamming woke Caleb up and he rolled out of bed. More sober than usual, but not feeling much better. He staggered to the window, pushing back the curtain. A couple of cars were parked in the driveway next door. One was clearly a real estate agent as the face plastered on the side of the car matched the short, blond-haired woman who was waving her hands around at the yard. The Hanovers had been avid gardeners and some of their handy work was still present, although overgrown. Caleb watched as a thin man and a petite, long black-haired woman looked to where she was pointing. A small boy clung to the woman's hand, no older than about four. As the couple trailed behind the woman, Caleb recognized the man when he turned.

Trevor fucking Strickland. One of the biggest dicks from high school. Caleb remembered Trevor was always talking down to everyone else and rumor had it he was heavy-handed with his girlfriends. Until he hit the wrong girl and her lacrosse-playing, older brother beat the crap out of Trevor after school one day. After graduation, Trevor left town and Caleb didn't ever expect his weasely ass to come back. However, there he was, looking at the house next door. Fuck.

Caleb dressed and made his way downstairs. Tammy was making pancakes while her two children played Slap Jack with their grandfather. Their normally quiet house was filled with screams and peals of laughter. Caleb poured a cup of coffee and watched his father entertain the kids. He had to admit, having the two children around seemed to make his father more cognizant and aware of his surroundings.

Tammy put a stack of pancakes on the table with butter and syrup, effectively drawing the children's attention away from the game, which had gotten out of control. The children filled their plates, poured way too much syrup on their pancakes, and proceeded to make everything within their grasp sticky. Tammy gave them each a damp paper towel and gestured for them to wipe their hands. Her son, Drew, dutifully wiped his hands and helped Sara clean hers. Drew was eight and sometimes too serious for his age. Sara was five, almost six, and the spitting image of Tammy. Like Caleb and Tammy's father, she was red-headed with pale skin and freckles. Caleb took after their mother with dark golden hair and a year-round tan.

"No school today?" Drew asked, his voice sounding hopeful.

Tammy finished rinsing the dishes and rotated to face them, leaning against the counter. "Let's have a hookey day with Grandpa. I need to call the school about having the bus pick you up here, anyway."

"Mommy says we are going to live here with you and Grandpa," Sara said as she shoved almost a whole pancake in her mouth.

"That so?" Caleb replied, meeting Tammy's eyes for confirmation. He hadn't wanted to say anything in case she hadn't told the kids yet.

"Plenty of room," his father muttered, staring out the window. "Looks like some people are viewing the Hanover house. Have a little boy with them."

Tammy craned her neck to peer out the window. "He seems like he's about Sara's age, maybe a little younger."

"You know who that is, right?" Caleb asked.

"The little boy?" Tammy answered, scrunching her face in confusion.

Caleb snickered at her response. "No, the guy. That's Trevor Strickland. From school?"

"Oh! He was such a jerk. I hope he's grown up," Tammy said, watching the family touring the yard.

Caleb agreed but didn't have much faith *that* leopard could change its spots. Men who hit women didn't often see the error of their ways. He glanced back toward the family at the Hanover house and shook his head. The woman wasn't much bigger than a child herself and although Trevor wasn't a big man, he outsized her dramatically.

"Asian," Tammy whispered from the window.

"What's that?" Caleb asked.

"I think she's Asian."

Caleb squinted to try and see better, but the lady led the boy over to an old playset and had her back to them. She was crouched down, pointing at something in the dirt. The boy tipped his head up to her and laughed. He could definitely be Asian. Feeling bad for spying on them, Caleb turned away and saw his father teaching the kids another card game. Poker. Was he seriously teaching them poker at eight o'clock in the morning?

"Alright, I need to head to work. You good here, Tam? You going to work today?"

Tammy waved him off. "Took a couple of days off to get situated. The kids will keep Dad entertained and I was going to clean out that old guest room, so I don't have to share a room with them again tonight. Nothing but feet and farts."

Caleb chuckled, not doubting that one bit. He gathered his work tools, then headed for the door. Tammy caught him before he went out and handed him a bag.

"Lunch."

Caleb peered into the bag and grinned. "Thanks, Tam. See, maybe having you around won't be so bad."

Tammy shoved him and laughed. "It's the mother in me. Anyway, have a good day. We'll keep Dad busy and I'm making stew and biscuits for dinner. So, come straight home."

Caleb knew what she was getting at and he couldn't make any promises. Regardless of them being at the house, he still felt an undeniable urge to drink right after work. He shoved the lunch bag into his pack and nodded. "Yeah."

As he loaded his things in his work truck, he glanced over at the people viewing the Hanover house. The dark-haired woman smiled at him and waved, drawing the attention of her husband, who didn't look happy about it. The guy, Trevor, eyed Caleb. As a shadow of recognition passed over his face, he smiled and waved. They'd never personally had issues in school, but Caleb wasn't looking to make any friends. Especially not Trevor fucking Strickland. That guy was bad news and Caleb hoped they'd pass on the house.

As he backed out of the driveway, he saw the small boy watching him. His dark, almond-shaped eyes followed Caleb's movements, but he made no gestures or expressions showing he had any interest in the man in the truck. Even so, Caleb felt exposed and frowned. The kid made him feel weird. The child's mother ran over and took the boy's hand, leading him back to where the real estate agent was waiting to show them the inside of the house. The woman's eyes darted to Caleb and a small smile played on her delicate lips. She was definitely Asian, making Caleb wonder how Trevor met her.

He wondered if Trevor hit her.

As if sensing Caleb's thoughts, Trevor grabbed the woman's arm, clearly perturbed, and guided her into the house. Caleb paused and for a moment felt protective of the woman and child. Then, reminding himself he couldn't even save the woman he loved, he put the truck in gear and pressed the gas pedal a little too hard, causing the tires to squeal. He noticed Tammy observing from the window with a grimace on her face.

Again, Caleb hoped Trevor and his family wouldn't buy the house next door. It was bad enough Tammy and her kids were moving in, disturbing his privacy... his drinking time. He didn't need a family with a kid all up in his business, too. His bubble was very quickly getting crowded and knew it would send him over the edge.

As that little bit of reality sank in, Caleb found himself detouring away from the job site and toward the liquor store.

He'd never let his drinking intentionally affect his work, but something about that day broke the rules. He drove in and cut off the truck, striding with purpose for the door... as if he was convincing himself it was urgent. He yanked the door open too hard, causing the bell at the top to smack against the glass.

"Whoa!" Mo exclaimed, startled. "Oh, Caleb. What are you doing here at this time?"

Caleb refused to be made to feel ashamed and grabbed his go-to bottles of vodka, practically slamming them on the counter. Mo watched him, his mouth frozen between words. Caleb threw money on the counter and growled, "Keep the change."

Before Mo could bag the bottles or reply, Caleb snatched them and stormed back to his truck. He didn't allow any emotions to surface and cracked one of the bottles, guzzling about a quarter of it before stopping. He sat in the truck, staring at the door of the liquor store. He saw Mo move past the door a couple of times, clearly seeing what Caleb was up to. A wave of shame came over Caleb and he quickly drank more before it could take hold. It was none of Mo's business, anyway. He saw Mo on the phone and he knew Mo was calling Tammy. Caleb fired up the truck and jerked out of the parking lot before Mo came out or Tammy showed up.

He drove out to the river and parked. The first bottle was rapidly becoming history and he released the tension he'd been carrying. That was better. Nothing really mattered. He opened the next bottle, ready to put it to bed when movement caught his eye on the other side of the bank. Fear froze him for a second when he realized it was just a deer. Not a creature. He pretended to shoot it with his hands, then felt guilty. He'd never been much of a hunter, even though his friends all were. He dropped his hands and watched the deer as it drank from the edge of the water.

All of a sudden, the deer jerked its head up and stared past Caleb, then bolted into the woods. Caleb sensed something behind his truck but was too afraid to turn and see some sort of beast coming for him. He put the truck in gear, ready to book it out of there when a pounding came on the back window, causing him to jump and spill some of his vodka all over his lap.

"Godddamnit!" he yelled and realized he couldn't go to work smelling like a distillery. He whipped around, expecting to see Bigfoot. Instead, he saw Stephan grinning like an idiot beside the bed of the truck.

Caleb jumped out of the front seat, pissed and ready to fight Stephan. Stephan put his hands up and shook his head.

"Cool down, Caleb. Your sister sent me to look for you. Mo called her, worried. I figured you'd come here. Small town, there aren't a lot of places to hide. Didn't mean to scare the shit out of you."

Caleb felt stupid standing there with a patch of vodka continuing to spread across his pants. He leaned against the door and eyed Stephan. "That's how you get yourself shot."

"Man, you've never carried a gun, I think I'm safe. You want to talk?"

Caleb shook his head. "Not really."

Stephan peered across the river. "Well, if you aren't going to work, let's go for a hike. You down?"

"Alright, fine. Can't go to work smelling like booze, anyway."

Stephan frowned for a second, then nodded. "Dude, that ship has sailed. You always smell like booze. You aren't fooling anyone."

Caleb wasn't sure why that surprised him but it did. Did everyone know? True shame came over him and he pushed down the burning tears threatening to come out. That was it, then. He was the town drunk. More fodder for the gossip hounds. He grabbed his pack and pulled out a bottle of water not able to meet Stephan's eyes. He shrugged.

"Let's go."

Up the Steep Hills

They hiked in silence, Caleb stumbling from the morning booze. He wasn't sure what Stephan's point was, but the last thing he wanted to be doing was traversing the thin trail up the hill. He stopped to vomit and heard Stephan chuckle. Glaring at his friend, he wiped the spittle off his mouth and stood up.

"Fuck off," he muttered, pausing to decide if more was coming out. When it seemed his stomach was empty, Caleb grasped a nearby tree and coughed the rest of the phlegm out of his throat.

"You need a break?" Stephan asked, knowing Caleb didn't like to be challenged.

Caleb shook his head as he cleaned his mouth by spitting and pushed on. "Why are we doing this, anyway? Doing Tammy's bidding?"

"I figured since you weren't going to work today, might be good to spend some time together."

"Don't you have somewhere you need to be?" Caleb questioned with bitterness in his voice.

"Well, I was on my way to work when your sister called. This wasn't my plan, but it is what it is," Stephan said, holding a branch back from smacking Caleb in the face.

"Geez... Tammy. I don't know why she has to get all in my business."

"You don't? Seriously? She's trying to keep it together and you're doing your best to tear it all down. You're quickly becoming the town drunk and Tammy is doing her best, trying to save your soul."

Caleb stopped at this, getting a brief view into her side of things. Stephan was always good at that, playing the devil's advocate. He shrugged and peered out over the edge of the trail down to the river. "You remember when we used to come up here as kids? Play hide and seek on steroids?"

Stephan laughed and grinned. "I remember you getting bored and stopped looking for me. I came down at dusk and you were sitting at the bench in the parking lot, eating all our snacks."

Caleb had indeed done that. Stephan always had better snacks than him. He snickered, then nodded. "Well, I found you in the end."

"Ha. If by 'found' you mean because I came out of hiding, then I guess you're right."

"All ends the same, anyway. Hey, have you ever seen anything weird out here?" Caleb inquired, scanning the trees.

"Weird how?"

"Like unexplainable weird. Creatures, monsters, things like that?"

Stephan stroked his chin and shook his head. "Not really. A couple of times, I thought I saw hunters, then wasn't sure. Figured the light was playing tricks on my eyes. Why are you asking?"

Caleb shrugged. "I thought I saw something the other day. Sort of like a man, but too big. Moved through the trees like it was part of them."

Stephan watched him, his face serious. "Were you drinking?"

"Not yet, went to the liquor store after. You're probably right. The light in the trees likely made it look creepier than it was," Caleb explained, doubting himself.

"You want to keep hiking or turn around?" Stephan asked, peering up the trail.

"I never wanted to hike in the first place, so let's turn around."

"Look, man. I know you have things to deal with, but drinking isn't helping. You can't be missing work and your sister has more than she can handle. Do you want to stay with me for a few days? A detox of sorts?"

Caleb felt his face get hot and Stephan's well-meaning words came across more like judgment. "Just stay the fuck out of it, alright? It's not that bad."

"It *is* that bad, but if you won't accept help, I won't push. The offer stands. You okay to drive?"

Caleb nodded. "Yeah, I think I puked up whatever I drank. I need to eat something."

"Waffles?" Stephan offered. "I'm buying."

"Waffles sound good. Especially if you're buying," Caleb joked, in an attempt to lighten up the conversation.

They headed back down to the parking area and Caleb followed Stephan out to the twenty-four-hour diner that served decent food for the price. Greasy, primarily fried food, but a whole plate was just a few dollars and more than most people could eat in one sitting.

After chowing down on waffles, grits, and coffee, the morning's booze had released its grip on Caleb and he sat back in the booth, satisfied. He stared out the window and dreaded going home to face Tammy. She was going to be livid. He sighed. "Ever since our mom died, Tammy has treated me like one of her kids."

Stephan cocked his head and pushed his plate away, sipping on his coffee. "You act like one."

That stung. "Whatever, man. I go to work, I take care of Dad. I'm doing the best I can. This isn't where I wanted to be in my life, you know?"

"I know. However, it is where you *are*. Like it or not, you need to suck it up and start acting your age."

"Like you?"

Stephan laughed, then shrugged. "Fair. However, I don't have anyone depending on me. I get to act a fool."

Caleb couldn't argue there. He slid out of the booth and grabbed his keys. "Well, I suppose I need to go home and face the firing squad."

"You want me to come along, create a buffer?"

"Nah, this is my bed, I need to go lie in it."

They walked out together when Stephan put his hand on Caleb's shoulder. "I know this sucks. But every single one of us needs you around, Caleb. Can you maybe stop trying to slowly kill yourself?"

Caleb turned to his friend and felt the walls going up. "Yeah, man. Sure thing. On it."

Stephan sighed, dropping his hand. "Don't have to be a dick about it. I don't need to be missing work to come and find your drunk ass at nine in the morning. Fuck."

Caleb felt his cheeks flame and knew Stephan was only trying to help. "Sorry."

They each headed to their trucks and Stephan pulled out first, not looking back. Caleb spied the other bottle of vodka and considered picking up where he left off that morning. Then, thinking better of it, he shoved it under the seat and headed for home.

Tammy wasn't waiting for him at the door like he expected. The house was oddly quiet when he went in. He found Drew and Sara watching television with their grandfather, but Tammy was nowhere to be seen. Caleb paused at the door.

"Hey, Drew. Where's your mom?"

Drew glanced over, breaking the trance of the show he was watching, and shrugged. "She was crying and told us to stay with Grandpa. I think she went upstairs."

Caleb would've taken pissed off Tammy any day over crying Tammy. He made his way up the stairs and pushed open the guest room door. Tammy was sitting cross-legged in the middle of the floor with boxes around her. She stared at him through red-rimmed eyes, then went back to sorting. Caleb went over and sat down next to her, picking up a dusty photo album she had open. It was from when they were kids at Christmas.

"I'm sorry, Tam. It won't happen again."

Tammy sighed and took the album, placing it in her lap. "Yes, it will. You are a fucking disaster and it appears everything is on me now."

"That's not fair..." Caleb began.

Tammy slammed the album shut, causing Caleb to flinch. "Not fair? Ever since Mom died, I've been trying to fill that role. Now, with Bob running off with someone else, I also will fill both roles for my own kids. I can't fucking do it all, Caleb. I need you to stop bleeding me dry!"

Caleb watched her face and could see the years had taken their toll. She was right, he just didn't know how to get himself out of the hole. He sat in silence, thinking of words that might make her feel better. She threw the album in one of the boxes and stood up. Caleb got up next to her, wanting nothing more than to embrace her and apologize. Instead, he stood frozen in his own shame. Tammy went to the window and peered out.

"The real estate agent told me that family put an offer in on the house next door," she said softly, waving her hand at the Hanover house.

"Already? The house just went on the market," Caleb replied, surprised.

"Apparently, they need something fast. That's what she told me."

"Well, fuck. I can't stand that guy."

"Me either. However, they're about to be our neighbors. Maybe we can invite them over for a barbeque," Tammy responded, her voice lightening with humor.

"I'd rather drown myself in the river," Caleb responded, making them both laugh.

"Please don't. Oh, I did invite Stephan over for dinner since he left work to go find you."

"Is that the only reason?" Caleb teased.

Tammy's eyes got wide, and she shot him a dirty look. "Yes! I'm about to be a single mother. I don't need any more children to raise. Stephan is almost as big of a fuck up as you, minus the booze."

Saying it out loud made the air in the room heavier and Caleb took an unintentional step back. It was easier when it was his dirty little secret. "Okay, well, I can help with dinner. What are we having?"

Tammy shrugged. "Didn't get that far. I think there's a casserole in the freezer. Unless you do want to throw something on the grill?"

Caleb smiled and bobbed his head. "I can do that. Not sure a casserole will feed all of us."

"I'll make a shortcake, then. Kids will be thrilled."

As Tammy prepped the dessert and side, Caleb ran to the store and cleaned the grill. As he was laying out the utensils next to the grill, he heard a man's voice and glanced over to see Trevor with another man at the Hanover house. Trevor was instructing the man on tasks he wanted done on the house. As if he knew he was being watched, Trevor said loudly that money was no matter. He glanced over at Caleb with the biggest, shit-eating grin on his face and gave a curt wave. Caleb cut his eyes back to the barbeque and fought the prickly rage forming in his chest.

God, did Caleb ever hate that weasel of a man.

Down, Down the Valley

C aleb rolled over and blinked a few times. Either he was
dreaming or had completely lost his mind. Shannon sat
across his bedroom, perched on a stack of dirty clothes
in the corner of the room. Blood ran from one of her eyes and
she had her arms wrapped around her petite frame as if the
room was freezing. Caleb sat up and squinted, still trying to
figure out if he was awake or dreaming. He'd never had a visit
from Shannon since she died. He'd begged her to come to him,
but she never had. Until now.

"Shannon?" he croaked out of his sore and dry throat.

She sat watching him, her face unreadable. Caleb
glanced around the floor at the empty liquor bottles and
became convinced this was his mind in its saturated stupor
fucking with him. He flopped back on the bed and threw his
arm over his eyes. Not quite sober, not quite hungover.
Somewhere in between two realities. He peered out and
Shannon was gone, if she'd ever been there.

He shifted onto his side carefully to face the window, attempting to keep the room from spinning. His stomach did consecutive flips, threatening to let loose. The breeze from the cracked window helped settle the turmoil and he breathed in and out in tiny increments. That was better.

The sensation of something pressing on the bed next to him made him open his eyes a slit. What the fuck was that next to the bed? His eyes flew open when he realized Shannon was standing beside him, her mouth twisted in horror. Her once vibrant blue eyes, now large, dark pools of emptiness.

Caleb's feet hit the ground and he scrambled to the door, terrified by the vision before him. As his hand hit the cool, metal knob and he twisted, his heart gave him pause. If this thing in the room was Shannon, she needed him. He let the handle go and eased around slowly, afraid of what he might see. Shannon was facing the window now, her back to him. Caleb waited but she didn't move.

"Shannon? Is that you?"

The breeze kicked up through the window, blowing the curtains, however, nothing on Shannon stirred. Her arms were rigid at her sides and she was staring at the house next door. Caleb moved closer, but she turned to him and put her hand up. A mixture of blood and tears ran down her face, rising in Caleb the need to go to her, to protect her. She shook her head, still fixated on the house outside. He stood in place, sensing she'd disappear if he went any closer.

All of a sudden, she whipped around, her face contorted in a scream but no sound came out. She was like a funhouse mannequin. Caleb felt his bowels loosen and stepped away involuntarily. Her hand raised and her finger pointed out the window. Caleb tried to see what she was gesturing at but the street was dark and quiet. Her finger was pointing up the street. To where she used to live. Nothing moved in the night, yet Caleb was still petrified. When she spoke, he almost screamed.

"He's back." That was it. That was all she said.

"Who, Shan? Who's back? The person that killed you?" Caleb asked, trying to make sense of the message.

She dropped her hand, letting it fall slack at her side. Caleb went in her direction, hoping to enfold her in his arms. As soon as he crossed the room, she was gone. He ran to the side window and stared out. Shannon was standing in the road on the crest of the hill by the Hanover house. She turned and wandered into the darkness toward her old home.

Caleb threw on clothes from the floor and ran out of his room, down the stairs. He hit the front door and flung it open, not wanting to lose sight of Shannon. He could see her outline moving up the road, almost to the bend going to her house. He cursed himself for not putting on shoes and ignored the pebbles digging into his feet.

"Shannon!" he yelled at the top of his lungs but she didn't turn back.

As he got to her road, he lost sight of her. A small light bobbed up the hill as if she was carrying a flashlight. She was not visible, however, the light continued up the hill and disappeared. Caleb ran after it, hoping to catch her at the top, but when he got there, she was nowhere to be seen. Her old home sat dark and there was no sign of life. Her mother still lived there but had become a recluse, never leaving or speaking to almost anyone.

"Shannon, where are you?" he hollered into the dark. Light from a nearby house clicked on and Caleb could see the outline of one of the residents staring at him. They shook their head and closed the curtain.

Caleb spun around, not ready to give up yet. She *had* to be there. He trudged to her house and wandered around the outside. What was she trying to tell him? He headed into the woods where her body had been found, but nothing except an owl in the distance greeted him. Caleb crouched down and wrapped his arms around his legs, shivering. Was he losing his mind? The sun was beginning to add light to the sky, so he stood up and headed toward home. His feet were hurting and he was confused by what happened.

Was Shannon really there? Was she trying to warn him of something? He thought of the creature he saw in the woods and shuddered. Was it watching him? Was that who she was talking about? He was in his thoughts as he neared his house, unaware of the man standing on his porch, observing Caleb's trek back home.

"Hey, Caleb. What brings you out at this hour?" a voice cut through the dark.

Surprised, Caleb jerked and stared to where the sound was coming from. Trevor. His family had moved in a few weeks before and Caleb had done his best to avoid them. "Trevor. Just taking a walk."

"That so? You usually take jaunts at the crack of dawn without shoes on?" Trevor replied, sarcasm in his words.

Caleb ignored the question and kept going home. He could see the light on in his father's room and didn't want him calling out and waking up the kids. He raised his hand in a sort of wave at Trevor, hoping that would be the end of the unwelcome reunion.

"I see your sister is living back home? Things not work out between her and her beau?"

Caleb gritted his teeth, wanting to go back and punch Trevor in the mouth. It was pointless. Even in school, Trevor tried to stir up trouble with classmates. He was a shitty, little dick, who delighted in other people's unhappiness. Caleb ignored the question and made his way to his front door. As he pushed it open, he heard Trevor laugh and mutter in his direction.

"Fucking drunk."

Caleb blew out the anger building in him and went inside. He put on a pot of coffee, then went to his father's room. His father was sitting in bed, reading.

"Hey, Dad, you're awake. You alright?"

His father nodded and eyed him with such lucidity, Caleb was taken aback. His father waved to the window. "I thought I heard someone outside."

"Oh, I was out there and Trevor from next door was trying to talk to me."

"Hmmm. Maybe, but I heard a woman's voice."

"You did?" Caleb shuddered. "What was she saying?"

His father sat the book he was holding down, then frowned. "He's back."

Caleb gasped, then tried to cover it, so he didn't alarm his father. "Was that all?"

His father nodded and considered. "I believe so."

Caleb wanted to tell his father he saw Shannon, that she told him the same thing. However, as soon as his father told him, his face returned to his confused state and he stared mindlessly at the book he was holding.

"You want some coffee, Dad?"

"Sure, that would be nice."

Caleb left the room and stopped by the dining room room window before heading to the kitchen. The street was lighter now, but still empty. He glanced at Trevor's house, relieved to see his neighbor was nowhere to be seen. His interaction with Trevor that morning was weird and confirmed even more how much he despised Trevor.

After he poured his father a cup of coffee, Caleb gazed out the living room window, which faced into the woods. Their house sat on a hill that meandered down to a small creek weaving its way through the trees at the rear of the property. When they were kids, they'd spend hours back there, playing war games, playing hide and seek. Back when the neighborhood was full of kids, riding their bikes everywhere until dark. Before they'd grown up and moved away, leaving their parents to rattle around homes that were far too big for them alone.

Caleb thought back to the first time he ever remembered seeing Shannon. They could't have been older than six or seven at the time. He and some other boys were throwing rocks at each other from behind trees when she and another girl came upon them. They'd made daisy chains for their hair and were each carrying a doll. One of the other boys snatched Shannon's doll and threw it in the creek. Her blue eyes flooded with tears and Caleb was ashamed to remember he'd laughed along with the other boys and called her a baby.

She'd run home sobbing.

Later that day, Shannon's father showed up at the door with the ruined doll. Caleb received a whooping because of it and resented Shannon for telling on him. He avoided her in the years to come, even though they were often forced together for neighborhood and school activities.

Caleb felt his cheeks get hot at the memory and wished he could go back and undo it. To tell her he was sorry. Even after they'd started dating, neither mentioned the incident and pretended it never happened. However, it did and he felt like shit about it. Caleb watched the sun change the world around with its ascent. The creek began to glitter through the branches and colors in the landscape reemerged into view. He held the coffee for his father and started to turn when something caught Caleb's eye.

Standing in the tree line was a tall, man-like creature with red eyes. Caleb was frozen by the sight and shook his head. It was what he'd seen in the woods at the river. The creature seemed to be staring right at him and caused his blood to run cold. The being spun around and vanished as if it had never been there.

"He's back."

From Afar

His clothes were soaked. Caleb roused himself and peered around, confused by what his eyes were seeing. His head was pounding and the world was unstable around him. Great. He was in the backyard, fully clothed, lying in a pile of wet and rotting leaves. He tried to get up, but his head had other ideas and he wretched violently into the slimy mass next to him. He wracked his brain, trying to remember how he got there when it came back to him.

He'd been drinking, even more than usual. A lot more since he'd seen Shannon in his room. The night before, he was attempting to find happiness and decided it was a good idea to go out and look at the stars. Lay on the ground like he and Shannon used to do. He must've passed out there.

Bracing his elbows on his knees, he rested his head forward and groaned. It was going to be a rough day. He tried to get up, falling forward into the leaves, then heard a giggle. His head snapped toward the sound and he saw the young boy from next door watching him. Trevor's son. The boy was clutching some kind of action figure in one hand and had his fingers from his other hand in his mouth as he watched Caleb. He took his fingers out of his mouth and waved at Caleb with a shy smile.

Caleb shook his head and used a nearby shrub to help him get to his feet. As he stabilized, he saw the boy's mother come out and call to her son. She caught sight of Caleb's hunched figure and her eyes narrowed. Caleb gave her a weak wave and her face relaxed when she realized it was only him.

She raised her hand at him and called to her son, who begrudgingly turned away from Caleb. The child ran toward his mother and excitedly told her something, his chubby hand pointing toward their wet and hungover neighbor. The woman stared as Caleb made his way back to the house.

She went inside for a moment, then called out to him from her yard. Caleb couldn't understand what she was saying and wasn't looking forward to a neighborly chat. He nodded and smiled, hoping that was enough to end the conversation, however, she was heading in his direction with something clasped in her hands.

As she neared, she extended her hand. Caleb frowned and stared at the small mesh bags she was holding out to him. He shook his head in confusion and looked at her in question. Up close, she was smaller than she appeared from far away. Her deep, dark eyes twinkled and she was saying something with a slight smile on her lips.

She pointed at her skull. "Trà Đắng. For headaches."

Caleb realized the bags were tea and took them from her. The writing on the tea bags wasn't English and he wasn't sure what magic she was trying to give him. He smiled. "Thank you. I'm Caleb."

"Lien."

It sort of sounded like Leigh Anne but if it was all one syllable. Caleb was afraid to mess it up if he tried to say it with his southern drawl. He motioned to the boy. "What's his name?"

The boy met his eyes and smiled shyly. "River."

His mother shook her head and pointed to her lips, sounding out his name slowly. "Trevor."

Caleb cringed. He'd never been a fan of naming kids directly after a parent, but especially since that parent was Trevor. He liked River better. "Nice to meet you, River."

The boy giggled again, clutching onto his mother's leg. The woman didn't correct Caleb and shuttled the boy toward home. She turned and smiled as she guided the boy through the door. Caleb couldn't help but smile back. She seemed much too nice to be with such a dick like Trevor.

Caleb made his way inside, hoping no one was awake yet. Unfortunately, Tammy was at the table sipping coffee and eyed him as he made his way to the pot. She was silent as he poured a cup, but motioned for him to sit down. Her eyes were hard and frustrated as he stumbled to the chair across from her and plopped down.

"Caleb, this can't go on like it's been. I'm not going to watch you throw your life away for a bottle."

"Then, look away," Caleb replied, his voice harsher than he intended.

Tammy sighed and pursed her lips. She set her coffee cup down hard, splashing some over the rim, then stared at him. "Nice. Or how about we fucking talk about this like the adults we are?"

"Fine, Tam. What do you need to tell me about my life? What's your great sisterly advice?"

"Jesus, Caleb. It's no mystery you're an alcoholic. It's getting worse day by day. I woke up this morning and saw you weren't in your bed. I searched for you and panicked when I couldn't find you. I went to the front door, then saw you talking to the neighbor lady. Your clothes are a mess, you reek like booze, and look like complete shit."

"Gee, thanks," Caleb muttered.

"You made the bed," Tammy whispered. "Look, I have my own kids and Dad to worry about. I can't be mothering another grown-ass man."

Caleb got up and shoved his chair in. "Then, don't, Tammy. Fuck. I never asked you to step into my life or to worry about me. Just leave me the hell alone."

"What are you? Twelve? Stop being petulant. Of course, I'm going to worry about you. You're my baby brother. But that doesn't mean you get to step all over us. For fuck's sake, Caleb, don't you see what you're doing to yourself? To Dad? How do you think he'd feel if you drank yourself to death?"

At that, Caleb felt the steam building inside him release. He pulled the chair back out and sat down. His father already lost so much and was basically helpless. If Caleb were gone, it would probably force Tammy to put their father in a home. "You're right. I'll fix it."

"Will you, though?" she asked, her voice soft but tense with honesty.

Caleb met her eyes and they both knew he wouldn't. At this point, he wasn't sure he could. Not on his own, anyway. He tried to think of words to say to convince her, however, they didn't exist. As he fumbled out an insincere promise, Sara and Drew came running in ready for breakfast. Caleb took this as a chance to leave and went to take a shower while the children diverted their mother's attention.

After a shower, Caleb dressed in clean clothes and glanced at the time. He'd need to hustle so he wasn't late for work. His father had joined Tammy and the kids in the kitchen, and was showing the children a magic trick. Caleb frowned at the doorway, not remembering his father ever doing magic tricks. Tammy met his eyes with a bemused smile and shrugged.

He grabbed his keys off the counter. "Hey, Tam, I should be home at four. What time is your shift?"

"Three, but the nurse will cover the gap. The kids get off the bus at four, so should be fine. Just don't be late. We're running out of approved hours from the insurance and will have to start paying out of pocket."

Luckily, their father worked for decades at a steel mill, so he had a pension and insurance. However, the nurse's hours quickly drained that. Caleb sidled past the kids and filled his travel mug with the last of the coffee. He glanced at his father, who was pulling a napkin out of his pocket and covering his hand with it. Mesmerized, Caleb watched as his father made a toy appear out from under the napkin, much to the children's delight.

His father winked at him and Caleb wondered who this strange man was. His father had always been loving, but serious when they were growing up. This goofy guy was a side of his father he'd never really known.

Tammy handed him a bagged lunch and tapped her watch. Caleb nodded and hurried to the door. He'd been late too much and couldn't afford to lose this job. Once he got to his truck and put his gear in the back, he began to feel a little less hungover. He could push through the day.

A crash from the house next door stopped him in his tracks as he was about to get into the truck. He strained his ears and peered over at the house. He thought he could hear yelling and a woman crying. He paused with his hand on the door and slowly shut the truck door.

Should he go over there?

Just as he was about to head in the direction of the house, Trevor came bolting out the door, his face twisted in rage. He saw Caleb and his face shifted. Almost as if he was resetting it into a mask. He stared at Caleb, then grinned.

"Howdy, neighbor."

Caleb cringed. "Trevor. Everything alright over there? Thought I heard something falling."

Trevor's eyes darted back at his house, then he shrugged, the same plastic smile on his face. "Ah, not the handyman, I'm afraid. A shelf I put up fell off the wall and broke everything on it. The wife was upset some of her favorite teapots got broken."

Plausible explanation, but Caleb didn't like how it was delivered. "I'm sorry to hear that. Is she okay?"

"Oh, you know... women. She'll be fine. Nothing a new teapot and some flowers won't fix. Anyway, need to get on to work. Nice chatting, Caleb."

Trevor got in his car and drove off. Caleb waited for a moment and observed the house next door. Deciding it was none of his business, he climbed in his truck and let it idle while he fiddled with the radio. As he was backing out, he saw Lien come out of the house with a trash bag. She had her head down and was clutching the bag tightly. If she knew Caleb was watching her, she didn't show it as she threw the bag in the can and turned to go back in the house. The boy, River, was at the door, tears streaking down his tiny face. His eyes caught Caleb's own and Caleb read something in them.

Fear.

As Lien got to the porch, she stopped for a moment where Caleb could see her face. It looked slightly misshapen, puffy. Swollen. Caleb squinted his eyes to try and get a better view, but she whipped around and scurried inside, pushing River in with her. Not before Caleb saw something that made his blood boil.

She was bleeding.

Up Close

Caleb couldn't get the image out of his head. Of the neighbor lady, Lien, with blood running from her nose.

He didn't think she realized it was there when she went outside. Sure, a shelf falling could hit someone in the face and make them bleed, but why then was Trevor in such a rush to leave if his wife was injured? That seemed insensitive at best, and downright cruel in reality.

Over the next few weeks, Caleb tried to pay extra attention to the house next door. He knew damn well Trevor liked to hit women. He'd been that way since they were kids. Trevor was smaller than most of the other guys, but he was smart. For some reason, girls saw his moody sullenness and intelligence as intriguing, so he dated a few girls out of his league in high school.

Most of them stayed quiet when the bruises began to appear, however, one finally told her brother, who made sure to set Trevor straight.

He showed up at school with a black eye, busted lip, and a lot less cocky than he'd been before. He faded into the background, then disappeared right after graduation. Apparently now, he'd found a woman who not only didn't know his dirty secret, but one that was also quite a bit smaller than him. Caleb guessed Trevor was up to his old tricks again.

One day after Trevor left for work, Caleb hung around a bit, thinking of a way to approach Lien, so he wouldn't spook her. He fiddled around with his truck hood up, checking all the hoses and wires as he eyed the house. Finally, summoning the courage, he thought of a way to approach her and went inside. Tammy was cutting out coupons at the table and glanced up. Caleb leaned on the door jam, watching her.

"Hey does Drew have any toys he's grown out of?" he asked conversationally.

"Probably. Why?"

"I was thinking the little boy next door might like them. He only ever seems to have that one action figure he carries around with him all the time."

Tammy eyed him, trying to read if there was an ulterior motive. "Sure, I think there is a box in the back of the closet in their room upstairs. That's awfully thoughtful of you. Strange, even."

Caleb could see her mind ticking away and he shrugged. "Being neighborly, is all."

Tammy got up and moved past him to get the box. She stopped and turned, putting her hand on his arm. "Be careful. I don't trust Trevor and he seems to want to isolate his family from everyone. I offered to take their little boy with us to the park and he laughed in my face."

"He did what?" Caleb could feel the anger rising in him, as he imagined elbowing Trevor in his little rat chin.

"Don't worry about it. Simply letting you know, something isn't right over there. He was always an asshole, but his wife seems like she might be trapped."

Caleb nodded. That's exactly what it seemed like. She had limited English, was clearly not from around town, and he'd never seen anyone visit them, so he assumed her family was nowhere near. Exactly the way Trevor wanted it. She had no big brother to turn to, like Trevor's high school girlfriend did. He shuddered and gripped the door jam so hard it made the tips of his fingers hurt.

Tammy left to grab the box and Caleb dug in the cabinets, finding a box of chocolate chip cookies. When Tammy came back with the box, he threw them on top and headed for the door. He paused, wondering if he was making the right decision going over there. The image of Lien bleeding and River crying popped into his mind and he knew he could never live with himself if Trevor hurt them again. Or worse.

Lien was surprised to see him at her house, not opening the storm door as she stared at him blankly through the screen. Caleb lifted the box and showed it to her.

"Hey, my nephew outgrew some of his toys and we thought River might like to have them."

Lien glanced at the toys, then down at River, who was now standing in front of her. He grasped her skirt with his small hand. He tugged her hem and smiled up at her. "Mama, please?"

Lien nodded and unlocked the storm door, peering past Caleb to their empty driveway. It was obvious she was making sure Trevor was long gone. She pushed open the door and took the box as Caleb extended it to her.

She met Caleb's eyes. "Tea?"

Caleb wasn't sure how appropriate it was for him to go into her house without her husband home but knew he needed to find out what was really going on behind closed doors. He followed her back to the kitchen as she put the kettle on. The home was sparsely decorated and none of it looked like it was hers. It didn't feel like a home. Lien pulled a tin out and measured tea into a basket that fit into a ceramic teapot decorated with birds and branches.

"I'm sorry about your teapots," he offered, making conversation.

Lien turned and frowned. "Teapots?"

"Trevor said a shelf fell and broke your favorite teapots?"

Lien's eyes were glazed with confusion as she tried to make sense of his words. As if a memory surfaced, she touched her face, then nodded.

"Ah, yes."

Caleb could tell she was scrambling to cover what happened and he pushed further. "I'm a carpenter. Do you want me to look at the shelf? See if I can mount it better?"

Her eyes darted around the kitchen. Caleb's followed. Not only was there not a shelf that had fallen anywhere visible, there weren't any shelves at all. She shook her head. "No, fine."

River was digging in the box of toys, pulling out colorful pieces that didn't seem to make any sense to him. He stacked them next to him and peered in. Caleb sat on the floor next to him and picked up the discarded pieces.

"These are Legos. Do you know what Legos are?"

River shook his head and watched mesmerized while Trevor began snapping the pieces together into a tower. When he was done, he gestured for River to hand him his action figure and proceeded to knock the tower over with the legs of the action figure. At first, River looked terrified, but as Caleb began to laugh, so did the boy. They repeated the cycle over and over until Lien set the teapot and cups on the table. Caleb got up and ruffled the boy's hair as he went over to sit across from Lien.

"Thank you," she said, motioning to the now scattered toys. She poured him a cup of tea and slid it over to him with cream and sugar cubes.

"Sure, they were sitting in a closet, anyway. Toys should be played with. Oh, and I brought cookies." Caleb fished the container of cookies out of the toy box and set them on the table between their cups.

River jumped up and stared at the cookies, his eyes never blinking. Caleb opened the cookies and took one out, then met Lien's eyes. "Can he have one?"

Lien bobbed her head, seeming unsure. Caleb handed the cookie to River, who could barely contain his excitement. The boy nibbled the cookie and did a little dance as he polished it off in a flash.

Caleb laughed and faced Lien. "It's like he's never had a cookie before."

Lien watched her son, then met Caleb's eyes. "Trevor doesn't like sweets."

"Good thing he isn't here then, isn't it?" Caleb replied, not able to hide his irritation.

A car door slammed nearby and Lien jumped to her feet, almost knocking over the teapot. Caleb followed suit, startled by her reaction. She went to the window and peered out, then sighed in relief. Caleb understood. She thought Trevor was home.

"Are you alright?" he asked, concerned.

She twisted the knot on her blouse and smiled. "Yes."

"I mean, like always. Are you safe?"

Her face turned red as she cut her eyes away. "Need to clean. Thank you for the toys."

Caleb couldn't deny he was getting the brush off and stood awkwardly, not sure what to do with himself. He grasped the teacup she'd poured and drank it in one large gulp. "I guess I'd better get on to work. I hope you enjoy the toys, River. Thank you for the tea, Lien. If you need anything, we are right next door."

Lien began to tidy the kitchen and Caleb took it as a message it was time to leave. He slipped past River and went to the door, glancing back as he opened it to go outside. Lien had her back to him and didn't turn around. He could see her back was rigid and even River was watching his mother, his face worried. The boy shifted his eyes to Caleb and smiled, holding up a brightly colored tower of Legos. Caleb smiled back and stepped out into the sunlight. He couldn't shake the feeling he'd done something wrong and headed for his truck. He let the hood slam shut and climbed in the front, his eyes still on the neighbor's house. He'd done the right thing by giving River the toys, hadn't he?

The question gnawed at him all day while he was working. Driving home, he forgot to swing by the liquor store as he considered the interaction between Lien and him early that day. Had he pried too much? Her mood shifted after he asked if she was safe, and he knew the answer to begin with. Trevor hadn't changed, and worse, Caleb noticed a gun sitting on the mantle of their home when he was there. High enough to be out of River's reach, but it wasn't River Caleb was concerned about.

He pulled in the driveway and saw Trevor's car parked next door. Anger rose in Caleb and he squeezed the steering wheel. He hadn't done anything wrong, he was only being neighborly. The toys were just sitting in the back of a closet and River obviously needed toys to play with. All children did. Caleb breathed out the hotness forming in his chest and pushed his truck door open. He was overthinking it. Even Trevor couldn't begrudge his son some free toys.

As Caleb headed for the door of his house, he thought he heard yelling coming from Trevor's house and paused, straining to see if he could hear what was going on. He heard River crying, then it fell silent next door. Caleb waited a moment but there was nothing else coming from behind those doors. He rubbed his head and stepped onto his porch. Trevor was a dick, but how could he be mad about some hand-me-down toys?

The next morning the box of toys was sitting on Caleb's porch, the container of cookies crushed to bits and placed on top.

The Door Opens

For the next few weeks, Lien and River weren't around much. Or they were around, but not visible from the outside. Caleb tried to see when he might observe Lien taking out the trash or playing with River outside, but it was like they weren't there. He wanted to go knock on their door and make sure they were alright, however, the message of getting the box of toys back let Caleb know it wasn't only not welcome, it was dangerous for them. He could easily take Trevor with one hand tied behind his back, but Trevor liked to prey on those weaker than him. Lien and River. Those who couldn't fight back.

One day, Caleb decided to swing home on his lunch break and was surprised to see Lien outside with River. River was collecting fallen leaves, bringing them to his mother, who appeared exhausted and worried. Caleb pulled in and got out of his truck, hoping to speak to her before she disappeared back inside their home.

"Good afternoon, Lien. How are you?"

Fear crossed her face and her eyes darted senselessly around. Almost like she expected an attack to come from anywhere. Caleb put his hand up, attempting to let her know he meant no harm. But she knew that. It wasn't him she was afraid of. It was Trevor's wrath that controlled their every move. He stopped in his tracks, afraid to go any closer.

"Hey, River," he said gently. The boy met his eyes but didn't smile. "Can I see one of your leaves?"

River glanced at his mother for approval and she gave a quick nod. River cautiously approached Caleb and handed him a large, gold-red leaf. Caleb flipped it over in his hands and smiled. He knelt in front of the boy.

"Thanks. It's beautiful."

River didn't reply but a tiny smile twitched at the edges of his mouth. Caleb noticed faded bruises on the boy's arms. Small ovals. Fingerprints. He glanced over at Lien, who was standing with her arms wrapped tightly around her. When she looked over at Caleb, he noticed the same faded bruises on her face. He stood up and took a step toward her. She seemed like she might run, so he paused. He tried to make himself as soft as possible to not scare her away.

"Lien, it's not okay that he's hitting you. You need to go somewhere safe." Caleb spoke as if he was calming a skittish horse. "Do you have any family nearby? Anyone you can stay with for a while?"

Lien shook her head, tears pricking her eyes. "Vietnam."

"You're from Vietnam? Do you know anyone over here?" Caleb asked, considering what it would be like to be in another country, not knowing anyone, not speaking the language well.

"No family here. Alone." Her words sounded resigned to her fate with Trevor.

"I see. What about Trevor's parents, River's grandparents? Can they step in?"

Lien laughed with bitterness and met his eyes, hard this time. "Say I'm dirty. They don't like me."

"Oh. Do they see River?" Caleb asked, trying to remember Trevor's parents from when they were in school. He seemed to recall they had a lot of money and moved away after Trevor graduated.

"No."

Caleb gazed at the boy, who was attempting to fill his pockets with leaves. So, Trevor's parents were shitty just like him? Not surprising. He got the feeling from Lien they were not part of their lives, likely because Lien was Asian. "Can I ask... why did you name him after Trevor?"

Lien peered at him in a way that said she didn't have a choice in the matter. Her eyebrows twitched but she didn't answer. She called out to the boy, "River, lunchtime."

Caleb noticed she was also calling him River and a smile crossed his lips. He watched River run to his mother and take her hand. A strange feeling passed over Caleb that reminded him of the night Shannon was killed. Like they weren't alone. He turned and stared into the woods, half-expecting to see the creature stalking them, but nothing was there. Lien followed his eyes and frowned.

"Must go. Not supposed to talk to you," she whispered. "I'm sorry."

Caleb's head turned so fast, he felt a muscle in his neck pull. "You aren't supposed to speak to *me*? Why?"

Lien touched her face like she had the time before in the kitchen and dropped her head. "Trevor said."

River observed the exchange and squeezed his mother's hand. The two of them were prisoners in their own home and had no way out. Nowhere to go. Caleb was fuming, but he had no suggestions to help. If he confronted Trevor, Trevor would take it out on them. If he ignored what was happening, they could end up dead. He pressed his forehead and grimaced.

"What about the police?" Caleb asked.

Lien's eyes got wide and she shook her head. "Trevor kill me. No police."

"Fuck. He can't just do this to you and get away with it. There has to be something we can do!"

"No. Nothing."

They stood staring at each other and Caleb wondered if he could get away with murdering Trevor and dumping his body in the mountains. The imagery gave him some satisfaction. As if she was reading his thoughts, Lien stepped over and placed her hand on his arm. She shook her head as her eyes cut into his. It was clear she didn't want him to get involved.

"Go. Don't worry." She turned and led River inside, not looking back.

Except that was all he could do. Caleb watched them go, feeling hopeless and trapped. He went inside and made a sandwich, racking his brain for a solution. Everything he considered had a bad ending. Tammy came in and set down some paint cans on the counter.

"Forget your lunch?" she asked as she rinsed her hands in the sink.

"Something like that. Hey, do you ever see anything strange next door?" Caleb replied and scarfed down the sandwich in a couple of bites.

"Slow down, Caleb, you'll choke. Next door... like Trevor and his family?"

Caleb tipped his head, then glanced out the window toward the house standing silent and lifeless. "Yeah. Like do you ever hear anything out of the ordinary?"

Tammy cocked her head, thinking about it. "No, if anything, it's too quiet. I mean, who has a four-year-old who isn't laughing, crying, or screaming most of the time? It's weird. Like, they just sit inside all day staring at the walls, you know?"

Caleb knew what she meant. When his own niece and nephew were around, there was constant noise, laughter, and arguing. "Yeah. I spoke to her outside and it looks like they both have been knocked around."

Tammy narrowed her eyes, then sighed. "It's no secret Trevor likes to beat up girls. I guess he hasn't changed his ways. Did she call the police?"

"No, seems like she's afraid to. Someone needs to give Trevor an old-fashioned beat down."

"Probably, but don't get any ideas, Caleb. We don't need that kind of trouble. Can you call in an anonymous tip?"

Caleb shrugged. "I think that would just make it worse. Cops show up, Trevor plays Mister Nice Guy and Lien doesn't speak enough English to let them know what is really going on. Then he takes it out on them after the cops leave."

Tammy leaned against the counter, chewing her lip. "No family or friends?"

"Doesn't sound like it. She's pretty isolated and maybe that was his plan all along."

"Abusers usually fit the same pattern. Isolation is a big part of that. Keeping secrets. I don't know, Caleb. I want to help, but I need to look out for Dad and my own kids. Maybe see if there is some kind of organization that can help. Let me ask at work."

"Yeah, do that. I need to get back to work. You working today?"

"No, I'm off, painting my room. Figured when the kids got home, I could take them and Dad out for ice cream. You want to come?" Tammy offered.

"Maybe. Let me see if Stephan wants to come along."

Tammy's eyes lit up at the suggestion and she grinned. "The more the merrier."

Caleb chuckled, recognizing the schoolgirl crush. "I'll ask him. What time?"

"Say five to be safe. Takes a bit to wrangle this crew up to go anywhere."

"Five it is. If I'm not home yet, leave me a note and I'll meet you there." Caleb checked his watch and sighed. "Fuck, going to be late. I'll see you later."

He hustled out the door and paused for a moment to stare at the neighbor's house. From the outside, it looked nice and quiet. Like any other home in any other neighborhood. Except, this home hid a dirty secret. One where a man thought it was alright to use his fists against his family. Caleb groaned as he got in his truck.

What power did he have to stop it?

By the time he was off work, Caleb had thought of and exhausted every possibility in his mind on how to save Lien and River. Outside of killing Trevor, everything had the potential to come back on Lien and make it worse. Besides, Caleb didn't think he had it in him to kill another human being. Even Trevor.

At home, he found the note from Tammy with where they were going and called Stephan to see if he wanted to go with them. Like Tammy, Stephan was a little too eager for the meet-up and said he'd be there as fast as he could. Caleb stood in the empty house after hanging up with Stephan and gazed around. He fished a bottle of vodka out of one of his hiding places and took a huge swig. What he really wanted to do was sit in the dark and drink, but he'd promised Tammy. He took another gulp, allowing the liquid to warm him up and create a nice fuzzy cloak around reality.

Stephan was already there when Caleb arrived and was talking up a storm to Tammy. Caleb noted she didn't seem to mind too much. Stephan was a mess, but he was kind and funny. Always cracking a joke. Bob was so serious, pursuing everything he wanted with doggedness until he got it, then moved on to something else. Like he did with Tammy. At least Stephan was transparent and didn't play any games.

Caleb joined his niece and nephew and pretended to try and steal bites of their ice cream, which ended up with peals of laughter and more than one spilled drink. Tammy eyed Caleb as she cleaned up the spills and shook her head.

"Kids," she said, pointing at the children. "Adult," she said as she pointed at Caleb. "See the difference?"

Stephan laughed and patted Caleb on the shoulder. "Caleb will always be a kid."

"Ha, you're one to talk," Caleb replied and winked at his nephew, who was still cracking up.

As they finished, Caleb helped his father out of the booth and they walked together to his truck. His father watched Tammy attempting to gather her sugared-up children into her car. Stephan stepped in to help. Being quicker than the children, he had them scooped and loaded up in no time.

"He's a nice boy," Caleb's father said quietly. "She deserves a nice boy."

"She does," Caleb agreed.

His father faced him, his eyes filled with sadness. "You deserve a nice girl."

"Dad..." Caleb started but his father put his hand up.

"You'll always love Shannon. However, being alone comes at a cost."

Caleb didn't have the energy to fight and helped his father into the truck. They drove home in silence and all Caleb could think about was getting to his room and finishing off a bottle. Shut down his brain.

After his father went to bed, Caleb did just that. He drank until he couldn't keep his eyes open and let the sensation drag him down under the layers. A living death, he thought to himself as he gave in to the dark.

The sound of a gunshot woke him up with a jerk and he listened, panting heavily. Was it just from the dream? All of a sudden, three more gunshots cut through the air and he realized it was coming from next door.

Trevor was killing them!

Father's Son

C aleb bolted out of bed and ran down the stairs, the alcohol causing him to lose his balance and fall on the landing. His knee smacked against a stair edge, sending shooting pain up his back. Yanking himself to his feet, he ran outside across the wet lawn, dreading what he might find. He made it to the house and began pounding on the locked door.

"Is everyone okay in there? Hello?"

To his surprise, Lien threw open the door with River in her arms. Her face was battered, her right eye swollen shut. Blood ran from her nose down her chin. She shoved the shaking child toward Caleb, who wrapped River in his arms and stared at Lien for what to do. The child clung to his neck as if he was drowning.

Lien's eyes were desperate and frantic. "Take River. Hide him, please. Run!"

Caleb did as he was told, but not before he saw Trevor's body splayed out on the floor of their living room, half his head missing. Blood pooled around Trevor's body and Caleb saw the gun on the ground near Trevor's lifeless form.

He ran toward his house, clutching River to his chest as sirens filled the air. Caleb spun around to see where Lien was. She was watching him from her doorway, her face covered in blood and an expression Caleb tried to put his finger on. Something which made him catch his breath.

She was relieved.

By the time Caleb made it to his front door, River was sobbing uncontrollably and had his fingers dug into the back of Caleb's neck. He was trying to climb up Caleb's chest as if he was attempting to get away from what he'd witnessed. Caleb got in and slammed the door shut, catching his breath as he listened to the sirens drawing closer. Lights flashed outside the windows and a glance out, showed Caleb Lien standing on the front lawn with her hands above her head. A police officer ran into the house and came back out, radioing for an ambulance. Neighbors were coming out to their front lawns to get in on the spectacle.

Caleb turned around and saw Tammy on the stairs, her eyes wide and concerned. She stared at him, then at the small, terrified child in his arms. Caleb put his finger to his lips to let her know to not let anyone know River was with them and she frowned.

"Caleb, what the hell is going on and why are you holding the neighbor's boy?"

Not wanting to say too much in front of River, Caleb carried him to his room and set the boy down on his bed. River didn't want to let Caleb go and whimpered when Caleb pried his tiny fingers loose.

"It's okay, River. You are going to hang out with me for a bit. You're safe here," he assured the boy, not being able to imagine what horror the boy had just witnessed. A quick check of the child didn't show any new bruises, but his eyes were empty and he didn't speak. Caleb laid him down and tucked him in. "I'll be right back. I just need to talk to Tammy, uh, my sister for a minute. I'll be right outside the door."

River never took his eyes off Caleb and clutched the blanket to his chin. Caleb got up and joined Tammy in the hall, closing the door so River couldn't hear them. Tammy peeked in on her own children, who were still fast asleep, despite the flashing lights and noise outside their window.

She came back to Caleb. "What the fuck happened?"

"I woke up from a dead sleep to gunshots. Like three or four. The first one was a little bit before the others, then it was like bang, bang, bang."

"Did Trevor shoot his wife?" Tammy asked.

Caleb shook his head. That's exactly what he'd thought at first when he heard the gunshots, too. "No, she shot him it looks like. He's dead. It appears he beat her up pretty good first, though. I think she was trying to survive."

Tammy sat down in the hall, pulling her robe around her. "Shit. How did you end up with the boy?"

"River. I ran over to their house, thinking Trevor was killing them, and banged on the door. Lien opened it and shoved River into my arms. She told me to hide him. I ran with him home, then."

"Why?" Tammy asked, crinkling her brow.

"I don't know. I guess cause his father is lying dead in a pool of blood and his mother killed him. I know she doesn't

85

have family and his won't accept her or River. Maybe to keep him out of social services? Foster care?"

"Maybe," Tammy murmured and rubbed her temples as she tried to piece it together. "Is this even legal? Having him here with us?"

Caleb shrugged and joined her on the hallway floor. "I have no clue. I just reacted. She told me to take him, so we have permission to have him here from a parent. Clearly, the other parent can't weigh in."

Tammy chuckled without humor and leaned her head against the wall. "Now what?"

Caleb didn't respond. He got up and went to a nearby window, facing the neighbor's house. An ambulance had arrived and the paramedics were rushing in with a gurney. They were too late to do anything, anyway. Trevor was most definitely dead, half his head blown away. Lien was cuffed in the front yard and a police officer was trying to get a statement. Lien stood quietly, not offering any explanation. Her eyes darted to Caleb's house and he moved his hand in the window to let her know he was there. If she registered his presence, she didn't show it.

A loud knocking came at the front door and Caleb felt his stomach drop. He met Tammy's eyes and gestured with his head for her to keep an eye on River. He checked his clothing for blood and not seeing any, headed down the stairs to the front door. A check of the eyehole showed a rather young police officer standing outside, holding a pad of paper.

"Fuck," Caleb whispered to himself, working out a story in his head. He opened the door and did his best to look sleepy and confused. "Hey, what's going on out here?"

The police officer looked at his notepad, then over to Lien still cuffed in the front yard. "Uh, there's been an incident. Did you hear anything unusual tonight?"

Caleb peered over at Lien, then shook his head. "Not that I can think of. I had a little too much to drink, to be honest, and passed the fuck out. What happened?"

The police officer leaned in close. "That lady shot her husband. Dead. Did you know them?"

"Um, I believe I went to school with the husband. Been a while, but I recognized him when they moved in. We didn't talk much. Just a hello in passing, really."

The officer jotted down some notes."Do you know if she speaks any English? We can't get a word out of her."

Caleb shrugged. "I wouldn't know. Like I said, just hello here and there. Why'd she shoot him?"

The officer looked like he was spilling a secret and blushed. "I may have said too much already. So, you didn't see or hear anything?"

Caleb acted like his fist and thumb was a bottle and pretended to drink from it. The officer laughed, then slammed his mouth shut. In this instance, being the town drunk was in Caleb's favor.

The officer stood awkwardly, then made his way off the porch. "Thank you for your time. If anything comes up, can you let us know?"

Caleb bobbed his head, glancing over at the flashing lights. He saw the coroner's car pull up and watched as the ancient man climbed out of the front seat, clutching a black medical bag in his hand. The police officer followed Caleb's gaze and sighed.

"Going to be a long night. Thanks again. Oh, one of the other neighbors said she thought they had a little boy living there. Have you seen a little boy? We checked the house and didn't find anyone else or any toys, things like that. There are a couple of bedrooms, but nothing specifically for a child, we can see. No sign of a child living there. Have you seen one?"

This is where it got sticky. Caleb didn't want to lie to the police, but his gut told him to do exactly what Lien asked him to do. Hide River. He cocked his head and frowned as if he was recollecting. He wondered where River's clothes were, or if they'd even looked.

"A child? Doesn't ring any bells. Girl? Boy? About how old?" Caleb asked, doing his best to seem helpful.

The police officer scanned his notepad, then shook his head. "Doesn't say. Only maybe a child living at the house."

"Hmmm, oh maybe the neighbor saw my niece or nephew. They recently moved in here. Their mother's going through a divorce. They're eight and five and play outside a lot. They may have wandered over into the neighbor's yard and been spotted by someone who thought they lived over there. Not too many kids here anymore, so that neighbor may have thought they moved in when Trevor and his wife did."

"Could be. Thank you, er... what was your name?" the officer asked. It was obvious he was new to the job and didn't know the protocol.

"Caleb Lache. My father also lives here, his name is Gary. He's got memory loss, though, so wouldn't be of much help. My sister is Tammy. She didn't see anything, either. She woke up with the flashing lights and asked me what happened. Sorry, we can't be of more help."

The police officer stepped back and stared up at the house. He pointed to the windows facing the neighbor's house. "What rooms are those?"

Caleb came out and looked up with him. "Oh, the hallway window, the bathroom window, and the kid's room."

"Do you think they saw anything?" the officer asked, digging for anything that might help.

"No, sir, we checked on them and they're sound asleep. Kids, you know? Will sleep through anything," Caleb joked.

The officer peered up at the windows, then shrugged. "Wouldn't know. Alright, Mr. Lache, thank you for your time, and if anything else comes to mind, please give us a call."

"I surely will, have a nice night, officer."

Caleb went in and shut the door, his heart pounding in his chest. He ran up the stairs and peeked in on River, who was lying with his eyes wide open, staring at the ceiling. Caleb went over and sat with him. The boy's eyes flicked over to Caleb, then back to the ceiling. Caleb rubbed River's arm and went to the kids' room. He snagged a stuffed dog out of a toy net and brought it into River. The boy took the dog and tucked it under his arm, his small face still expressionless.

Caleb stared out the window to the trees behind the house and wondered what mess he'd gotten himself into. A shifting in the trees caused his heart to skip a beat. Something was back there. He peered hard, trying to see what was out there, but it was too dark. He sighed and turned back to River. The boy had his eyes on Caleb, tears streaming down his cheeks. Caleb went over and lay next to River, wishing he could make it better.

Maybe now that Trevor was dead, it would be.

Beyond Words

The following morning, Caleb woke River up for breakfast. The boy sat up and peered around Caleb's room, confused as to why he was there. He rubbed his eyes with his balled-up hand, then grabbed the dog toy and climbed out of bed. Caleb had been around his niece and nephew their whole lives, however, this was different. River wasn't related to him and Caleb was about as far from being a parent as he could be.

"Hey, River. You want some waffles for breakfast? Tammy is making some downstairs. She's my sister and her two children are here, as well. Drew is eight and Sara is five. You can play with them."

River watched Caleb without expression, his dark, almond-shaped eyes peering out from under a shock of shiny, black hair. He looked just like his mother, lacking the pointed weasel face of his father. Caleb stuck his hand out and River grasped it. At least, that was something.

They made their way down the stairs to the kitchen, where Tammy was knee-deep in waffle making. A large stack of waffles was on the table and she had another going next to the waffle maker.

"Uh, Tams, I think that's enough waffles for now. We'll have waffles for days," Caleb teased.

Tammy faced him and smirked. "Well, considering you rarely cook, I thought I'd freeze a bunch so they can be popped in the toaster later on these busy mornings. Are you hungry?"

"I am. River, do you want a waffle?"

The boy didn't speak but clambered up in a chair and set his toy on the table. Sara recognized the dog and was about to claim it as hers when her mother gave her the eye that stops every child immediately. Sara pouted and eyed the stuffed dog with resentment. Caleb put a waffle on a plate for River and poured syrup on it. The boy stabbed the waffle and picked it up whole, attempting to eat it like a candy apple. Tammy chuckled and came over with a knife.

"Caleb, you have to cut it in bite-sized pieces for him," she explained as she took the waffle and expertly divided it up into equal small pieces. "He can't eat it like that."

"Oops, sorry. Not used to this whole being a responsible adult thing," Caleb replied and winked at River.

"Well, this isn't usually how it happens," Tammy said, then eyed him. "You have a minute to talk in the other room?"

Caleb followed her out to the living room, knowing she was going to ask more questions than he had answers to. He glanced out the window toward the neighbor's house, now abuzz with activity. Caution tape was tied around certain areas and police were putting markers around the yard. The front porch was blocked off with yellow tape, but the door was wide open as different people in suits went in and out, carrying plastic bags.

"Hey, Caleb? What are you going to do about the child? His mother could be going to prison for a long time and he needs stability. He needs a home."

Caleb turned from the window and chewed the inside of his mouth. "Tammy, I don't know. This wasn't anything I planned or was expecting. For now, I guess I'll just keep an eye on him until I hear otherwise."

"What if you never hear otherwise? What if she gets locked away for twenty years? The boy needs a family, someone to protect and look out for him. An adult who can make sure he's taken care of," Tammy insisted.

"Are you saying I can't?"

"Are you saying you can?"

That stopped Caleb in his tracks.

Tammy was right. Caleb couldn't even take care of himself. The bottles littering his trail were hard evidence of that. Besides, River wasn't old enough to go to school, so what would Caleb do with him when he needed to work? It wasn't fair to put that burden on Tammy. She already was overwhelmed with her job, her own kids, and Dad. Adding a small child to the mix was just too much. He supposed he could call social services.

Another child lost to the system.

"Fuck, Tam, just let me think on it a couple of days, okay? Maybe something will come of it and we won't have to worry. For now, he's fine. I can take a few days off work, we are caught up and I have a ton of sick days."

Tammy didn't look happy with the way the conversation went and picked at the wood on the fireplace mantle. "Why does this even matter to you? You barely knew them before all this happened."

Caleb shrugged. "I don't know. It just does. He's a kid who basically lost both his parents and had to wake up scared and alone. I guess I can relate."

Tammy stared at Caleb, then her face softened. "Fine. A couple of days, but after that some serious thought needs to go into that boy's future. You're no father and he must be seriously traumatized by what he saw over there. Has he said anything?"

"Not yet. He'll come around."

At that, they heard giggling coming from the kitchen and headed that way. Caleb's father was doing a magic trick for River, who was delighted. The boy clapped his hands together with joy but still didn't speak.

"Hey, Dad. This is River, he's going to be spending a few days with us. He's the neighbor's boy," Caleb explained.

His father turned to him and smiled. "Just showing him some magic. He seemed like he could use it."

Caleb again wondered who this fun old man was. Silly, goofy. River giggled again, making Caleb relieved for the distraction. He looked at Tammy.

"I hate to ask this so soon after our conversation, but I need to run to the store and grab River some things. Clothes, toothbrush. Can he hang out with you until I get back?"

Tammy frowned but nodded. "That's fine, but hurry back. I don't want your crazy promise to become my responsibility."

"I will, thanks."

Caleb left and made sure to not make eye contact with any of the law enforcement in the neighbor's yard. He was terrible at keeping secrets and this was a big one. As he got to his truck, he overheard a conversation that made him pause and his heart squeeze painfully.

"You know this is the second murder in this neighborhood? Some girl was killed back about a decade or so ago and they never caught her killer. Probably a disgruntled boyfriend. Heard she was knocked up," a skinny, red-faced officer, who looked like he was still in high school, said to one of the detectives.

The detective caught Caleb's eye and raised a hand. "Get back to work, we're here to gather information, not gossip," he told the younger officer.

Caleb ignored the gesture and climbed into his truck, fighting the urge to deck the skinny officer. He gripped the steering wheel and gritted his teeth. How dare they talk about Shannon like that? Like she brought it on herself? He turned the key and did his best to ease out of the driveway when he really wanted to gun the engine and squeal the tires out of frustration with what he'd just heard. That would only draw attention to him and he didn't need that while his neighbor's child was holed up in his house.

At the store, he quickly realized he was in over his head. He always just got Tammy's kids toys as presents, and probably not appropriate ones. He'd never bought children's clothing and stood in the middle of the racks, not knowing where to start. He tried to imagine River standing with him and pulled pants and shirts off the hangers to see if he thought they'd fit, holding them like an invisible child in front of him. A woman strolled by Caleb and snickered at him, causing his ears to flame.

"Fuck off," Caleb whispered under his breath and threw what he'd picked in the cart. He grabbed a few extra pieces and a jacket since the weather was starting to turn cooler. The toy aisle was easier and Caleb made sure to add a few things for Sara and Drew as well, so they didn't feel left out. He even bought Sara a new stuffed dog to hopefully smooth things over about the dog he'd taken from her room.

The gifts were well received, though River seemed unsure what he should do with them. Caleb bought a small bed to put in the corner of his room, as he didn't think it would be acceptable if the child slept in his bed. He went upstairs with the bed and a trash bag, then proceeded to clear the bottles and garbage out of his room. Once he was done, he put the bed frame together and added sheets with puppies on them. He didn't know if River actually liked dogs or was just clinging on the first thing he was handed, but when it was done, the bed was welcoming and fit for a little boy.

Caleb hauled the bag of bottles out to the trash and side-eyed the law enforcement still working next door. Other neighbors were finding reasons to stroll by and chat with the officers. Caleb overheard them talking about Trevor and his "foreign wife", how "you can't trust those people." He shook his head and walked to the backyard, not wanting to bring his anger back into the house with River around.

He wandered down a path toward the creek, letting the sound of the water over rocks drown out the sound of bigotry. Once he got down to the creek, he sat on a boulder and stared at the water. What would he do about River? Where would a child that was half white and half Asian find an accepting home with one parent dead and the other in jail? Poor kid didn't even know what was ahead of him.

Off in the distance, a long, sorrowful moan rose into the air, causing the hair on Caleb's arms to stand up. He scanned the area but didn't see anything. The wail erupted again, farther away this time. Whatever made the noise, was moving from the area. The sound brought a sense of déjà vu to Caleb and he listened to see if it would come again. It didn't and he shrugged it off. Something about the sound reminded him of another time. Of Shannon.

It hit him as he made his way back up the hill to the house. It was the noise he'd made when the police told him Shannon was pregnant. It was the sound of all his dreams shattering the universe. Tears sprung to Caleb's eyes and he wiped them away. Movement at the top of the hill caught his eye and he expected to see the creature.

Instead, River was standing at the beginning of the path, watching Caleb emerge from the woods. The boy clung to the stuffed dog and waited as Caleb drew closer, his dark eyes fixed on Caleb. He didn't make a sound but as soon as Caleb drew near, River extended his hand toward him.

Caleb took River's hand and squeezed it. That's what they had in common. They woke up one day to a world where everything they knew and loved had been destroyed.

Caleb wouldn't let River get lost like he was.

To Rise Again

O ver the next couple of weeks, things fell into a sort of routine. River continued to stay with them and Tammy didn't bring it up again. Maybe because Caleb was drinking less, or perhaps she was too tired to fight about it. The investigation into Trevor's murder continued and while the newspaper ran an almost daily section on it, nothing really came out as to how Lien was being charged.

What did come out, and Caleb wasn't expecting, was the rehashing of Shannon's murder. The town itself didn't have many murders and two in the same neighborhood, thirteen years apart, got people's tongues wagging. Was the neighborhood cursed? Could the murders be connected? Of course not, but people wanted drama where they could find it. Shannon's picture resurfaced and was run in the paper with various articles. The town's only known cold case.

Caleb did his best to keep his head down and focus on work and River. However, it seemed everywhere he went, he heard Shannon's name in the whispers on the wind. Some were kind but pitying, others still managed to blame her for her own murder. It was disgusting,

River hadn't spoken since before his father's murder and Caleb didn't push it. He and the boy seemed to form a way to communicate, which didn't require words. Tammy agreed to have River home with her when Caleb worked and Caleb in turn made sure her children were fed dinner, bathed, and did their school work. The once quiet house now had bodies at every corner. Children running through the halls, dishes always to be done. Caleb couldn't deny he preferred it that way. It was a lot easier to drink when it was just him and his father. He didn't want River seeing that, so he often stopped on the way home to have a couple in his truck. Either way, it was less because he didn't want to be drunk in front of the boy.

After work one day, Caleb was tossing his gear in the back of his truck when a man in a suit came up to him, carrying a briefcase. Caleb frowned as the man approached, wondering if he was a detective. The man smiled and stuck out his hand, holding a business card.

"Are you Caleb Lache?"

Caleb froze and his mind raced, thinking if he should tell the truth or tell the man to fuck off. He still had trust issues with law enforcement since they put him through hell over Shannon's death. "Uh. Maybe. Who are you?"

The man chuckled and put his hand up in mock defense. "Not a cop if that's what you're thinking. My name is Frank DeRossett. I represent Mrs. Strickland."

Caleb stood staring blankly at the man. Who the hell was Mrs. Strickland? He shook his head and put his hands up in confusion. "Sorry, I don't know who that is. You must have me mixed up with someone else."

"Oh. Caleb Lache? Doubt there are two of those in this town. I'm the public defender for Lien Hue, she was married to Trevor Strickland?"

Caleb nodded, understanding, but didn't say anything to the man. He wasn't sure what the lawyer was trying to dig at but if he represented Lien, maybe it was to help. Caleb took the business card the man was holding out and flipped it over. Public Defender. That couldn't be good. If that's all Lien had on her side, she was going to get splattered.

"Look, Caleb. I don't have much time and don't want to discuss sensitive topics out in the open. Can we go somewhere to chat for a bit?"

Caleb scanned the lawyer's face, searching for any signs of deceit. Not finding them, he squinted up at the sky and sighed. "I suppose. Mary's Diner has some back booths. Do you want to meet me over there, Mr. DeRossett?"

"Call me Frank. Sure thing, I'm famished. I won't take much of your time, however, there are some delicate matters that need discussing."

"Alright, follow me over. I can't stay long, I have..." Caleb stopped himself. He was about to say he had a little boy at home he needed to get to, but anyone familiar at all with Caleb knew he'd not been in a serious relationship since Shannon, much less fathered a child. "I have things at home to attend to."

"Right behind you."

They drove over to Mary's and found a back booth away from any prying eyes. Frank ordered a slew of food, Caleb only coffee. He glanced at his watch and waited for the waitress to disappear. Once she was out of sight, Caleb leaned forward. "What is this about?"

Frank bobbed his head and opened his briefcase. He withdrew a stack of papers, meeting Caleb's eyes. "Everything we're about to discuss is strictly confidential. Any word of this could affect Mrs. Strick-, uh, Ms. Hue's case. Do you understand the importance of discretion?"

Caleb agreed and tried to scan the papers Frank was holding upside down. Frank deftly moved the papers and put them in a neat stack next to him.

"First, let me explain her defense. Mr. Strickland had a history of abusing his wife and son. She never filed a report out of fear they wouldn't arrest him and he'd come after her. She's from Vietnam and has no friends or family here. So, she was trapped and said things became much worse after they moved in next door to you. Trevor became violent at the drop of a hat and what had once been shoving and slapping, became punches and brandished weapons," Frank explained.

Caleb shifted uncomfortably in his seat, not sure he should be told all of this information. "Okay?"

"Okay, so we are pushing for a plea deal that she was acting in self-defense. That evening, Ms. Hue says her husband became enraged at his perception she was trying to leave him. He found a small bag with some toiletries and the such, then confronted her. She claims he began punching her in the face. She heard their son, Trevor Jr., wake up and didn't want him coming out and seeing what was going on. Or worse, end up part of his father's rage. She grabbed the gun off the mantle and fired it once to try and stop Trevor. This only made him angrier and he ran at her, saying he was going to kill her and the boy. She shot him three times as he came at her. Missing once, striking twice."

"Why are you telling me this?" Caleb asked, his eyes darting around the restaurant to make sure no one was listening to their conversation.

"You need to know all the facts, so what I ask you makes sense. Let me first say, the plea deal would still lock Ms. Hue away for up to ten years, less for good behavior. If she doesn't take it and gets convicted, she could be imprisoned for life. Do you understand?"

Caleb bobbed his head. "So, ten years to life is what she is facing?"

"Yes, less for good behavior with the plea deal. Possibility of parole at seven years. She has a son, right?"

Caleb narrowed his eyes and stared at Frank. "I wouldn't know."

Frank smiled and shuffled the papers in front of him. "Trevor Jr., four years old. She told me everything. The boy is currently in your custody? At your home?"

Caleb wanted to get up and run out of the diner. At that moment, the waitress came back with Frank's full platter and Caleb's coffee. The two men dropped the conversation and thanked her. Once she left, Caleb waited for Frank to pick up where he left off. Frank took a bite of smothered hashbrowns, then wiped his mouth. He met Caleb's eyes.

"Look, let's not dance around this. Ms. Hue told me she asked you to take her son after the incident. To hide him. I hope he is still in your care?"

"He is. No one knows and I'd like to keep it that way."

"Is he well?" Frank asked.

"No, Frank, he isn't. He's fucking traumatized. He isn't speaking, he wakes up crying most nights. He walks around like a zombie, clinging onto a ratty, stuffed dog I gave him that night."

Frank tipped his head. "I imagine so. He needs therapy to work through what he saw. What he lived through."

"Yeah, well, since I'm having to hide him, that isn't a possibility, is it?"

Frank reached over and slid the stack of papers toward Caleb. Caleb glanced down at the pile, however, most of the legal language was above his head. "What's this?"

"Ms. Hue has asked if she could make you Trevor's legal guardian. She says she has no one else and doesn't want him getting absorbed into the foster care system."

Caleb began seeing spots behind his eyes and fought the urge to vomit. He swallowed back bile and fixed his eyes on the paperwork. Guardianship paperwork. He'd become River's guardian while Lien was locked up. Which could end up being River's whole childhood.

"How does that work?"

"You'd be given legal custody of the child until his mother is either released from prison or relinquishes the guardianship. This would give you the same rights as a parent. However, she has made it crystal clear that until she is released, you're the only one she trusts with Trevor."

"Stop calling him that."

"What? Trevor? That's his name, right?" Frank appeared confused and rifled through the papers in front of him. "Yes, Trevor Michael Strickland, Jr."

"His name is River. If we're going to continue this conversation, please call him that and not the name of his piece of shit father who beat him."

Frank gazed at Caleb for what seemed a moment too long, then sat back in the booth, sizing Caleb up. "Well, I can see now why she wants you to watch over the boy."

Caleb did his best to squash the irritation rising in him and shoved the papers back toward Frank. "Not to be a dick, but what's in this for me? I currently have my sister and her kids living with me and my father. River is sleeping in a bed in my room. We're barely getting by and to be honest, I'm not the ideal candidate here."

Frank leaned forward. "Oh, I think you are. Besides, you are currently the *only* candidate. I spoke to Mr. Strickland's parents. They want Ms. Hue to be punished to the extreme and they see the boy as an abomination. They think he was sent back to Vietnam, for whatever reason. They made it clear they do not recognize the boy as their grandchild."

"So, if I say yes... what happens next?" Caleb asked, feeling defeated.

"If you agree to be the boy's guardian, we'll fill out the papers here, then I'll file them. That's it. She is appointing you as the guardian and there are no contesters. In essence, you'll take over raising the boy and all his care. On the positive side, you wouldn't need to keep hiding him as you would be considered his stand-in parent."

Caleb drew the papers back toward him and considered the options. He either did this and protected River until his mother came back, or River would be removed and placed in foster care. "Fine, I'll sign the papers. I'm not thrilled about this, mind you, but I don't want River to end up being shuffled around until his mother gets out. You'll need to explain all the legalities to me, though. I haven't so much as opened a credit card in my name, much less agreed to be a guardian for someone else's child."

"Sure thing. We can go page by page and you'll get copies of all of this once it's finalized," Frank explained.

They went through each page, Frank making sure Caleb understood the language before he signed anything. At the end of the document, Frank double-checked the signatures and slid the paperwork into his briefcase, clipping it shut. He paid for his food and Caleb's coffee, then the two men headed out to their vehicles. A thought crossed Caleb's mind and he turned to Frank.

"What happens if she's sentenced to life?"

"We're doing our best to make sure that doesn't happen," Frank answered and placed his briefcase on the passenger seat. "We're trying to assure the minimum sentence, considering the circumstances."

"I mean, what happens to River? What if Lien is sentenced to say even fourteen years, making him eighteen when she gets out of prison?"

Frank paused and rubbed his chin. "Not sure what you are asking here specifically, but River will stay with you as long as you and she deem it necessary."

Deem it necessary. So, if Lien was locked up for the next fourteen years, Caleb had just agreed to watch over River for the rest of his childhood. Even if the plea deal was accepted, he'd agreed to the next ten, or so, years.

Tammy was going to kill him.

It Comes

"**Y**ou fucking did what?" If Caleb had expected Tammy to be angry, he had no idea just how angry she could be.

Her face was almost as red as her hair and her chest heaved with rage.

"Tam, I had to. He has no one. Lien asked me to," Caleb feebly replied, trying to get his sister to calm down.

"What *is* this woman to you? Did you have something going on with her?"

Caleb laughed at this, then instantly regretted it, as Tammy's eyes narrowed to such a tight slit, he expected her to leap at him and rip his throat out. "No. I hardly knew her. She made me tea once and we said hello in passing. That was it."

"So, that was it, but she basically handed her child off to a complete stranger? Something doesn't seem right here," Tammy spat.

"What choice did she have? It was pretty much me or social services."

"Did you ever consider maybe social services would be better for him? He could find a stable family, not a raging-" Tammy stopped herself, but Caleb knew where she was going with that.

"An alcoholic. I get it and I'm doing my best to keep that under control if you haven't noticed."

"Oh, I noticed, but I also know all it takes is one small shove to push you back over the edge. Raising someone else's child is definitely that shove. Right off the cliff," Tammy replied, her eyes opening a little more but her mouth held in such a tight line, it looked like she didn't have any lips. "Caleb, can you honestly say this has nothing to do with what happened to Shannon?"

Caleb froze, discomfort stirring in him over her asking such a horrible thing. He took a deep breath and decided not to answer her last question. "Look, Tam. It's done. I signed the papers. It's legal. I can't go back on my word now and leave River in this world all alone."

Tammy blew out her anger and gripped the counter she was standing in front of as if she was going to vault over it and come at him. She shook her head. "Now what? I can't keep watching him while you are at work."

"I'll look at childcare," Caleb responded.

Throwing her head back, Tammy roared with laughter. "Will you, then? Do you even have a clue how much that costs? Even with all of us living here, we're just getting by."

Caleb didn't have a reply and hung his head. She was right. With both her and him working, they had the bills covered, but that was about it. He couldn't swing day care, at least not a good one. "I'll figure it out, alright?"

Tammy turned her back to him and began slamming pans onto the stove. Caleb waited for her to come at him again but she ignored his presence. He got up and peered into the living room where River was playing with Drew and Sara. Well, Drew and Sara were playing, River was sitting watching them as he clutched the toy dog to his chest.

Caleb sighed and went out to him. "Hey, River, you want to take a ride with me?"

The boy stood up and nodded, still not having said any words since the night Caleb brought him home. Caleb put his hand out and River took it. Drew's eyes lit up.

"Where are you going, Uncle Caleb?"

"Oh, just heading into town for a few things. You want to come along?"

Drew considered it, then shook his head. "Nah, I'm going to help Mom cook dinner."

Caleb watched his nephew and was proud of the kid he was. He was wise beyond his years and seemed to comprehend the pressure his father's choice put on his mother. "I'll bring back dessert, okay?"

"Dessert?" Sara yelled, her attention fully on Caleb now. "What kind?"

"What do you want?"

Sara scrunched her nose and tipped her head as if that was the most difficult question. Then she smiled. "Triple chocolate cake!"

"Triple chocolate cake it is! That sound good to you River?" Caleb asked the boy. River stared at him, not understanding the question. Oh, yeah, that's right. Trevor didn't let him have sweets.

Caleb squeezed his hand with a smile. "You'll love it."

They loaded up into the truck, then headed into town. As Caleb walked around the store with River in the shopping cart, he got some weird stares from the townsfolk. *Town drunk and possible girlfriend murderer Caleb Lache now has a half-Asian child?* Caleb ignored the prying eyes and gathered groceries, including the much-requested triple chocolate cake.

After checking out and loading River into the truck, Caleb fought a battle within himself. He could see the liquor store from the grocery store parking lot and it was calling to him. He'd tapered off since taking care of River, but couldn't deny the taste of vodka would hit home at the moment. He could almost taste it already. He'd wait until the boy was in bed asleep, then only have one.

His mind set, Caleb drove over to the liquor store and parked. How would he explain River to Mo? All of a sudden showing up with a child in tow... to buy booze. Fuck. No matter how he imagined it, he looked like a horrible person bringing a small child into a liquor store, in the middle of the day, to buy alcohol.

He turned to River. "I just need to run in here real quick. You can see me from the front window. Stay buckled and I'll be out in a few seconds. Alright?"

River stared at him, silent, but a flash of concern crossed his tiny face. He hugged the stuffed dog close and nodded. Caleb ruffled his hair and got out of the truck.

"I'll be back in the blink of an eye."

Caleb went straight back to where his drink of choice was and grabbed two bottles. Made sense to stock up so he didn't have to come back anytime soon. He grabbed a third bottle with that reasoning and made his way to the register, peeking out on River in the truck. River's eyes were locked on the liquor store door and he looked terrified.

Feeling guilty, Caleb slammed the bottles on the counter and dug his wallet out. He threw a newspaper in with the bottles, pretending he was not there only for the alcohol. Mo came up and raised his brows.

"In a rush?"

"You could say that," Caleb replied. "Got ice cream melting in the truck."

Mo cocked his head, clearly reading the lie but choosing to ignore it. "Don't want that. Here, you're all set."

Caleb scooped up the bag of bottles as they clanked together and headed for the truck. River appeared relieved to see him and Caleb slid in next to the child, handing him a lollipop he'd bought. "See? Just a few minutes."

As he drove out of the parking lot, he saw Mo watching him from the window, his eyes fastened on River in the passenger seat. Shame washed over Caleb as he realized Mo would know he'd left River alone in the car. Caleb raised his hand in a wave, but Mo shook his head and disappeared out of view. Even the owner of a liquor store doesn't want his products to be the reason a child is neglected. Caleb wanted to be angry about Mo's judgment, however, he couldn't blame him. It was stupid to leave River alone in the truck.

As he eased the truck into the driveway at home, he noticed Stephan's car parked on the road. He'd been spending a lot more time with the family and Caleb was glad for the distraction. Tammy avoided heavy conversations when Stephan was around. Helping River out of the truck, he handed the boy a light bag to carry in. River clutched it in one hand and the stuffed dog in another.

Stephan was chatting with Caleb's father when they came in. He jumped up and grabbed a couple of bags out of Caleb's hand. Caleb made sure to keep his bottles with him. He ran upstairs and shoved them under his bed for when River went to sleep. He could do this, he could moderate his drinking.

However, during dinner and the small talk after, all Caleb could think about was the bottles under his bed. He could practically taste the booze sliding down his throat. When it was River's bedtime, he had to slow himself down from speeding through the books he read to the boy. Tempted to skip pages, he reminded himself River needed stability. He made it through the last book and watched River, who was starting to doze off.

Once he was sure River was asleep, he went over to his bed and opened the newspaper he'd bought. Like a punch to the gut, there was Shannon's picture and an article rehashing her murder. Knowing better, but doing it anyway, Caleb scanned the article. Maybe for a new tidbit in her case. Or for absolution. Instead, he was raked over the coals once again. The article never mentioned his name, however, it alluded to their relationship and her unknown pregnancy. Caleb closed the paper with more force than required and eyed River's sleeping form.

Maybe Tammy was right, maybe some of this was about Shannon and him seeking forgiveness. He reached down and eased a bottle out from under the bed. He gently turned the cap so it didn't make a crackling sound and took a gulp.

He was surprised when he went to take a sip a bit later and the bottle was empty. River was still out, so he pulled another bottle out and opened it. He wasn't sure when he finished that one and opened the third bottle, but when he opened his eyes to the sun creeping into the sky, his head was pounding and all three bottles were empty.

Caleb groaned and sat up, placing his feet on the floor to gain some stability. The room spun and his stomach threatened to spew as he glanced over at River's bed. It was empty. Caleb frowned and looked at the time. It was still early and River usually waited for Caleb to wake up before leaving the room. Caleb rose, ignoring the waves of nausea that greeted him and went to the children's room. Both Drew and Sara were still asleep. He checked on his father, who was also dead to the world. Where the hell was River?

Caleb went through the house, checking all the rooms, but River was nowhere to be found. Panic set in and he started calling the boy, softly so as to not wake up the rest of the house. Caleb stepped outside and peered across at the neighbor's house. Had River gone back over there? Maybe searching for his mother? Caleb made his way across the lawn toward the house when something down at the creek stopped him in his tracks.

The creature was standing on the other side of the creek. In the daylight, Caleb could see it had an almost grayish cast to its skin. Its arms hung low at its side and it didn't seem to have any fat on its body. Its long legs ended at almost claw-like feet. Human-shaped feet but with sharp, thick talons at the end. It caught sight of Caleb and its red eyes narrowed, as if it was sizing up fresh prey. Caleb froze in place, not sure if he should run and hide or stay perfectly still. His decision was made when he spied something else by the creek.

River was standing on the other side across from the creature. He had his stuffed dog extended out to the monster, his other fingers tucked in his mouth. The creature extended its arm to River and took one single step over the creek toward the boy. Caleb heard yelling and realized it was coming from his own mouth.

"Get the fuck away from my child!"

In the Light of Day

C aleb ignored the rocks and thorns ripping at his bare feet as he ran as fast as he could toward the boy and the creature. River was mesmerized by the huge beast and didn't turn to see Caleb bearing down on them. The creature paused crossing the stream and observed with a mix of interest and what seemed like humor as Caleb made his way down the hill to the creek. It bent down to the boy, placing its long taloned fingers on River's shoulder, then scooped him up in its massive arms.

"No!" Caleb screamed as he watched the boy being enfolded to the monster's chest.

The stuffed dog fell out of River's hands as he was transported off the ground in the creature's arms. This snapped the boy out of his stupor and he began to cry, reaching down for the toy with both arms. Distracted, the creature froze, staring from Caleb's impending form to the soft blue and white toy on the ground. Caleb took the opportunity to snatch a branch off the ground and ran at the monster, swinging full force.

The first swing landed squarely on the creature's elbow, causing it to lose grip on River. The boy began to tumble from the long arms, but the creature quickly recovered and snatched the boy's waistband, preventing him from hitting the ground. Caleb took another swing, this time lower so it hit the beast about midleg. It stumbled back, clinging onto River as it regained its footing.

"River, jump!" screamed Caleb as he used all of his energy to come at the creature. He swung the branch as hard as he could, except this time the monster caught the branch midswing and yanked it away from Caleb like a toothpick.

At that moment, River thrust himself out of the creature's grasp and hit the ground. Caleb grabbed the boy and his toy dog and ran back toward the house, his feet slipping on the wet, muddy path. River clung to his neck, making it even harder to move, but Caleb pushed on. Afraid to look back, he kept scrambling up the hill, refusing to let go of River. When he got to the top of the path, he glanced back. The creature wasn't there, or if it was, it was camouflaged by the trees. Caleb set River on the front porch and leaned over, vomiting until he could do nothing but dry heave.

River began to sob at Caleb's feet. Caleb knelt down and wrapped his arms around the small child, feeling tears trying to fight their way out of his eyes, as well. He handed River the stuffed toy dog and pressed his head against the boy's forehead as he composed himself.

"I'm sorry, River. I shouldn't have... I need to stop fucking up. Are you okay?"

River stared up at him with large teary eyes and nodded. He pointed back down to where the creature had been and rubbed his nose.

"I know. I'm scared, too. You can't leave the house without me. Do you understand?"

River sniffed, hanging his head. Caleb held the boy close to him and took a deep breath. What the fuck was that thing? He'd realized as he was swinging on it, it had to be a minimum of fifteen to twenty feet tall. At least. It seemed as tall as their house, though his perception might've been skewed by fear. What he did know, is he was nowhere near hitting it in the head and he stood six feet tall himself.

Caleb rose and picked River up, holding him to his shoulder. More than a promise to Lien, he genuinely cared for the boy and couldn't imagine anything happening to him. They went inside and Caleb set River on the couch.

"Just going to put some coffee on. Stay right here. Don't ever go anywhere without me again." His voice sounded more stern than he meant it to, but if it scared River to stay close, then so be it. Caleb couldn't lose him, too.

After he put on coffee, Caleb brought River juice and a pastry. He clicked on cartoons and sat next to the boy on the couch. River placed his tiny hand on Caleb's leg and moved in close to him. Regardless of how they came together, they were a family now. River quickly became distracted by the bright characters on the screen and nibbled mindlessly on the pastry. Caleb glanced out the window to see if he could spy anything out there, but the woods sat empty and quiet. The creature was gone from sight.

For now.

He thought again about his dream with Shannon and her message, "He's back." Had the creature grabbed her when she got close to her home, then dragged her into the woods? Murdered her? If so, why? Her body was intact and hadn't been gnawed on or desecrated. The police had ruled out a wild animal attack because of that. So, if the creature *had* killed her, it wasn't for food. Caleb shook his head, he didn't want to think about that.

However, now he couldn't deny what he saw was real... and it seemed to be stalking him. Or River. He saw it at the river in town, and multiple times in the neighborhood. This was the first time he knew for sure it wasn't a shadow or trick of the eyes. He'd fought it with a branch. It was trying to take River. He gazed at the boy, whose eyes were following the characters on the television as if nothing happened. Caleb did a quick check to make sure the boy hadn't been injured. Other than a few scratches, he was fine.

As the rest of the family began to wake up, Caleb shook off the anxiety and considered if he should tell Tammy or not. He didn't want the children playing outside, but he also knew she'd never believe him. Blame it on the booze. The booze. He'd been drunk even when he woke up. He felt better after puking, however, could still feel the wooziness of the alcohol in his system and doubted himself for a moment. The scratches on River reminded him it was real. The creature had been there.

Drew and Sara came in and sat in front of the television, immediately absorbed into the action and Caleb got up to talk to Tammy. She was in the kitchen making breakfast. She turned when he came in and smiled.

"Thanks for putting coffee on. I need it this morning."

"No problem. Hey, don't let the kids play outside, right now. I thought I saw a mountain lion this morning. Down by the creek," Caleb fibbed, figuring that was more believable, yet still scary enough to keep the kids inside.

Tammy set the spatula she was holding and frowned. "Really? Damn. I wonder why it's coming so close to homes."

Caleb shrugged and stroked his prickly chin. "Maybe the new development they're building down the road. Pushing the animals up this way. Anyway, just make sure the kids stay close to the house. I'll take a hike back there later and see if I can find any tracks."

"That's smart. Stephan is supposed to come by in a bit. Maybe you can go together, for safety. Take Dad's shotgun."

"Good idea. You're spending a lot of time with Stephan. Something I should know about?"

Tammy blushed and grinned. "Not at this point. We're just talking. I could use any friends I can get right now. All Bob's and my mutual friends have decided to pick him in the divorce."

"Oh, shit, I'm sorry Tam. I'm here if you ever need to talk or anything."

"Well, except the bottle is your best friend and half the time I need someone, you're passed out."

Now it was Caleb's turn to blush. He shook his head, embarrassed. "Sorry."

Tammy turned back to the stove, flipping pancakes. Caleb watched for a moment, wanting to hug his sister and promise to do better, but he didn't even believe it himself. He didn't even know who he was half the time. Instead, he headed back to check on their father. He was still sound asleep, so Caleb went into the living room where the kids were glued to the television set. A soft knock came at the door and Caleb opened it to see Stephan standing there, holding a cantaloupe in one hand.

"Hey, Stephan, Tammy's in the kitchen. What you got there?"

Stephan held the melon up and tried spinning it on his finger, catching it right before it smashed onto the ground. "Cantaloupe delivery."

"Okay?" Caleb said and chuckled.

"I don't know, I just bring what she tells me."

"Tammy?"

Stephan grinned. "That's the one."

"Hey, you want to take a hike in the woods in a bit? I thought I saw an animal back there and want to make sure it's safe for the kids."

"Sure! Let me give this to your sister and we can go."

Caleb wasn't sure he was ready to go back into the woods so soon, but his family was everything to him and he knew it was necessary. "I'm going to go throw on some shoes and grab Dad's gun. Can you let Tammy know River will be with the kids and to keep an eye on him?"

"You got it. I'll meet you on the porch," Stephan replied, heading for the kitchen.

Caleb threw on hiking boots and a flannel over his t-shirt. He went to his father's room and removed the shotgun and shells from the locked closet with the key from the top molding. He walked over to his father's form and made sure he was breathing. His father rolled over and stared at Caleb for a moment like he didn't recognize his own son. His eyes came into focus and he smiled in recognition, placing his hand on Caleb's.

"Hey, Dad, it's me. I'm borrowing the gun. Thought I saw a mountain lion and am going to scare it off. Tammy's making breakfast."

His father nodded, then went back to sleep. Caleb met Stephan on the porch and they hiked down to the creek. Stephan was looking low for a mountain lion, while Caleb was scanning up. After an hour, they didn't find anything and started the trek back to the house.

Stephan stopped and crouched down, running his fingers through the dirt. "Hey, look at this crazy print."

Caleb came up beside him and shuddered. It was a long foot and at the end, indentions made deep holes in the mud. He considered telling Stephan what he saw that morning, however, it died in his throat. "Weird."

"Looks like a dinosaur or freaky bigfoot track, right?" Stephan said, laughing as he stood up.

"It looks like something. Probably where a large branch fell and made a strange impression is all," Caleb replied, forcing a laugh to make it seem like nothing.

"Well, at least it's not a mountain lion."

Caleb preferred if it *had* been a mountain lion. That would be easier to take down. "Let's grab breakfast."

Back at the house, the kids had moved on from cartoons to drawing with crayons and paper at the kitchen table Caleb checked on River, who was focused on his drawing. It was a crude drawing, but seeing what he'd created on the paper made Caleb catch his breath.

At first, it looked like a picture of a house in the woods. *Their* house in the woods. However, when Caleb leaned closer, the morning's events resurfaced.

Hovering in the trees was a large, dark shadow with red eyes and long arms reaching toward the house.

The Weight of It All

The public defender called about a month later to inform Caleb that Lien accepted the plea deal and was sentenced to ten years in prison. Caleb felt his knees buckle at the news and didn't try to stop the tears from streaming down his face. River was four, he'd be fourteen by the time his mother was released from prison. The public defender said she could possibly get out early on good behavior but nothing was guaranteed. Even so, she'd serve years before release. Years River wouldn't have his mother.

"So, what does this mean for the guardianship papers?" Caleb asked, fearing he already knew the answer.

"They stand as long as you want them to. Lien wants River to stay with your family. She understands the gravity of the situation and wants what's best for the boy."

"She doesn't even really know me. We only spoke a handful of times. How can she know this is what is best for River?" Caleb replied, his heart beating rapidly in his chest.

"The alternative is the boy gets absorbed into the system and as history shows, it's not always the most nurturing place for children. How's he doing?"

Caleb glanced over at River who was giggling with Sara on the couch. He still wasn't speaking but had bonded with the other two children. "Alright, considering the circumstances. He keeps drawing pictures of his mother. I think he wants to visit her."

"That can be arranged. She's being transferred to the women's prison tomorrow in Shelby County. As soon as she's been processed, I can let you know about visitation days. Look, Caleb, I know this is all a shock, but you're doing right by the child. I've seen children get lost in the system. Abused, neglected, and shuttled from home to home, then dumped on the streets at eighteen. He deserves better."

"I know he does. However, I won't lie, I have my own issues and financially we're struggling. Raising a child wasn't in the cards." When he said it, Caleb's thoughts went to Shannon's pregnancy. The child they never had. What if that child came back as River and he was about to hand him away?

"It's your call. No one is forcing you to raise River. I can have him picked up today if that's your wish," Frank replied, his voice hiding any emotion.

Caleb shook his head, imagining River being dragged off by another stranger. "I can't do that. He's finally starting to come out of his shell again."

"Do you want him to remain in your custody for the duration of Ms. Hue's incarceration?"

"Yeah. We're the only people he knows, now," Caleb answered, knowing he was River's only chance.

"Would you be open to adoption? Ms. Hue asked me to see if you'd be willing to adopt River. No obligation, but it would make him your son officially and protect him from the system," Frank said.

Adopt River? That would make Caleb his father. "What would happen when Lien got out of prison if I did?"

"She'd be his mother, and you'd be his father. You could do a split custody arrangement or whatever you both agreed upon. You wouldn't lose your rights after her release if that's what you are worried about."

Caleb was silent, running the options over in his head. He could just retain guardianship and Lien could have River back when she got out. By then, River would be a teen and wouldn't remember his mother much outside of visits in prison. Caleb would already be his father. He sighed and pressed his thumb on his temple, trying to push back the squeezing headache forming. If he adopted River, he'd legally be Caleb's son. He and Lien would act as co-parents at her release. This would allow River more stability and a family to call his own no matter what.

"I'll adopt him."

As he said this, Tammy was coming down the stairs and her eyes grew wide as she heard the words. She froze halfway down and glanced between River and Caleb, her mouth hanging open in an almost perfect circle. Caleb shook his head at her, placing a finger in the air to let her know to wait to flip her shit until he was off the phone.

"Great! I'll draft up the paperwork and have Ms. Hue sign her portion. If you want to meet later this week, we can finalize the paperwork and get it filed."

"Hey, uh... Frank? I have one request. I want River to take my last name and have his name officially changed to River. Can you ask Lien if she's okay with that? I don't ever want to see the name Trevor associated with him again."

"Sure, I can do that. Considering she calls him River, as well, I can't see how she'd have an issue with that, but I'll ask," Frank promised. "I'll call you as soon as I can to meet up. Thanks, Caleb, you're doing a great thing."

Caleb watched River playing with his now cousin and knew River was a gift to him. "Thanks, Frank. I look forward to hearing from you."

As he hung up the phone, Tammy made her way down the rest of the stairs and motioned her head to the kitchen. Caleb followed her in and braced himself to get reamed. Instead, she walked over and wrapped her arms around him. This being exactly what he needed at the moment, he let tears fall and took in the choice he'd just made. He was going to be a father, a single father, to a boy who was traumatized in more ways than one. Tammy stepped back and read his eyes, her own brimming with tears.

"I'm so fucking proud of you, Caleb. I was against this at first, but I can see how much River means to you. How much you mean to him. I'll help however I can."

Caleb was surprised by the shift in his sister but wasn't about to question it. "His name is legally being changed to River Lache, if Lien is okay with it."

Tammy tipped her head, then chuckled. "Lache means duck, so he'll be River Duck."

Caleb nodded, then glanced over at his son. "Even ducks make waves."

"That they do, and I have a feeling that little duck is going to make some pretty big waves in his lifetime."

Caleb went in and sat down next to River, drawing the boy close. "River, I need to tell you something."

River watched for a second and a flash of fear crossed his small face. He was used to bad news. Caleb shook his head. "Not like that. Your Mom won't be able to come home for a while. We can go visit her soon, though, okay?"

River dropped his chin and fought back tears. No child should have to face being away from a loving mother. Caleb pulled him onto his lap and hugged the boy tight. "I know this is hard, but I want you to know we're your family now, too. Your mother has asked me to be your daddy. You'll be my son. Do you want that?"

River sat back and wiped the tears off his cheeks, seeking Caleb's eyes for truth. When he saw it in Caleb's eyes he nodded and gripped his thin arms around Caleb's arms. Caleb kissed River on the head and held him in silence for a long time. Sara asked River to come draw with her and Caleb loosened his grip.

"Sara's your cousin, now. Drew, as well. You'll always have them. Tammy is your aunt and my father is your grandfather. You have family that wants and loves you very much. You don't have to call me your father, but know I love you and consider you my son."

River climbed off Caleb's lap and went next to Sara. He focused on his paper, so Caleb got up and walked outside. He found his feet carrying him down the road and up the hill to Shannon's house. He went back into the woods where they found her body and sat down near the spot. Gut-wrenching sobs overtook him, he missed her more than ever. He imagined holding her close and whispered.

"Shannon, I think our child came back to me. To us. I'll never let you go and will love you forever."

Wind blew through the tops of the trees and for the first time since her death, Caleb didn't feel so alone. So isolated. He took a deep breath and rested back on the pine needles, staring up at the sky through the branches. He was a father now. Someone needed him. Someone wanted him. The eighteen-year-old boy he'd once been felt some of the wounds heal a little as he wiped the tears off his face. After a while, he sat up and glanced around, feeling like he was being watched.

He jumped up, realizing he didn't tell Tammy he was leaving and worried River may have tried to follow him. He practically ran all the way home. He paused near the porch, peering down by the creek where they'd seen the creature. They hadn't seen it since that day, but Caleb couldn't shake the feeling it was stalking them and wanted to come for River. The creek area was empty, so he went inside and saw River sitting with his father in the recliner. His father was reading a storybook and River was pointing at the dog in the picture.

Caleb stepped back outside and scanned the area. He could feel it. The creature. The hair stood up on his arms and he turned, gazing up the road toward Shannon's house. Movement in the trees made him catch his breath. He knew it was the monster. It appeared as if the trees were moving and the creature paused, rotating to face Caleb. Its eyes watched him for a moment, then it disappeared into the foliage.

Caleb knew it wouldn't end until the creature was gone. He rubbed his face and thought about what to do. For whatever reason, it was drawn to River and the boy was too young to truly understand the danger. He'd be at risk every time Caleb turned his back. Caleb knew what he needed to do. He sat on the stoop and worked out a plan in his head. Tammy could stay with Dad. Caleb had weeks worth of vacation saved up. He had the time, did he have the courage?

He needed to go after the monster. If it killed Shannon and tried to take River, he had do to what needed to be done. The beast would continue to go after the ones he loved unless he killed it. Only then, would they be safe again. Caleb had never harmed anything, chickening out when his friends shot squirrels and rabbits. He could never make himself pull the trigger. He didn't have a choice this time around. This time, they were the ones being hunted by the beast. He'd have to make himself do it. Track the creature and take it out before it hurt anyone else. His stomach flipped at the idea and he took shallow breaths to settle himself.

He'd likely need to take River with him, so Tammy wasn't overburdened while he was gone with caring for their father, her two children, and River. One less mouth to feed could make a difference.

He'd say it was a camping trip, some father-son time to bond. The weather was turning cooler but still warm enough to camp as long as they had a fire, tent, and sleeping bags. The trick would be to not let the creature know he was hunting it. Just a camping trip. It'd be a risk with River in tow, but Caleb knew he couldn't leave the boy alone. The child would try to follow him, anyway, and that would put him in danger. At least with Caleb, he could keep the boy under his wing for safety.

Keep an eye on him.

Caleb hung his head with the weight of what he was facing. He was sensitive, had always been. He needed to find the warrior in him. To tap into his rage and stop running from it. He didn't want to harm anything, however, he'd promised to watch over River. To keep him safe. He needed to do this to move forward, to start fresh in life.

First, though, he needed to quit drinking.

Stay Still While Running

Stephan agreed to be Caleb's detox buddy. River was shifted over into the children's bedroom now that he'd formed a relationship with them. At first, Caleb thought the boy might resist, but once River saw his bed next to Sara and Drew's bunkbeds, he was excited and climbed into it even though it was the middle of the day. At least, that part went smoothly.

Stephan and Caleb completely cleaned out his room, searching for any hidden bottles and ridding the room of the new collection of empty ones. Without River's bed in the room, Caleb felt a little sad but knew it was time for the boy to bond with the rest of the family. He needed to get his shit together to be a proper father to River.

Stephan brought a camping cot with him and placed it next to Caleb's bed. Tammy made sure they had plenty of snacks, water, and blankets. Stephan brought a small television, as well, so they weren't bored out of their minds. The plan was to lock in, except for going to the bathroom and having family meals until Caleb cleaned his system of alcohol.

When nighttime came, they watched television in the room and joked around, remembering all the trouble they'd gotten into when they were younger. Caleb tucked River in, then went to the bathroom. From that point on, the door was locked. They didn't want the kids coming in and seeing Caleb in the state he was sure to be in. Tammy camped out in the children's room in case River went searching for Caleb in the middle of the night.

Nothing happened the first few hours and Caleb thought maybe he wasn't as bad off as he initially thought. He paced the room, read for a while, and listened to music. Stephen dozed off after a bit. That's when Caleb began to feel anxious. He should go check on River, he thought. As soon as his hand hit the doorknob, Stephan sat up.

"Dude, where are you going?"

"To check on River. Make sure he's alright."

Stephan shook his head and pulled a blanket over himself. "He's fine. Tammy's in there. You'll just make him feel like he's not safe if you keep checking on him."

Caleb sat on the end of his bed and placed his head in his hands. Man, he wanted a drink. He couldn't fall asleep without one. Perhaps, quitting cold turkey wasn't smart. Maybe it was better to wean himself off a little at a time. Give his body a chance to adapt. Yeah, that made more sense. He stood up and went to the door, intent on seeing if there might be a beer in the fridge.

Stephan cleared his throat. "Don't make me tackle you. It's all or nothing. We're in here until you detox."

"I just need to run to the bathroom," Caleb bargained.

"I'm going with you if that's the case. I'll stand right outside the door."

Caleb felt irritation bubble up inside his chest and let out a heavy sigh. "Fucking fine. I'll hold it."

Stephan waited until Caleb sat back on the bed, then moved his cot in front of the door and plopped down on it. "Just in case you decide to sleepwalk tonight."

"Dick," Caleb muttered and flipped through a magazine, practically tearing the pages out as he turned them.

"Dick or not, I'm staying with you as long as it takes," Stephan said as he lay on the cot. His long legs stretched out and his feet dangled off the end of the cot.

Caleb watched him and wanted to argue, but he'd known Stephan long enough to know he couldn't win that argument. Stephan never lost his cool. He flopped back on the bed and stared at the ceiling.

It was going to be a long night.

By morning, Caleb hadn't slept at all and was beginning to regret his decision. Stephan got up and they took turns going to the bathroom. Caleb considered running downstairs while Stephan was in there but could hear Tammy with the kids and Dad in the kitchen. When Stephan came out, he eyed Caleb.

"Thought you might have tried to book it while I was taking a leak."

"I would've if I had a reason to."

"You want to go down and grab breakfast? See River?" Stephan offered.

"Sure."

They headed to the kitchen and Caleb was happy to see River playing pick-up sticks with Drew. As soon as River saw Caleb, he ran over to him, wrapping his arms tightly around Caleb's legs. Caleb scooped him up with a chuckle and squeezed the boy to his chest.

"I missed you," he whispered in River's ear. River sat back and met Caleb's eyes but didn't respond. Caleb kissed him on the forehead and set him down. "I promise, I'm doing this for us."

Tammy handed him a plate of hashbrowns and sausages, chewing her lip with uncertainty. "You okay?"

"Fine, mostly bored. Tonight will be tougher."

"I'm just a room away if you need me," she offered.

"Nah, you're helping by making sure River feels safe. Stephan is annoying me with his persistence."

"Good," Tammy replied and winked at Stephan. "Thank you for keeping my brother in line."

Stephan grinned, his ears turning pink. "You got it. Besides, I like knowing you're just a room away."

Caleb groaned at their obvious flirting and sat down with his food. He didn't want it but ate it anyway. He glanced at his father who was reading the paper across the table. His father was mindlessly chewing on a sausage at the end of his fork as he perused the news.

"Hey, Dad?" Caleb asked.

His father put the paper down and looked over. "What's up, son?"

"Can I borrow the shotgun and the tent? I was going to take River camping in a few days before it gets too cold."

"Sure. Why the gun?"

"Oh, thought I saw that mountain lion a while back. Just to be safe, you know?"

His father stared at him with rare lucidity. He set his fork down and peered hard at Caleb as if he was reading between the lines. "A mountain lion, you say?"

Caleb nodded. "Something like that."

"Hmmm. Does this have anything to do with our conversation a bit ago? About Bigfoot?" his father inquired.

Caleb laughed nervously and did a quick scan to see if anyone else was listening. They weren't. Tammy and Stephan were huddled by the sink, having their own private conversation and the kids were trying to stick straws up their noses. "Yeah, sort of."

His father leaned in and rubbed his nose. "You be careful out there. There are things we don't see or understand back in those woods."

"Have you... have you seen it?" Caleb whispered back.

"When I was a young man, working on a tree trimming crew, I saw something. Big, Gangly. Not Big Foot. But something. Some people say it's the Kentucky Wildman, but it isn't. More like an alien."

Tammy paused her conversation with Stephan and glanced over, her brows knitted. "Dad, what on Earth are you talking about?"

Their father picked up the paper and shook his head. "Nothing, honey. Just tales from my youth."

"About aliens?" Tammy asked sarcastically, snickering at the thought.

"Oh, you know. Just crazy things we see in the woods," her father replied without batting an eye.

"Grandpa, did you see aliens when you were younger? In the woods?" Drew inquired, suddenly drawn into the conversation.

Sara stopped what she was doing for a moment to listen. River kept playing with the straws, unaware of the conversation.

"Well, let's not get ahead of ourselves, sprouts. Sometimes the trees make weird shadows is all," their grandfather replied, not wanting to scare the children. "After breakfast, do you want to help me pick some pinecones to make birdfeeders?"

The children readily agreed and the previous conversation was all but forgotten. The old man winked at Caleb and touched his nose. Message received. Caleb and Stephan went back to his room with packed lunches and a stack of books. They put the television on and killed time playing card games and reading. By nightfall, Caleb was feeling his body shaking and wrapped a blanket around him. Tammy brought them dinner, then went to give River a bath.

"You're sister is amazing," Stephan murmured as if he was speaking to himself. "A real gem."

"Ew," Caleb teased.

"I know, I know. But seriously, I think I've been in love with her since the eight grade."

"Your eighth grade or hers? She's got three years on us, remember."

"Mine. Older women, am I right?" Stephan joked.

"I wouldn't know."

They stayed up until about midnight when Stephan yawned and rested on the cot. "You alright?"

"I've been better," Caleb replied, trying to steady the shakes. He felt like his insides were in a blender and his hands were trembling so badly, he could no longer read.

"I'm not going anywhere and can stay up with you. You want to play another card game?"

"No, man. Go ahead and close your eyes. I'm going to listen to music for a bit."

Stephan pulled a blanket over him and closed his eyes. He was still blocking the door, so there was no way for Caleb to get out unless he wanted to climb through the window. Within minutes, Stephan was snoring and Caleb tried to focus on the song he was playing. After a few minutes, he realized he was tuning out the music and reached over to cut the cassette tape off, making Stephan open his eyes. Caleb waved him off and sat on the edge of the bed.

By early morning, he was shaking so badly, the bedframe was rattling. Stephan came and sat with him, massaging his back and whispering words of encouragement. Caleb vaccilated between wanting to sob and wanting to smash everything in sight. He refused food and vomited into the bowl next to his bed. Stephan never left his side.

This went on for a few more days, Caleb couldn't really track the time. At times, it felt as if his organs were disintegrating inside of him, other times, he felt as if he was an empty shell. The worst was the hallucinations and random loud sounds he was hearing... like bombs going off. He couldn't sleep more than small increments at a time or eat. Even keeping water down was a challenge.

On the fourth or fifth day, he dozed off for a couple of hours and woke up drenched in sweat. Stephan was crashed out on the cot and the room was bathed in moonlight. Caleb's eye caught a familiar shape in the corner of the room as he sat up, bracing himself on the bed frame.

"Shannon," he whispered through cracked lips.

She was beautiful, glowing in the moonlight. Her face was perfect and she placed her hand on her chest as she smiled at him. Caleb could feel her love radiating around him and he held onto it as his body released the poison that had taken hold since her death.

She blew him a kiss and mouthed, "I love you."

Caleb tried to get out of bed and reach her, but his legs collapsed as soon as he touched the floor. He went down with a crash, waking Stephan up, who was at his side within seconds.

"Caleb, you alright? Here, let me help you up." Stephan grunted as he lifted Caleb back up onto the bed.

Caleb gazed at where Shannon had been, but she was gone. He could still feel her near him and knew he'd defeated the beast within him. He sat on the edge of the bed and chugged a bottle of water from the nightstand. It was over. He'd faced and conquered that which held him down for years. He smiled at Stephan and nodded. Stephan clapped him on the shoulder, grinning.

"I'm so fucking proud of you, man. Now, you can be a real father to that little boy," Stephan said.

Caleb wiped the sweaty hair out of his face. He could be a father to River, the father he deserved. First, though, he had another task to finish to make sure they could all be safe.

He needed to find the creature in the woods and take it down. End its reign of terror.

Once and for all.

From One to Three

O ne more item needed to be completed before Caleb could take River camping. He'd called Frank and asked for a few days to work things out before signing the adoption papers. Things being his detox. He still wasn't feeling a hundred percent and knew it would be weeks before he truly had the effects of the alcohol flushed from his system, but since seeing Shannon that night, he'd no doubt he could stick with it. He had one more request of Frank to complete the process.

"I want to do this in front of Lien. I need to know this is what she truly wants before we make it final. Plus, River wants to see his mother. Can that be arranged?"

Frank coughed lightly into the phone. "Absolutely. Let me work out the details and call you back with a date and time. You'd need to come to the prison, you understand?"

"I understand. It's important we do this with Lien, so she knows I intend to make sure River sees her and communicates with her as he grows," Caleb replied adamantly.

"You're a good man, Caleb," Frank said. "I'll call you back in the next day with the arrangements."

"Thanks, Frank. How long do you think it will take to get this all set up?"

"I'll pull some strings to expedite the process. Hopefully, by the end of the week."

They hung up and Caleb went to find River. He was playing hide and seek with the other two children. While Caleb spied his hiding place right away, he didn't want to spoil it and waited for Sara to find him. When she did, River squealed with delight and began running through the house. Caleb went after him and scooped the wiggling child up into his arms.

"River, let's take a walk."

Caleb helped River get on his coat and shoes. They headed out and hiked in the woods. River stopped to pick up baby pine cones and put them in his pockets. They made it to the creek and sat on the bank. Caleb tossed sticks into the water, watching them bob and weave down the stream. He turned to River.

"Hey... uh, we're going to go camping soon. Have you ever been camping? Like sleeping in a tent?"

River shook his head and threw one of his pine cones in the creek. It ducked past rocks and disappeared out of view. Caleb put his arm around River's small shoulders and hugged him close. River nestled in and they sat in silence for a bit.

"We're going to see your mother in a few days, okay? We're going to sign some papers, which will make you legally my son. Your mother will always be your mother, but she wants me to look after you while she's away. To be your father. She loves you very much. As do I, River," Caleb explained, not sure what River was absorbing. He tried to keep the terminology as simple as possible. "Would you like that?"

River played with a pinecone in his hands and didn't respond. Caleb wasn't sure he was grasping his mother wasn't coming back anytime soon. It broke his heart to imagine what was going on in River's head. It was a heavy burden for such a young child to carry. Caleb turned the boy gently toward him, meeting his eyes.

"River, I need to know you want me to be your father... your daddy. Not like your other father, who was mean. I'll never hurt you, do you understand that?"

River watched him, then put his arms up and wrapped them around Caleb's neck. Caleb drew him close and sighed, that was about all the answer he was going to get. He stood and picked River up, placing him up on his shoulders as he hiked back to the house. River grasped Caleb on the face with his hands and giggled as Caleb began to run with him. Caleb was out of breath by the time they made it up the hill. He swung River down to the ground, holding the boy's little hand in his.

When he got in, Tammy handed him a scrap of paper. "The public defender called while you were out. He asked for you to call him back right away. It seemed important, he asked me to relay this as soon as I saw you."

Caleb took the paper and walked over to the phone. He quickly dialed, his nerves shooting up. What if something happened? What if he couldn't adopt River? What if Lien changed her mind?

When Frank answered, he almost yelled into the phone, "Frank, it's Caleb. What's up?"

"Hey, thanks for calling back so fast. Can you make it out to the prison tomorrow? I was able to swing a time due to the urgency of the situation."

Caleb breathed a sigh of relief. "Just tell me when and where, we'll be there."

Frank gave him the instructions, what was and wasn't allowed, and the time to meet up. They'd meet out front, then go in together. It wasn't a normal visitation due to the legality of the process, so Lien would be brought to a room with them to finalize the paperwork. Afterward, Frank and Caleb would go straight to the courthouse and go before a judge to make it official. Frank told Caleb to dress in a suit if he had one and bring any required documentation.

The following morning, Caleb and River got up early to drive to the women's prison. Caleb dressed in a suit of his father's and made sure River had a nice outfit to wear. They looked like they were going to church. He gave River crayons and paper to keep him entertained on the long drive. Caleb was incredibly nervous and expected something to stop him from adopting River.

At the prison, Frank met them outside and guided them through a series of locked gates and doors. A few guards greeted Frank by name, which put Caleb more at ease. Frank knew the inner workings and seemed relaxed as they made their way through the maze to where they were meeting with Lien. Finally, they were shown to a room with a table and window. Caleb and Frank sat on one side of the table and Caleb held River in his lap. River colored on the paper, drawing a house and what looked like Sara playing outside, due to the bright red hair of the girl in the drawing.

When Lien was brought in, River's head snapped up and he began to cry. She was escorted to a chair across from them, but her hands remained cuffed. Her frail form seemed almost childlike as she faced them. She placed her hands on the table and stared at River with such longing, it broke Caleb's heart. River tried to crawl across the table to his mother, but the guard shook his head at Frank. Lien's face was crushed, being able to see her child but not allowed to hold him.

Caleb pulled River back and whispered in his ear. "It's okay, little man. Your mama is right there. You have to sit on my lap, right now." Caleb turned to the guard. "Can she at least hug him? He doesn't understand."

The guard pursed his lips and glanced at the door. "For one moment."

Caleb put River down and smiled at the boy. River ran to his mother and tried to climb in her lap. She struggled with the cuffs but managed to loop her arms around her son and hold him close. River pressed his face to her chest and sobbed. Caleb fought back tears and could tell Lien was doing the same as she cradled her son for the first time in months.

Frank cleared his throat. "We don't have much time, so let's get these papers taken care of. Are you both ready?"

Caleb looked at Lien for assurance. "Are you sure about this?"

Lien nodded and tried to wipe tears from her eyes. "Yes. River needs a home. A family to care for him."

"With me?" Caleb asked, needing her to say it.

"With you," she replied.

"Are you okay with changing his name? To my last name and legally to River?"

Lien smiled painfully, then tipped her head. "Of course. He is River now. He is your son. Frank told me about your girlfriend. Shannon?"

Caleb wasn't sure what that had to do with any of it and he stiffly cocked his head. "Yes. She was murdered when we were teens."

Lien's eyes told him she understood his sadness. "River Shannon Lache. I would like this to be his name."

Caleb's mouth hung open in shock. He glanced at Frank, who gestured that was totally acceptable. Caleb stopped fighting the tears he was holding in and let them flow freely down his cheeks. Using his sleeve to wipe his face, he composed himself. He watched River and it all made sense.

"River, would you like that?" Caleb asked, knowing the boy wouldn't respond. River leaned his head against his mother and nodded. Caleb rubbed his chin and cleared his throat. "Lien, I promise I'll take care of him until you get out."

"I know," she whispered and tried to stroke her son's head. "I trust you."

Frank pulled out the stack of documents and began explaining the process. He made sure each of them signed in their designated spots and kept the sheets in order. By the time they were done, River had dozed off in Lien's lap and the guard had thankfully turned a blind eye. He motioned to Frank, letting them know their time was up. Frank carefully slid the papers in his briefcase. He turned to Caleb with an apologetic expression.

"We need to go. They were being gracious in giving us this much time to get this finalized. Caleb, do you want to take River from Lien?"

Caleb wanted to scream, "No!", but knew it wasn't really a question. He met Lien's eyes with sadness and she fought back tears. She lowered her head, resting it on River's.

When Caleb went to ease River out of his mother's arms, the child woke up and clung to her, whimpering. Caleb felt like shit having to pry River from his mother's arms. He got River loose and held him to his chest as the boy cried. Lien murmured something in Vietnamese to River and he wiped his nose, shaking his head. Caleb stroked the boy's back and looked at Lien.

"He hasn't spoken since that night."

She frowned. "River?"

River turned to her and listened. Lien spoke to him in Vietnamese for a moment and River nodded, his chin quivering. She met Caleb's eyes.

"I told him he doesn't need to speak until he is ready but you are there to protect him. I told him you love him and will be the father he needs."

"Thank you, Lien," Caleb replied, knowing he was taking River away from his mother, yet again. "We'll visit as much as they allow. We'll write."

The guard tapped his watch and Frank got up. "We'd better get to the courthouse to meet with the judge. Thank you, Brad," Frank said to the guard. He turned to Lien. "I'll be in touch."

She dropped her head, staring at her cuffed hands. She didn't want to see them leave. Caleb walked out with River, who felt heavy in his arms. Like he was transferring his pain to Caleb. As they left, Caleb could hear Lien sobbing in the room and anger filled him. She was being taken away from her son for defending her life from a monster. For defending River's life, as well.

At the courthouse, they met in the judge's chambers and finalized the adoption. It seemed like it should be a bigger deal than it was. After the ceremony, Caleb said goodbye to Frank and took River to the truck. When he buckled the boy in, their eyes locked for a second and that's when the monumentality of the situation hit him. River was his son. Not just for a while.

Forever.

Caleb climbed in next to River and sat in disbelief at the circumstances. Once, he had a dream of marrying his high school sweetheart and starting a family with her. One night changed all that. For the last thirteen years, he'd been trapped between that dream and the stark reality of being alone in the world. He had his father, Tammy, and her kids. However, at the end of the day, he felt isolated, seeing them live their lives. Now, he had a son. A son he believed was meant to come to him. For them to find each other after all this time.

River Shannon Lache.

The Tender Journey

I t was before dawn when they got up and organized their gear. The house itself sat on the edge of the national park and it went miles back into the forest. Caleb didn't know how long they'd be gone but mapped out a couple of different directions, which would allow them to come by the house and regroup before heading another way. Each trek would go out for miles but bring them back when food and clean clothes ran out. Even so, he packed a week's worth of supplies for the initial run.

By the time they had everything tightened up, the sun was beginning to rise. Caleb made sure River was dressed warm enough and had his stuffed dog. River was too little to carry anything, so Caleb loaded the large pack with a tent and sleeping roll on his back, groaning at the weight. Even minimizing what they needed, still left so much to carry. Not wanting to lose track of River or have him fall, Caleb connected them together with carabiners and rope.

They left before the rest of the family woke up, not wanting to be held up by unsolicited advice and goodbyes. Stephan offered to go along, however, Caleb knew this was a journey he and River needed to take alone. Begrudgingly, Caleb packed the shotgun and shells, hoping he'd have no reason to use them. He brought an extra rope so he could suspend the gun in the branches when they stopped. He didn't want to risk River touching it.

Meandering down the worn path to the creek, Caleb paused and searched for tracks. It'd been a few weeks since he'd seen the creature and hoped it had moved on. His gut told him otherwise. Whatever it was, the beast was drawn to their family. He found one print but it looked worn, like it'd been there for some time. Even so, he glanced at what direction it was heading and tracked it along the creek. River walked behind him, mesmerized by all the sights.

By lunchtime, they stopped and Caleb was relieved to set down the pack. He worked manual labor but the constant carrying of the heavy bag was giving him a backache. They ate sandwiches and Caleb told River about how his own father used to take him on long hikes as a child. He left out the fact they were hunting trips and ended with them hauling a dead deer back through the woods. Caleb hated that part and refused to look the deer in the eyes.

River pointed off into the distance and Caleb followed his finger but didn't see anything out there. He gazed back at River, who had his eyes locked on something Caleb couldn't see. Caleb squinted and a flash of movement caught his eye. It was gone as quickly as he saw it. Probably just a deer. He gathered up their trash and shoved it in his pack. He made sure everything was wrapped in paper, so when they stopped for the night, he could start a fire.

They hiked until evening, Caleb noting a few tracks that could be the creature's. He marked their trail on his map and checked the compass to make sure they were staying on course. River began to get cranky, so Caleb figured it was as good time as any to set up camp. He slid the pack off and handed River a cookie.

"I'm going to set up the tent. You sit here on this log and have a cookie, okay?"

River took the cookie, clutching it in his hand as if it might vanish. He nibbled the edge all the way around. Caleb found flat ground and erected the tent. It was starting to get dark and he wanted to get a fire going before they were in pitch blackness. Once he started gathering twigs and branches, River was done with the cookie and wanted to help. As they piled what they found, Caleb felt a sense of pride in River. He showed River how to get the fire going, then they sat and ate a dinner of canned beans and rolls.

That night after they ate, Caleb could see River was running out of steam and took his hand, leading him to the tent. The light from the fire cast an orange glow through the tent walls, making it seem homey. They climbed in and Caleb told River a couple of stories before the boy dozed off. Caleb still couldn't sleep, so he read a book he'd brought to pass the time. There was something soothing about reading in the tent with River curled next to him. He wasn't sure when he dozed off, but a horrible, screeching sound jolted him awake.

"What the fuck?" he yelled and put his hand out for River. The boy was tucked in his sleeping bag, however, Caleb could tell the sound had woken him up, as well. "It's okay. Maybe just an owl."

He pulled River toward him and put his own body between the tent flaps tent and the child. All of a sudden, a loud thudding tore through the campsite, making River cry. Caleb peered out of the zipper but couldn't see anything. Something had been there, though, because their packs were strewn about. Bears. It had to be. He'd secured the food up high, but something had gone through their packs. Caleb sat back, steadying his breathing. Bears... that was all.

As soon as that thought settled him, the sound came roaring through again, this time knocking out most of the fire. Squinting out of the tent, Caleb could make out a large shape by the diminished fire. Too big to be a bear.

"Get the hell out of here!" he yelled, hoping to scare whatever it was away. The form froze, then rotated slowly toward the tent. Caleb realized his mistake and wished he'd kept the gun with him. The shape moved the direction of the tent and hovered over the top of it, its breath loud and rough. River whimpered and clutched Caleb's arm. Caleb rubbed the boy's head, putting his finger to his lips.

They stayed like this for a few minutes, not sure if whatever was out there had left or was still standing outside. Caleb opened the zipper a couple of inches and looked out. He could see the tree-trunk-sized legs of the creature outside the tent. Fuck. He should've kept the gun on him.

He scanned the tent for anything that might serve as a weapon. A pot, hiking pole, bear spray. Nothing would make a dent in something so big. Just as he was about to open the tent and confront the being, he heard it shift away. He peered out the small opening and could see its retreating form disappearing into the darkness.

Once he was sure it was gone, he let out a ragged breath and loosened his grip on River. The boy crawled into his lap and sobbed. Caleb felt like shit. He shouldn't have brought River with him. He should've hunted the creature alone. However, something told him River needed to come. Some instinct deep within him, let him know in order to end this, River had to be with him. Once River settled, Caleb laid him down and tucked him in.

"It's okay, little man. It's gone. Go back to sleep."

River hugged his stuffed dog and stared at Caleb intently. It was dark but Caleb could see his small, brown eyes in the bits of light. They were scared. Caleb leaned over.

"Do you want me to take you back to Aunt Tammy in the morning? To be with Sara and Drew?" Caleb asked.

River shook his head and placed his hand on Caleb's arm. Like Caleb, he knew they needed to stay together. Caleb squeezed his hand, then leaned over and kissed the boy on the forehead. "Go back to sleep. I'll keep an eye out."

Once River dozed off, Caleb slipped outside and stoked the fire. The creature had clearly trespassed straight through it, scattering coals and wood everywhere. Caleb gathered everything up and made sure the fire would hold until morning. He went to urinate on the edge of the trees and scanned around. It was dead quiet and nothing stirred. The creature had made itself scarce.

If it wanted to hurt them or take River, why didn't it? It could've crushed them in the tent. Caleb shook his head and made his way back to the campsite. Outside the tent, he tripped over something hard but couldn't see what it was when he searched the ground. It didn't feel like a rock or wood. It seemed to have moveable parts that shifted under his foot. He peered down, however, he couldn't see anything.

Inside the tent, River was fast asleep and Caleb curled in next to him. No matter what, he needed to make sure River wasn't easy to get to. He clipped the rope and carabiners on their pant loops and closed his eyes. He couldn't get the image out of his head of the large, gray, hairless legs standing outside the tent. Again, he wondered why the creature went through their things but didn't come after them.

By morning, Caleb had managed a couple of hours of sleep and woke to see River playing with his stuffed dog. He rolled over and watched the boy immersed in make-believe. Still, even when playing and not knowing he was being observed, River made no sound. It was like seeing a television program on with the sound off.

Caleb sat up and stretched, peeking outside the tent. The fire was low but still had coals burning and nothing else appeared disturbed. He unclipped the rope between them. "Do you need to go to the bathroom?"

River nodded and they climbed out of the flaps. They went to the tree line to relieve themselves, then Caleb set to making breakfast. He wrapped two potatoes in tin foil with sausage and threw them in the coals. For himself, he brought instant coffee and gave River juice. After a bit, the potatoes began to smell delicious, so Caleb fished them out and opened the foil. The juices from the sausage permeated the potatoes, making them moist and soft. They polished off the food and began cleaning up the campsite.

Caleb considered his options, knowing the creature was aware they were out there. Should they keep tracking it? If they found it, what could he do? Shoot it? He sighed, understanding he'd struggle to pull the trigger. Regardless, he needed to do something. If this thing killed Shannon, it would come back again. Setting his resolve, he decided they'd continue to follow the prints. He'd need to find the courage to take the beast down once they found it. It was the only way to keep them all safe.

As he broke down the tent, his foot hit something in the dirt and he bent to pick it up. "What the fuck?"

He brushed the mud off the item and his mouth hung open. It was something he hadn't seen since before the night Lien killed Trevor. It was the only thing he knew for sure belonged to River up until that point.

Covered in dirt, with a limb missing, was the action figure River carried around with him when Caleb first met the boy and his mother. The only toy Trevor let the child have. Caleb hadn't seen it since prior to that night and assumed it'd been left in their house.

The question was, how did it end up miles from the house in the middle of the woods?

In Circles

For the next few days, they hiked, camping at night. The creature didn't come again but left enough tracks for Caleb to follow it deeper into the forest. Part of him felt like it was too easy. Almost as if he was being set up, but he continued on. He decided to leave River back home on one of their trips to restock, then come out once he figured out where the creature's main lair was. He marked everywhere they went on the map. After a week, they needed to head back home to regroup and get more supplies. He marked where they left off, making sure he could find his way back quickly. From there, he'd close in on the beast and take it out.

Hopefully.

Once they got back to the house, Caleb gave River a bath, then took a shower himself. He threw their dirty clothes in the washer and packed enough food for only himself. This would allow him to stay out longer if needed. He hadn't told River he was leaving him back and was happy to see the boy playing with Sara. It might be easier if he was distracted and didn't notice Caleb leaving again.

Caleb's father was reading in the living room recliner, so Caleb came and sat next to him. His father put the paper down and gazed at Caleb over his reading glasses, sensing Caleb needed something. Caleb couldn't tell how lucid he was and wasn't sure it mattered.

"Dad, can I tell you something? Ask your advice?" Caleb asked, hoping his father wouldn't think he was nuts.

His father took his glasses off and watched Caleb. "Sure thing. How was camping?"

"It was fine. Listen, will you believe me if I tell you something? Something really weird?"

"I'll do my best."

"I saw something out there. I've seen it before but this time I saw it really close."

"Like a bear, or something like that?" his father inquired.

"No, like what we talked about before. Dad, I saw a monster. A real living one. It stood as tall as the house. Hairless, gray skin, red eyes. Its arms were too long. They hung down well past its knees. I guess they were knees. It looked like all muscle, no fat. It moves as if it isn't totally here. Like it's part of the vegetation."

His father listened and passed no judgment. "What do you think it is?"

"I don't know. At first, I thought it was like the stories people tell of the Kentucky Wildman, but it's not hairy and not a man of any kind. It's not of this world, I think. Have you ever heard of anything like that?"

"I can't say I have, however, as I said before, I saw something out there when I was young. Back in the day, people talked about a tree creature that wandered the national forest. Said it was as if a tree came to life."

"Did they say if it harmed people?" Caleb asked, his curiosity piqued.

"Not that I remember. People said they saw it off in the distance or sometimes crossing a road. Never heard of it attacking people. That's not saying much, though. People are found dead all the time. Hikers, campers. Word is they get lost and die from exposure, but some have been found with their bodies torn open."

This made Caleb's skin crawl. One swipe and that creature could rip him open. He imagined his body lying in the woods with his insides spilling out and doubted what he was doing chasing that thing. Then again, if he didn't, the creature already made its presence known near their home. He chewed his thumbnail and sighed. This was way more complicated than he'd planned.

River needed to stay home for the next journey. That much he knew. Even though he felt he was supposed to bring River with him, he couldn't take the risk. Whatever was out there was powerful and determined.

"Thanks, Dad. Did people ever call it anything you know of? A name I could use to search it up to learn more?"

"No. Only the tree monster. Is this what you think you saw out there?" his father asked.

"Maybe. Sounds about the same. I saw it in our woods by the house," Caleb answered.

"Hmmm, I see. What do you plan to do?"

"I've been tracking it to see if I can corner it. Shoot it when I do, I guess."

His father stared at him, then shook his head. "If it is what folks said they saw, bullets might not stop it. I know people said they shot at it, but it kept moving, anyway."

Caleb considered this and it confirmed what he was worried about. What if he took a shot at it and only made it angry? It could run faster than him, he'd have no escape. He leaned back in the chair and closed his eyes. He needed to have an alternative plan. A way to take the thing out while keeping his distance.

He got up and went to the phone, dialing his friend Keith who worked out at the quarry. Relief washed over him when Keith answered. "Hey Keith, it's Caleb. You got a moment?"

"Sure thing, Caleb! Haven't heard from you in a long time. What's up with you these days?"

"You know, staying busy. By any chance, can I buy some explosives off you? Something I can carry easily in my backpack?"

Keith was quiet, then asked, "You planning on blowing some shit up? Nothing illegal, right? I can't have this tie back to me if you get yourself in trouble."

"No, nothing illegal, I think. I've got to clear some rock fall back in the woods and they're too heavy for me to move by hand," Caleb lied.

"Ah, yeah. I have some you're welcome to. We've switched to a newer product at the quarry and have a backstock of some C-4 if that should work for that. When do you need it?"

"Thanks, man. Can I come by today? Your house or the quarry?"

Keith laughed hard at this. "The quarry. I'm not storing that shit at my house around my kids. How much do you need?"

Caleb had no idea, he'd never blown anything up. "Uh, enough to remove say a full-grown tree-sized amount of blockage?"

"Okay, I got you. Come by the quarry, I'll be there in about an hour and I'll hook you up. I'll give you a little extra in case the first blast doesn't clear it. It can take a couple of rounds, " Keith offered.

"Thanks, man. Can you give me a quick lesson on how to use it?"

"Probably smart. Don't want you blowing your fingers off out there," Keith joked.

After they hung up, Caleb let Tammy know he was heading to the quarry to meet up with Keith and told her he was thinking of leaving River back this time around.

She squinted at him. "Why? I thought you were just camping?"

Caleb shook his head. "He was getting tired with all the hiking, and I saw some fallen trees and stuff back there I was going to clear while I'm out there."

Even to him, it sounded like bullshit. Tammy shook her head. "Don't lie to me."

"Look, Tam, I need to deal with something. Shouldn't be more than a couple of days." The lies were coming easier.

"That little boy doesn't want to be away from you," she reasoned.

"I know, but this is a question of safety. I'll bring the flare gun and set it off to let you know I'm alright if it takes longer than I expect. Okay? It's just not safe for him to be with me," Caleb explained.

"Is it even safe for you to be out there?"

"Probably not, but I'm being careful. I'll buy walkie-talkies at the store, so I can communicate with him. With you. Please, help me out here."

Tammy leaned against the doorframe and chewed her bottom lip. "I don't like this, Caleb. All this mystery. Why can't you just stay home?"

"I just can't."

"Fine. Two days, then you need to come back, either way. I have a lot on my plate."

Caleb wasn't sure that was enough time, however, he needed her to keep an eye on River. "Alright."

River had dozed off on the couch near Caleb's dad, so Caleb went over and kissed the boy on the head and turned to his father. "He can sleep. I'll be right back."

His father gave a small wave and went back to reading his newspaper. Caleb snuck out the door and headed for the quarry. On the drive, he considered the options. If he was going to try to explode the creature, he'd need it to be still. Maybe he could figure out where it slept and wait until it was out. *If* it slept.

Keith met him at the storage shed and they went inside. Keith grabbed some C-4 off the shelf. "Have you ever used this stuff before?"

"I haven't. Is it a risk to carry in my backpack?" Caleb asked, wondering if he was going to blow himself up.

Keith shook his head. "Don't let Hollywood movies fool you. It's stable until detonated. You'll need to place it where you want, then stick the detonator into it. Move away, then fire the detonator. This gives you more control over it."

"Okay, sounds easy enough. Do you have a detonator?" Caleb asked, handling the C-4 gently.

"Yeah, but you can't tell anyone I gave that to you. The C-4 is backstock we don't use. The detonator is not. Here let me go over showing you how to do this," Keith said and took the C-4 from Caleb. He set it against the wall and pretended to put the detonator wires into the C-4. "See, like this. I won't actually do it but once you put these in, go as far back as you can and push this to detonate. Make sense?"

Caleb was still nervous about handling the C-4 but nodded. "I think I got it."

"Look, if it doesn't detonate right away, don't go running over there to see why. You need to stay back for a bit. If it still doesn't after a while, you can check it out after say thirty minutes. Maybe the wires came loose."

Caleb was pretty sure if it didn't detonate, he'd just haul ass and forget about it. "Got it."

"Okay, well, you should be all set with this amount. If you get hung up, reach out and I can meet you out there to get those rocks moved."

Those rocks. Really, a giant, tree-like creature. Caleb muttered, "Thanks, man. I owe you one. I think I can get it done by myself."

Keith walked him back to his truck and leaned against the hood, lighting a cigarette. "I hear you're a daddy now? How'd that ever come about?"

Caleb didn't want to discuss his private life and shook his head. "A kid needed a home and we decided we could provide it for him."

"Yeah? I heard his mother killed his father. Shot him to death, right? That's fucked up," Keith replied in a joking manner.

Caleb felt his cheeks flame. "Goddamnit, Keith. I don't know where you get your gossip, but maybe just let it die. The boy's mother was defending her life and the child's life. It's nothing to joke about!"

Now, it was Keith who looked embarrassed. "Damn, dude. Sorry, I didn't mean to piss you off. I'm glad you took the boy in. You come from good family."

Caleb shrugged and climbed into the cab of his truck. "Thanks. We're trying to set things right, make sure the boy has a safe and loving home until his mother is released from prison. He deserves that."

"How long has she got?"

The words wanted to die in his throat when Caleb spoke. "Ten years."

Keith whistled and slapped the hood of the truck. "Hell. The boy won't even remember her by the time she sees the light of day again."

Caleb was over the conversation and stuck his key in the ignition, firing it up. "I'll make sure he does. Thanks for the C-4. I'll call you if I need any help. Good to see you again, Keith."

Keith took the hint and backed away, waving as Caleb pulled out. Caleb raised his hand in a wave and swallowed the peppery anger in his throat. This town was all about gossip, no matter who it hurt. He refused to let River be on the shit end of that. Like he'd been after Shannon's murder.

He had a feeling he'd be fighting a lot more monsters than the tree creature in River's life to make sure the boy didn't suffer. The boy trusted him and he'd damn well make sure no one hurt River on his watch. He couldn't be everywhere with him, but Caleb would be the buffer from a cruel world when he could.

Starting with the monster in the woods.

Can Run

C aleb rose before the sun made its way into the sky and peeked in on River. He was curled up in his bed next to Sara's with his thumb in his mouth. Caleb couldn't think of a time he saw River with his thumb in his mouth and his heart warmed at the sight. Not wanting to wake the boy, he quietly shut the door and took a step back.

Tammy was up, knowing he was leaving early. She wanted to be ready when River asked for Caleb. They crept down the stairs and Tammy put coffee on. While it was brewing, she fiddled with the CB radios Caleb bought. They had farther range than walkie-talkies and were designed more for this type of situation than kids playing out together between houses.

"Keep yours on, Caleb. I don't want to worry more than I already am. Do you want to tell me what you're actually doing out there? I don't buy the mountain lion or fallen tree reasons. You wouldn't leave River for that," she insisted.

Caleb knew he needed to come clean, as much as he could to his very practical and grounded sister. "I saw something in the woods."

"The mountain lion?"

"No. Something worse. I...uh... please trust me when I say this. I saw a creature in the woods. I think it's what might have killed Shannon."

Tammy squinted one eye at him, reading his face. "What kind of creature?"

Caleb played over different descriptions, but they all sounded crazy. He pulled the drawing River had done out of his pack and showed it to Tammy. "River drew this after the first time we saw it. It's big. Not human, not animal, either. I think, anyway."

Tammy took the paper and peered at it, her face doubting what he was telling her. "Kids draw all kinds of make-believe. Maybe he heard you talking about it and drew what you were describing."

"I saw it, Tams."

"Maybe you saw something. The light playing off the trees, a buck with stuff caught in his antlers. I mean, Caleb, come on. You can't expect me to believe you saw a monster out in the woods. Now, you're leaving to go chase something that is smoke and mirrors."

"Tammy, listen. I'm not loopy and I know how this sounds. River and I saw it up close the other day. It was trying to snatch River down by the creek. I went after it with a branch. It was tall, like tree tall. It grabbed River but dropped him and we ran back to the house. We saw it again the first night we camped. It stood right outside the tent. This isn't smoke and mirrors. It's real and I need to kill it before it comes back and hurts one of the children."

Tammy bit her lip, the idea of something snatching one of the children enough to make her listen. She handed the paper back. "I hope you're wrong. I know you don't think so, but what's scarier than you going off the rails, is the possibility that you aren't. I don't know what to say here. Please, just be careful out there."

"I will," Caleb promised. As safe as he could be chasing a monster, anyhow.

"Why don't you see if Stephan can go with you?" Tammy asked.

"No. This is something I think I'm supposed to do alone. The creature comes around when it's just me. I think it would hide if Stephan was with me," Caleb explained. He filled his thermos with steaming coffee and shoved some cracker packs in his bag for breakfast. He packed more food this time to stay out longer if needed, not having to bring supplies for River, as well.

Tammy walked him to the door. Caleb tested his CB and put it in the outside pocket of the pack, so he could hear if she called him. They hugged briefly and for a moment, Tammy reminded him of their mother. Always making sure everyone was alright. He drew back and met his older sister's eyes.

"I have the flare gun and will keep my radio close in my pack. Don't let the kids mess around with yours. I want to make sure I'm tuned in to any sounds in case there's an emergency."

"Got it. Only I'll use it. What do you want me to tell River when he wakes up and you're gone?"

Caleb felt his heart tug and sighed. He hated to be another adult who disappeared on the boy. "Tell him I'll be home as soon as I can. I'll get on the radio with him after bathtime and tell him a story."

Tammy nodded and peered outside. The sun was casting an orange glow over the hills. "Alright, get going before he wakes up and we have a temper tantrum on our hands."

Temper tantrum, that was something River never had. He cried, but even then seemed to turn into himself to do so. Probably the effect of Trevor's abuse. Caleb shifted his pack and stepped through the door, rotating to Tammy. "Thanks, Tam. For keeping an eye on River. For not treating me like a nut case about this."

Tammy smiled and touched his arm, still not saying she believed him. "Be safe."

Caleb headed down the worn trail to the creek and stopped to peer at his map. He was following the same trail they'd taken before, now having an idea what he might find the beast. He sipped his coffee and glanced at the hills. There was something invigorating about the early morning when the sun hadn't quite broken its slumber.

He hiked along the creek for a while, scanning the ground for any fresh prints. He wanted to find the creature but didn't want it to see him coming. If he tracked it, he might be able to keep the element of surprise. A few yards farther down the creek, he thought he spied a sort of footprint and knelt down to get a better look. Behind him, he heard a branch snap and turned to look. Nothing was there and the sound was too light for the creature. Probably only a possum or other small animal. He rose and continued along the creek.

By the time the sun was hanging in the sky, he was hungry and stopped to eat one of the packs of crackers. He'd traveled at least a few miles from the house and was ready to head deeper into the woods. He set his pack down, fished the crackers out, and washed them down with coffee.

He sat for a few minutes, peering at the map and the trails he'd marked. The one thing he considered was the creature was hiding in the extensive cave systems back in the woods. Every few years, a hiker would get lost and would later be found, alive or dead, in one of the cave tunnels. They were a maze and reached far into the hills and underground. People had no idea what they were getting into when they went in to explore. All the turns looked the same and it was easy to get disoriented and lost.

Caleb marked on the map everywhere they'd seen the creature or any of its tracks. They all seemed to be around the cave openings. Except the ones by the house and he believed those were from the creature watching them. Stalking them. A rustling caught his attention and Caleb scanned around, trying to pinpoint its source. Nothing seemed out of the ordinary, however, he got the distinct feeling he was being watched. Being followed.

Gathering up his gear, Caleb headed up one of the trails leading to the cave system. He didn't want to get trapped by the creature inside the cave but figured he could narrow down where it was dwelling and go in at night. The rustling sounded again and Caleb whipped around, ready for a fight. Still, there was nothing.

Was he being paranoid or was something following him through the woods?

Moving along the trail, Caleb tried to tune into the sounds around him. It was quiet, except for the wind in the trees and the creek burbling. He was losing his mind. He began to hum a song to refocus and scrambled over boulders and fallen branches. By lunchtime, he forgot about the sounds and considered finding a place to stop for lunch before the trail was completely absorbed by the dense vegetation. He found a clearing in the sun and sat down, leaning against a boulder. His back was sore from carrying the pack and he was glad to slip it off for a little while.

He closed his eyes and let the sun warm him. He chugged water and polished off two sandwiches. When he was ready to go on, his eye landed on the radio and something felt wrong. It hadn't made any sounds. No static, no chirping. Nothing. He tugged it out of the pocket and realized when he'd shoved it in there in the morning, the power button had been accidentally turned off.

"Fuck," he whispered as he turned it on and switched to the channel he and Tammy agreed on. "Hello? Tammy, you there? Hello?"

He was greeted by silence and waited. Hopefully, she hadn't tried to reach him. River would be up by now and would know Caleb was gone. Caleb sighed in relief and slid the radio back into the pack. He made sure the power was on and slung the pack over his shoulders.

As he made his way up the hill the radio crackled and he thought he heard something. He pulled it out. "Hello?"

"Caleb! What the fuck? I have been trying you on the radio for hours! Why weren't you answering?" Tammy's voice screamed through the black plastic.

"Sorry, it had gotten turned off when I put it in the pocket of my pack. Is everything okay?"

"No! Caleb, River is missing. I thought he was sleeping in and went to wake him up for pancakes. His bed was empty. We searched all over the house and yard. We can't find him anywhere!" Her words were frantic and made the hair on Caleb's arm stand on end.

"What the hell, Tammy? Where is he? Did the other kids see him this morning?" Caleb tried to contain his panic.

"Drew said his bed was empty when he got up."

Caleb sat down hard on the ground. He couldn't think straight. Could River have gone back to his house? Or the creek? "Did you check down by the creek?"

"Yes. Stephan came over and has been scouring the property. The police are on their way."

The police? Caleb swallowed hard. He could lose River. How could this have happened? He wracked his brain, trying to think like a scared little boy. If River woke up and Caleb wasn't there, what would he do? The image of the creature reaching out for River made Caleb want to vomit and he massaged his forehead. Did River go to the creek and the monster got him?

Caleb got up and began heading back up the trail. It would take him hours to get home. He didn't know what else to do at this point. He'd failed River. He left him and now he was gone. Gone. Shannon's face flashed in his mind and the guilt was uncontrollable. He began to bawl as he staggered back toward the house. He tripped and fell, smacking his chin on a rock. Caleb grabbed the rock and pitched it as hard as he could into the woods. It thudded as it hit a tree trunk and bounced away. Another sound caught Caleb's ear and he jumped up, rage filling him.

"Not fucking now. I don't need any more shit to deal with, right now!"

The sound grew louder through the trees and Caleb thought he saw movement. He snatched a branch off the ground and held it like a sword in front of him, expecting the creature to appear in front of him.

The movement came closer and Caleb could feel his heart pounding in his chest. His hands were slippery from sweat and he gripped the branch as hard as he could. At that moment, every fear he'd ever had was heightened, then immediately dashed. The branch fell from his hands as the movement took form. Caleb dropped the pack and ran toward the figure. His arms swept the boy up and pressed him to his chest. River cried into Caleb's neck, almost dropping the stuffed dog on the ground.

Caleb squeezed his son as hard as he could, relief and disbelief taking over. "River, how did you find me? Did you follow me?"

River rubbed his nose and nodded. Caleb sat down with River in his lap, rocking back and forth. He reached over and took the radio out of the pack. "Tammy?"

"Caleb! Are you on your way home? The police are here, they're asking a lot of questions."

"I have him. I have River. He must've followed me."

"What? How?"

"I don't know. I kept hearing noises around me but didn't see anything. He just wandered out of the woods to me. He's in my arms as we speak."

"Oh, thank God. What should I tell the police?" Tammy asked, her voice unsure.

Caleb rubbed River's back and thought. "Tell them I'd changed my mind and took him with me, but forgot to let you know I did."

Tammy was silent on the other end of the line. Caleb was about to speak again when she came through. "Caleb, that boy needs to be with you."

"I know." Caleb knew it now more than ever.

"I'll send the police away. Are you coming home with him now?" Tammy asked.

Caleb looked at his son, then up the trail. "No. We have to finish this."

Can't Hide

C aleb set up camp for the night, needing to count supplies and figure out clothing for River. Since the boy followed him, all he had on him was his stuffed dog, his pajamas, and his light jacket. Caleb was relieved to see his son at least put on shoes. Caleb only packed for himself. One sleeping bag, a couple of changes of clothes, enough food for one. It either meant they'd need to go back for supplies, which wasn't an option if he was to get this done. Or move faster and make do with what that had.

He rifled through his clothes, but nothing he'd packed as a six-foot-tall man would work for a four-year-old child. They were deep in the national forest, so nowhere near anything where they could get food or clothing. He took out a sweatshirt and slid it over River's head once the sun dropped. It went to the ground but would work to sleep in. He'd need to figure out something in the morning. Maybe he could cut some of his clothes to fashion something for River to wear.

They ate and climbed into the tent. Caleb opened his sleeping bag and crawled in, motioning for River to get next to him. It was a tight squeeze, however, the nights were too cold for either of them not to be in the sleeping bag. He left it partially unzipped so they weren't sardines in a can, but River curled in next to him, clutching his dog. Caleb wasn't comfortable, yet was tired enough to fall asleep.

By morning, he was so cramped, his back locked up and he moved like an old man. He woke River and they eased out of the sleeping bag, stretching out the kinks. Caleb stoked the fire and put water on for coffee. He didn't have anything other than water for River to drink, but the boy didn't seem to mind. Caleb stared at the map, trying to decide if he should head back or keep pushing on. He felt they were close to the cave openings and could get there by the end of the day. He cut the extra length off the sweatshirt and used the cut piece to fashion a belt around River's waist. It was still too big, but the boy would be able to walk now and stay warm.

They packed up camp after breakfast and headed for the entrance of the cave system. Caleb hadn't seen any signs of the creature, however, his instinct told him he was going in the right direction. By early evening, they made it to an opening of the caves and Caleb doubted himself. What if the creature had gone back to the house?

He picked up the CB and pressed the button. "Tammy, are you there?"

He was greeted by silence and sighed. She was probably at work. The home health nurse wouldn't know to listen for the radio. He wondered if Tammy had taken it with her to work when the radio crackled and a voice responded.

"Caleb? That you?" Stephan responded.

"Hey! I wasn't sure if anyone had the radio," Caleb replied. "Is everything okay there?"

"It is. Tammy told me not to tell you this, uh... the home health nurse quit. Your father's health insurance ran out for the year."

Caleb froze and stared up at the trees. Damn. He knew they were using the home health nurse more since River came, but he thought they were good until the end of the year. "Fuck. Is that why you're there?"

"Partly. Helping out, right now. You alright out there?" Stephan asked.

"Yeah. Wasn't expecting River to follow me, so now we are going to run low on food and he has no extra clothes," Caleb explained.

"Do you want me to bring you some?"

"Nah, I think you are needed there more. I'm hoping to be done here after tomorrow."

"What exactly is it you're doing?"

Caleb chewed his lip, wondering how much he should tell Stephan. How much Tammy may have already told him. "Chasing ghosts, I guess?"

"What does that mean, Caleb? Is this about Shannon?" Stephan replied, his voice sounding worried.

"It's not *not* about Shannon. But not entirely, either. I saw something and am investigating it."

Stephan didn't reply at first and Caleb checked the radio to see if it was still working. Stephan cleared his throat. "Tammy told me a little. Said you thought you saw something big out there. Not human."

Caleb rubbed his face, wondering if they were all talking about how he'd lost his mind behind his back. "Something like that. Do you believe me?"

"I believe *you* believe you, which is enough for me. Caleb, you've always had your head on straight. If you say you saw something, you saw something. Just be careful. Is it safe to have River with you?"

"No, but he didn't let me leave without him, so here we are. I won't let anything happen to him," Caleb said, not convinced he was strong enough to make that true. "I'm more worried if I bring him home, he'll just try to follow me again and get attacked by an animal, get lost, or worse."

Worse, being the creature finding River wandering in the woods alone and snatching him. He glanced at River who was kneeling in the dirt and drawing with a stick. Caleb squinted to see what he was drawing but couldn't make it out.

"Damn, I wish I could help," Stephan replied.

"Don't sweat it. We should be home the day after tomorrow, I hope. I'm back at the caves and going to explore a little before dark. Hopefully tomorrow, I can find the monster and take it out. If not, I'm not sure I have enough supplies to get through. I'll make a decision, then. I just need clothes and food for River."

"Let me know if you want me to meet you somewhere with those," Stephan offered.

"Thanks. I think it's best if you keep an eye on the homestead. How's Dad?"

"Good. He's been napping today. About to wake him for dinner. Not sure he wants to eat what I cooked, but you know," Stephan said, laughing.

"Thanks, man. Our family owes you."

"Think nothing of it. Your family is my family."

They signed off and Caleb took a look around. The sun was dropping, so he wasn't brave enough to go into the caves until morning. He peered around and saw a flat area down the hill that would work as a campsite. He went over to River and touched his head.

"Hey, let's walk over there and set up the tent. Are you hungry?"

River nodded and stood up, the sweatshirt a large bubble around him. Caleb adjusted it and retied the cinch. Caleb caught a glimpse of River was drawing and shuddered. It probably wasn't what it appeared like, but it *looked* like large, angry eyes peering out of the cave. He glanced back at the cave, which stood quiet and empty. At least, as far as he could see.

River took his hand and they hiked down the hill to the clearing. They built a fire and ate some crackers and beans. Caleb frowned searching in his pack. They didn't have enough food for the whole next day and he considered if he should try hunting or fishing, neither of which he was good at. He had the shotgun but no fishing pole. Deciding to worry about it the next day, he closed the pack and strung it and the gun up in the tree above them.

Once the tent was up and the fire roaring, Caleb sat down with River and told him a story of when he was a little boy. How he believed if he built a boat big enough for him to fit in, he could put it in the creek and sail to Australia. He wasn't sure why he believed it, but he was convinced the creek would take him wherever he wanted to go. River listened intently, running his tiny fingers over the dog's ratty ears.

Caleb tucked River in, not ready to go to bed himself quite yet. He sat outside the tent by the fire, thinking about Lien and how lonely she must be behind bars. How much she must miss her child. The only person she had left. He could relate, he felt the same after Shannon died. Like he was in prison. In a way, she'd suffered a death, as well. Lost her freedom, lost her son, everything she knew. All because of that piece of shit Trevor. A memory of Trevor surfaced from high school and Caleb settled on it for a moment.

Caleb and Shannon had gotten into a lover's quarrel in the school hallway. They were by her locker and she was telling him in hushed tones he needed to respect her space because he was interjecting himself into her other relationships with friends. That she was his girlfriend but still needed her space. Caleb, afraid she was trying to break up with him, was getting louder and more insistent that he was her boyfriend, so she shouldn't be shutting him out.

It was a stupid argument and he knew he was wrong, however, his fear of losing her was making him irrational. She stormed off and didn't speak to him for the rest of the day. He called later and apologized after a heart-to-heart with his father, who told him he was dead wrong and needed to respect her as her own person.

That wasn't the part of the memory he was thinking about, though. It was the part where he watched her stomp down the hallway, clutching her books in her arms. As she got to the corner, Caleb saw Trevor standing there with a shit-eating grin on his face. He'd seen them fight and was enjoying it. As Shannon went past Trevor, he stepped out of the shadows to stop her.

"Hey, Shannon. Everything ok?" Trevor asked her as he eyed Caleb. He had every intention of turning a minor spat into a much bigger deal.

Shannon paused and stared at him for a second, then huffed and disappeared around the corner. That was it. The whole memory in Caleb's mind. He wasn't sure why it gave him such a crappy feeling in his stomach, but the look on Trevor's face then was the same one Caleb saw on his face that morning he'd seen Trevor outside his house when he followed Shannon's image to her house. Trevor was only happy when someone else was suffering. Caleb shook it off and got up, ready to bed down.

River was curled up into a ball in the sleeping bag as Caleb squeezed in next to him. The boy turned and placed his hand on Caleb's arm in his sleep. An overwhelming need to protect the boy came over Caleb and he put his hand over River's as he dozed off.

The next morning, he went out to stoke the fire and was stopped in his tracks. Stacked in a pile on the rock where he'd been sitting the night before were clothes and items in a blanket. A closer inspection revealed the clothes were River's size and the blanket contained packaged food and tea bags.

Caleb stared around the campsite, attempting to figure out where the items came from. Had Stephan come out with the stuff? No, he couldn't have. He couldn't have made it that far that fast and never would've left without talking to Caleb. There also weren't any clothes Caleb bought for River and the food and tea weren't from their house. The mystery only deepened when he took a packet of tea out of the bag.

It was the tea from Lien's house.

Devil's in the Details

Caleb played over different scenarios in his mind as he made them breakfast. River was now in his own clothes and the food they found was enough to keep them going for a few days.

How did it get there?

Caleb rubbed his face while he stared into the fire, swirling the tea around in his dented metal cooking cup. First, he found River's action figure out deep in the woods, now items from Lien's home showed up, as well. He couldn't wrap his brain around it. Trevor was dead, Lien was in prison. The house had been standing empty since that night.

Caleb waved River over and handed him the tea, now lukewarm. River sat next to Caleb on the log and sipped the liquid, a piece of bread smeared with peanut butter in his other hand. The stuffed dog sat guarding River as the boy ate his breakfast. Even though River was clearly hungry, he took his time, savoring the bread with small bites and sips of the tea.

Caleb peered down at his son. "Did you see or hear anything last night?"

River shook his head, taking another bite of bread. Caleb sighed and patted River's back.

"Yeah, me either. I want you to know, you can talk to me, River. I'm your daddy now, and I'll keep you safe. I know what you saw was scary that night, but I promise you're everything to me. I won't push it, however, as soon as you're ready, please talk to me. I miss your voice."

River watched him intently but didn't speak. He put his tiny hand on Caleb's leg and took a sip of tea, wrinkling his nose at the bitterness. Caleb laughed. The tea was bitter but he wasn't sure the proper way to make it. When Lien made it, it wasn't bitter, rather nutty and smooth. Maybe he left the tea bags in too long.

As he packed up the tent, a thought crossed his mind and he paused what he was doing. First, he'd found the action figure. River hadn't had it that night when Lien thrust the boy into Caleb's arms. So, it had been in the house. Like the clothes, food, and tea. Someone, or something, went into the house and took those items out. But why? Caleb told Stephan that River needed clothes and they didn't have enough food for the two of them. Then it appeared. Had someone heard him say that, intercepted their communication?

Caleb swung the pack on his shoulders and took River's hand. If someone overheard the conversation, what would it be to them to make sure Caleb and River had food and clothes? Enough to go all the way to the house and bring it to where they were camping. For what purpose? None of it made any sense. He was grateful for the food and clothes, however, wondered if it meant something more. Something sinister? Were they being stalked?

All of these thoughts were swimming around Caleb's head as they hiked up the trail. They came to the entrance of the cave and stopped. The image River drew of the eyes peering out of the cave popped into Caleb's mind and he shuddered. Was the creature in there watching them, now? Tucking the tent and extra supplies behind a tree, Caleb scooped River up onto his back and they headed in slowly, ready to bolt if something came out at them.

It was quiet inside. Dark as they moved deeper into the recesses of the cave. Caleb clicked on his headlamp and peered around. If he was expecting to find bones or other signs of the creature, he was disappointed. The cave was empty. Nothing. Some dirt and other rocks but that was it. He set River down and sat on one of the rocks. It appeared to be a bust, coming there. Caleb knew the caves went underground for miles, so there was still a possibility the creature was somewhere in the maze, but it didn't seem that way. The cave appeared vacant.

River began to whimper and Caleb looked to see at what. The boy had his eyes focused on one of the cave tunnels and the hair on Caleb's neck stood up. He couldn't see anything, but the air in the cave had changed. Become denser. Caleb pulled River close to him and stood up. They backed toward the opening, keeping their eyes on the tunnels. All of a sudden, a scream like no other echoed throughout the cave. Not human, but not necessarily an animal, either.

Caleb grabbed River and ran away from the cave, his arms trembling and his heart racing in his chest. River was crying into Caleb's chest and shaking like a leaf. The sound was like nothing Caleb had ever heard before. Painful, angry, lost. Whatever was making the sound wasn't happy. Caleb snatched the tent and pack from behind the tree, throwing them over his shoulder, and they went down where they could still see the cave, hiding behind a fallen tree trunk.

River refused to look up, however, Caleb kept his eyes trained on the cave entrance. About the time he was ready to give up and move on, a shadow fell across the opening of the cave. A long and large shadow. Caleb held his breath as the shadow molded into form and the creature came into the light, its head brushing the top of the cave. It was hunched and stepped out, standing to its full height. Caleb felt his blood run cold. In the broad daylight, the creature was even bigger than he remembered. If it was the same creature. Maybe there was more than one.

That thought was even more terrifying than the beast standing before him. What if he was seeing not one, but a family of monsters? Caleb glanced down at River, who still had his face plastered in Caleb's chest. He peered back at the large, gray form at the cave. It didn't seem to have spied Caleb, making him wonder what the scream was about.

In an effort to adjust River off Caleb's leg that was going to sleep, the canteen attached to the pack swung and banged against the tree trunk, making a loud thud. Panic set in as Caleb looked to see if the creature heard it. The creature had its head cocked in the direction of where they were hiding, its eyes scanning the area.

Caleb froze, not sure if it would make more sense to make a run for it or stay put. At that moment, a large hawk took flight from one of the overhead branches, distracting the creature's attention. Caleb ducked as low as he could to not be seen by the beast.

As the hawk broke the beast out of its stupor, it strode down the other side of the hill away from where they were hiding, its thick muscular legs crossing distance at a stunning rate. Caleb waited until the coast was clear and picked River up as he stood. They wound through the woods away from the caves, so Caleb could get his bearings.

Now, he was unsure of how to proceed. He could sneak back up there at night and detonate the cave opening, but there were openings everywhere. The monster could just escape through another tunnel. Outside of attaching the detonator and C-4 to the beast directly, he wasn't sure what to do. Did it ever sleep?

Caleb found he was heading away from the caves back toward the house. He was still days away, but his feet were taking him where his brain wouldn't. He was crazy to be out there, trying to take down a house-sized creature that looked like it was made out of trees. There was no way he could beat the thing. Especially not with River in tow. He was willing to risk his life, but not River's.

They hiked until the evening and set up camp in a grove of trees. Afraid to draw the creature to them, Caleb decided to forego the fire. They ate in the tent and Caleb told River stories. By the time they were both tired enough to sleep, it was pitch black outside and Caleb was sure they were covered enough to not be spied.

As he drifted off, his mind went back to finding the toy left in the campsite, then the clothes and food. Something meant to do that on purpose. Other than his family, only one other thing knew they were out there. The creature. Was it trying to lure them out? To get to River? Did it actually go to Lien's house and take those items? It was so big, it was hard to imagine it trying to get into the house. It would have to squat or crawl to get in and move through the house.

Yet, something in Caleb told him that's exactly what happened. The creature wanted River. For what reason, Caleb had no idea. Did it eat children? Shannon was murdered but her body was left pretty much intact in the woods. No children had gone missing in town for as long as Caleb could remember. So, that couldn't be it.

Did River hold the key to something?

Caleb dozed off, thinking about all the possibilities. He felt like he was missing something obvious. Something Shannon was trying to tell him. "He's back." The creature was clearly around if it had been before. What brought it back? Caleb's head hurt and he tried to push the thoughts away, so he could rest. River was curled up next to him sound asleep. Caleb placed his hand over the boy and let sleep take over.

They were awoken in the middle of the night by something moving in the woods. Caleb jolted awake and made sure River was still with him. River clung to his arm as the sound grew louder. It sounded like trees were being ripped up by their roots. Caleb went to peer outside when the tent began to shake. It felt like an earthquake, which would've been less scary. The tent felt like it was being lifted off the ground.

River began to bawl and Caleb wanted to join him. Whatever was outside was attempting to get into the tent and they had no escape. Caleb dug in his pack for the bear spray and shifted to the tent flap. The tent stopped moving and it became quiet in the area, Caleb unzipped the tent slightly but nothing was visible out there. It could've been a bear. They'd eaten inside the tent and the smell was probably still in there.

After a few minutes, Caleb was convinced the bear had moved on, looking for easier food, and he took a deep breath. He settled River back down and sang him the only lullaby he remembered his mother singing to him. His voice was terrible but River seemed to like it. River cuddled up next to Caleb and fell asleep. Caleb was just about to doze off again when a sensation woke him up. It was like the tent was driving down the road.

Then it hit him.

They were being dragged in the tent by something that was most definitely *not* a bear.

As Fast As They Can

C aleb wrapped his arms around River, who was now very awake and shaking. The tent bounced along the ground, sending everything inside scattering. Caleb scooped what he could into his pack, one arm still tightly around River. They'd have to try to make a break for it. Caleb got his pack on his shoulder and scooted toward the tent flap. He unzipped it, planning to leap out with River in tow. However, once he looked out, he knew he'd need to come up with another plan. The creature had the top of the tent in one hand and was pulling it along through the woods. The flap was facing the creature's legs. If Caleb tried to get out, they'd either be trampled by the creature's massive legs or would be caught immediately.

Caleb fished his hunting knife out of his pack and let gravity pull him and River to the far side of the tent. He sliced a hole in the floor of the tent, hoping he could move fast as soon as the creature realized they'd slipped out the bottom.

Caleb said a little prayer and gathered River close. It was now or never. Rolling them into a ball, Caleb pushed through the hole and felt the ground beneath them. They tumbled free of the tent and Caleb was up and running before the creature had a chance to turn. River clung to him as the branches whipped across their bodies. Caleb didn't care where they were going, as long as it was far away from the monster.

His foot caught a root and they both flew onto the ground, Caleb losing his grip on River. The boy cried out and Caleb lost sight of him in the dark. He sat up, rubbing his bruised chin.

"River," he whispered. "Where are you?"

He could hear whimpering in the dark and shifted the direction of the sound. He felt through the pack for a light and realized he must have lost the flashlight in the escape. That and the CB radio. Fuck. They were out there in the dark with no way to call for help.

"River," Caleb called louder. The boy was quiet and now more than ever, Caleb needed him to communicate. "Please, River, talk to me so I can find you before the creature does. Just say something."

He strained his ears and while he could hear River sniffling, he couldn't make out where it was coming from. They were out of time. The sound of the heavy footfall of the beast broke the silence and was bearing down on them. Caleb peered around, attempting to make out any sign of his son. A scream cut through the dark, making his stomach clench. River was screaming.

Caleb ran toward the sound and saw the creature scoop the boy up in his arms. River looked around desperately for Caleb, then spying him, stretched his arms down toward Caleb. Caleb had no weapons. The C-4 was still in the pack but he'd no way to attach it to the beast without putting River at risk. Even so, he ran at the creature's legs and hit them with a stick he found on the ground. The creature made a sound between a growl and irritation and kicked Caleb aside. Caleb tumbled down the hill but came right back at the beast.

One swing of the creature's arm, sent Caleb flying against a tree and he got the breath knocked out of him. The creature frowned and took a step at Caleb. Caleb felt his world going dark and struggled to move. As he slipped into blackness, he heard something he didn't think he ever would.

"Daddy!" River cried from the beast's arms. "Help!"

~

When Caleb came to, he was no longer at the base of the tree. He sat up and tried to make sense of where he was. There were rocks around him and he could see straight up to the sky full of stars. He shook his head, feeling a large knot on the back of his skull. Where was he? Where was River? Panic set in and he tried to get up, the world around him spinning with the effort. He leaned aside and vomited.

Every ounce of his body ached. From the leaves and sticks in his hair and clothes, he'd either been dragged there or carried through the brush. By the creature? Why didn't it just kill him and get it over with? It had River, which is what it was after, so why bring Caleb along, too? He remembered River crying out for him. Calling him daddy. Begging for Caleb to save him.

Caleb failed him.

The cave. He was outside the cave. How? Once the spins stopped, Caleb gazed around. The cave opening was about twenty feet away but was dark and quiet. No sign of the creature or River. Caleb stood up and eased over to the cave entrance. He peered in, grabbing for his pack. Good, it was still on his back. He dug around and felt the C-4. At least there was that. The detonator was tucked into an inside pocket. However, the rest of their food and supplies were gone.

A sound deep in the cave broke Caleb out of his searching and he moved to an inside wall. The tunnels were too dark to see, but he swore he saw a flicker of light coming from one of them. Like from a fire. Caleb crept along the wall, listening for any sign of life. River wasn't crying, which Caleb wasn't sure was a bad or good thing. He inched down the tunnel toward the flicker. As he drew closer, the light became brighter and Caleb could feel a warmth radiating up the tunnel from the space.

The tunnel fed into a larger opening that looked like a room deep in the cave. Light from the fire danced around the walls, creating a comforting glow. Caleb almost let his guard down when he remembered why he was there. To save River. He held his breath and pressed against the cool rock, leaning around the cave wall to get a better view.

The creature was crouched by the fire, half turned away from the cave opening. It seemed calm, peaceful, which put Caleb on edge even more. He scanned the cave for River but didn't see him, at first. Then a small figure came into view, curled up on the far side of the fire. The boy had his arms around his knees and was rocking back and forth. He didn't appear physically harmed but was clearly traumatized.

Rage filled Caleb and he considered running at the beast, trying to knock it off guard. However, common sense took over and he knew if he managed to push the creature over, it would only serve to enrage it and put both Caleb and River in danger. Caleb slipped back into the dark and weighed his options. He couldn't get to River without getting past the creature. He could hide and wait until the creature went to sleep. *If* it went to sleep. Or create a distraction. Caleb touched his pack and sighed. It was risky, but might be the only way.

Caleb retreated up the tunnel and assessed the area. He could set a controlled explosion, enough to distract the creature, then run in and grab River. It might not work, however, he needed to try. Caleb scanned the tunnels, gauging the safest way to blow shit up without completely blowing shit up. A thin tunnel ran off the second tunnel that wasn't attached to the room with the fire. Caleb pulled out a small amount of C-4, remembering what his friend told him. He placed it in a crevice and attached the detonator. He unwound the wires from the spool, hoping he understood what he was doing.

Stretching the wire out, he made his way back to the split between tunnels, wondering if it was far enough to be safe when the explosion happened. He knew it would scare River, but he needed to get the monster away from the child. From his son. The sound of River screaming for him echoed in his brain and set his resolve.

When the blast shook the caverns, Caleb doubted his decision. Rocks and dirt fell from above and the sound was deafening. Caleb's ears began to ring and every cell in him shook with the earthquake he'd created. Stunned, he stood in place, disoriented and confused. Which way was the other tunnel?

The sound of River crying snapped Caleb back to his senses and he ran toward the sound. The creature appeared at the entrance of the room, fury in every motion it made. It glanced back at River, who was pressed against the back wall screaming. Caleb caught a glimpse of River and hid in the shadows while the monster thundered past him, its head brushing the ceiling of the tunnel.

As soon as the creature disappeared down the other tunnel, Caleb bolted into the room. River saw him and stopped screaming, dazed by what he was seeing. Caleb dashed around the fire and gathered River into his arms. The boy rested weakly against Caleb's chest, not showing relief at seeing him again. River was emotionless, limp like a dishrag. Caleb hugged him tightly and moved toward the opening, expecting the creature to appear out of nowhere.

As he hustled down the tunnel, Caleb realized he'd left the pack with the rest of the C-4 in the other tunnel. He had nothing. No weapons, no supplies. Just him and River. He'd need to run all the way home. Now, he'd managed to piss the monster off. Even if he did make it home, it could come and kill them all. They'd never be safe again.

If they ever were.

Caleb could see the cave entrance looming ahead of him, stars twinkling in the sky beyond. He'd worry about everything else later. Right now, he needed to get River out of there. He could figure out what to do later once they were far from there. River hung on as Caleb ricocheted off the cave walls, stumbling as he focused on the opening.

They were in the clear, Caleb could feel the cool air on his face and a sense of elation came over him. He'd done it. He'd distracted the creature and saved River. As his feet hit the ground outside, Caleb felt his shoulders relax and scanned for a clear trail. It would take at least a day or two to get home, but if he kept moving, they could make it before not having food became a real issue.

"It's okay, River. I've got you. You're safe," Caleb whispered into his son's hair. River nodded and held on tighter. It was going to be okay.

A terrifying scream erupted behind them and Caleb couldn't help but turn to see. The silhouette of the creature blocked out the moonlight. The creature raised its arms and let out such a mournful wail, Caleb felt his knees get weak. The sound was what Caleb remembered making when he found out about Shannon and the baby. Like his very soul was being ripped from his body.

Caleb turned and continued down the trail, expecting the creature to come after him and snatch River away. Nothing came. He continued walking into the night toward home, holding his son in his heavy and tired arms.

Another wail cut through the night, the sound of despair calling to the stars.

Arise With the Sun

Without a map, compass, or general sense of direction, Caleb felt like he was going around in circles. His arms were exhausted from carrying River and his legs were shaking with exertion. Finally, lost and worn out, Caleb stopped to listen. He could hear water and knew if he followed the creek upstream, it would eventually lead them home.

Home.

Caleb imagined lying in his bed, hearing River playing with his cousins. The image brought tears to his eyes and he set River down. The boy cried and clung to him, afraid to be even an arm's length away from Caleb. Caleb sat on the ground and gathered River in his lap, soothing the child with his hands.

They had no food, no shelter, no clean clothes. They were miles from home. Even following the stream would take days and Caleb didn't know if he had it in him. River certainly didn't. It took everything in Caleb to keep it together and his eyes were fighting to close. River dozed off in his lap, so Caleb scooted to rest his back against a tree. If they could wait for the sun to rise, he could see where they were. Perhaps, he could figure something out, then.

Caleb let his eyes close and felt the heaviness of sleep come over him. When he jolted awake, the sun was creeping into the sky and his legs were tingling with lack of circulation. He stretched out his legs, which woke up River. The boy looked miserable, tired, and scared. Caleb kissed his forehead and helped River up.

"Let's go to the bathroom and I'll figure out something to eat. I was a Boy Scout, you know?" Caleb attempted a little levity. River just stared at him, clearly not knowing what a Boy Scout was. Caleb smiled. "Basically, I was taught how to get by in the wild."

They went to the treeline and relieved themselves. Caleb scanned the area for anything edible, however, nothing he recognized as safe to eat. He dug in his pockets and scored half of a candy bar from his inside jacket pocket. He didn't remember sticking it there and it seemed somewhat old. River's eyes lit up when Caleb handed it to the child. It wasn't much, but might settle River's stomach for a bit.

After they were done, Caleb began the trek along the water, River walking beside him. Caleb watched his son and admiration came over him. River had already been through so much in his life, yet looked to Caleb with such open trust. As they hiked, Caleb kept his eyes peeled for anything they could eat. This late into fall, not much existed. He did find a few small, somewhat shriveled apples, and hoped it wouldn't upset their stomachs. They needed to risk it as they would run out of steam if they didn't eat something soon.

After a couple of sawdust-tasting apples, Caleb felt a little better. They were heading home. He took time to show River different rocks and plants as they hiked, hoping it would keep the boy's mind off the incident with the creature. River kept stopping to stare behind them, but as far as Caleb could tell, nothing was there. However, he couldn't deny he felt like they were being watched. Being tracked.

By evening, Caleb couldn't ignore the blisters on his feet and had carried River the last few hours. He knew they were going in the right direction by the sun and moon, but it seemed endless. They stopped and Caleb gathered branches for a fire. He hoped his years in the Boy Scouts would pay off as he needed to ignite the fire, using what was at his disposal. He tried creating sparks with rocks, however, that proved fruitless. He then yanked the string out of his sweatshirt and gathered sticks. He set the contraption on top of a flat piece of wood and began to create friction by spinning the stick with the string. He almost gave up when he noticed smoke coming from where the stick met the wood and pressed on.

Once he saw a small glow growing from the ember he fostered, he grabbed pine needles and placed them on the heated area, blowing gently to get the needles to catch. When they did, much to his own surprise, Caleb whooped with joy. River, seeing Caleb happy, smiled and clapped his hands. Within minutes, Caleb had a small fire going and felt ridiculously proud of himself. They huddle by the fire, enjoying the glow of light.

Caleb knew it would draw attention to where they were, but he needed to keep River warm. He fashioned a shelter out of branches, leaves, and pine needles, aware even a strong wind would decimate it. They climbed in and Caleb sang songs to River until the child was sleeping soundly.

What he wouldn't do to go back and make a different choice. What was he thinking, chasing a giant, tree monster deep into the national forest? It was stupid and reckless, even if it *had* been just him, but now it was River, as well. If anything, he'd made things so much worse for all of them. Caleb slipped out to stoke the fire and sat watching the flames dance and jump. Movement across the stream caught his eye and he found himself staring eye-to-eye with the creature. It didn't move or attempt to cross the water. It observed him, then turned and became one with the night. Caleb found he was holding his breath and let it out.

The creature was following them, but not coming after them. Why? They were easy prey, now. It could pick them off and no one would ever know what happened to them. Just the town drunk and his biracial, adopted son disappearing into the woods, never to be seen again. It would be town gossip for a few minutes until something else happened.

Caleb sat outside the makeshift shelter and closed his eyes for a moment. His eyes were tired and felt hot and scratchy, but sleep wouldn't come easy. He was scared, yet part of him said the creature wasn't going to come after them, now. Or again. He was missing something. The creature seemed sad, lonely. Or maybe he was transferring his own feelings onto the sounds the beast was making, relating to when he learned about Shannon's pregnancy after her death.

Maybe that wasn't it, though. Perhaps in the creature's world, those sounds were anger. Maybe it wasn't coming after them because it enjoyed the game. Making them suffer, making them fear for their lives. Keeping the chase going for some sick game. Caleb was thinking about this when he couldn't fight off the drowsiness anymore. He let it take him under as he leaned back against the tree the shelter was braced against.

Caleb stirred a bit later and peeked in on River. The boy was curled up in a ball, shivering. Caleb pulled his coat off and laid it over the child. As he moved away, River's hand reached out for him. Caleb took his son's hand and climbed in next to him. Regardless, if the creature wanted to harm them, Caleb closing his eyes for a bit wasn't going to stop it. If anything, he needed to be rested and alert for what they were about to do.

He dreamed of Shannon. She was dressed in a long, flowing, iridescent gown, holding a small baby in her arms. She waved at him to follow her and they moved effortlessly through the woods until they came to the mouth of the cave. Caleb resisted, not wanting to go back in there. Shannon smiled, holding a secret in the curve of her lips, and motioned for him to go with her into the cave. They wound down the tunnel to the room where Caleb found River before and the creature. The fire was still raging, but the room was empty.

Shannon placed the baby in the center of the fire, however, it didn't burn. The baby levitated above the flames, sleeping peacefully. Caleb drew closer, staring at the tiny child. Its head was covered in blond ringlets and its tiny bow-shaped, pink lips were relaxed. Caleb reached out for the child, but the fire burned his hands and he jerked back.

Shannon stood on the other side of the fire, her eyes glowing with an understanding he couldn't comprehend. She wasn't harming or sacrificing the child, rather was releasing it.

Her eyes shifted to something behind Caleb and he turned to see what she was looking at, the hair on his neck standing up.

At the entrance to the room, the creature was standing with its eyes on Shannon. Watching the baby. Caleb felt his heart racing and searched for a weapon of some kind. The creature moved past him to the fire, as if Caleb wasn't standing there. It didn't see him. Caleb stared between Shannon and the monster, frozen in place. The creature extended its arms into the fire and scooped the child out of the flames, cradling it to its chest. Not to harm it, to keep it safe.

At that moment, Caleb was startled awake by River screaming and sat up so fast, he knocked the rickety shelter over. His eyes darted around, landing on River who was thrashing in his sleep. Caleb reached out, his arms trembling as he drew River close to him. The boy was shivering so hard, Caleb felt like his whole body was vibrating.

"River, wake up. You're having a bad dream. I'm here. You're okay," Caleb whispered, stroking the child's head.

River's eyes flew open, unfocused and still caught in the dream. When they landed on Caleb, they came into focus. His mouth quivered and he spoke for only the second time in months. "He's going to hurt me."

Caleb pictured the creature in his dream, clutching the baby to his chest. Not to hurt it, but like a parent would. "The monster we saw before?"

River dropped his head, tears spilling down his face. "No. Daddy."

"River, your father died, remember? He can't hurt you anymore. I'm your daddy now. I would never hurt you. I'll always protect you."

River rubbed his nose and shook his head as he gestured with his arms. "Mama made him fall. Loud. Red paint floor. Mama crying."

Caleb frowned. Lien shot Trevor. It was loud and Trevor fell on the ground in a pool of blood. River was telling him what he saw, the only way a young child could explain it. Caleb sighed as he considered how to delicately address the boy's trauma. "Your mother was protecting you. She didn't want him to hurt you. Did he hurt you, River?"

River nodded and acted as if he was hitting himself. He grimaced and shook his finger. "Bad boy."

Caleb felt his chest tighten and pictured Trevor hitting River, calling him names. Calling him a bad boy. Rage came over him and he felt hot tears sting his eyes. "You aren't bad, River. You're a good boy and he was a mean man. Your father. That's why your mother had to stop him from hurting you, from hurting her. She wanted to keep you safe. I want to keep you safe. Do you understand?"

River climbed into Caleb's lap and wrapped his fingers around Caleb's wrist. "Daddy."

"That's right. I'm your daddy and I'll keep you safe. Just like your mama did. Okay?"

"Okay."

Caleb fixed the shelter as best he could in the dark and added branches to the fire. He was sure he wouldn't be going back to sleep, but it was still dark and hiking wouldn't be smart until morning. River fell back asleep and didn't have any more nightmares. Caleb thought about his dream with Shannon and considered what it could mean. The baby looked like her, with golden, curly hair. Their child. Why was she putting it in the fire? Why was the creature cradling it like its own child? Caleb chalked it up to a weird dream and tried to not think about it too much. Maybe he was confusing his relationship with River, with what happened to Shannon and the baby.

However, in the morning, it made a lot more sense in the light of day. Seeing the creature across the water the night before, seeing it again in his dream told him something in his soul he'd been running from. He knew in order to get answers to what happened to Shannon, he needed to do something he was terrified to do. Something which could cost him and River their lives. Even as doubt flooded his mind, Caleb knew what had to happen next.

He needed to go back and face the beast.

To Face the Truth

For some reason, the way back to the cave seemed easier, as if the path had been laid out for them to go. Where they'd stumbled and gotten lost prior, the trail seemed clear and short.

Caleb also found packs of crackers on the path they'd either dropped or were placed for them to find. Caleb was grateful for the nourishment and River seemed in better spirits with food in his stomach. Now, Caleb needed to make a plan. Something told him this time was different. This time, he'd find the answers he was searching for.

By sundown, they were within sight of the caves, so Caleb paused and started a fire. He eyed the opening of the cave, but nothing went in or out. From what he learned last time, the caves went deep into the earth, probably miles, and the creature could be anywhere in the tunnels. It could be directly under their feet. Caleb shrugged off the thought. He opened a pack of crackers and handed River one.

The boy nibbled the side where cheese was seeping out and smiled. "Thanks, Daddy."

Caleb couldn't help but feel his heart swell at River calling him that. He grinned. "I like hearing your voice, little man. Are you doing okay?"

River nodded as he split the cracker apart and licked the bright orange cheese inside. His stuffed dog was sitting by his side and Caleb sat on the other side of that. He observed the cave and thought about what his next step would be. His pack with the C-4 was still somewhere in the tunnel unless the creature found it. The gun was long gone and clearly sticks were no match for a monster of that size. Caleb chewed his thumbnail and thought about what to do. A straight confrontation would mean he'd surely lose. When it came to brute strength, the creature prevailed. He'd need to sneak up on the beast.

Fashioning a rudimentary shelter hidden in the cover of the trees, Caleb pulled off his jacket for River to use as a blanket. They'd lost everything they'd brought along the way in the cave explosion. It was going to be a long, uncomfortable night, however, Caleb knew in his heart he still needed to face the creature. Confront it about what happened to Shannon.

Then he could go home.

Once River was asleep, Caleb slipped out and scanned the area for anything that might serve as a weapon. Luckily, he had his pocket knife in his pants and found a large branch. He began to shave the tip to a point until he'd fashioned a sharp spear. He couldn't take the creature down with a stick, but he might be able to incapacitate it with the spear. If he could hit it in the kneecap, if it had a kneecap, he could at least immobilize it to run in and grab his pack.

By the time the sun eased into the sky above the trees, Caleb had a large spear and a couple of smaller ones ready to go. He hoped his inclination was right and he wouldn't need to use them. He jostled River awake and guided the boy onto his lap. Now, the goal was to keep River safe.

"River, I need to go into the cave. I don't want to leave you here alone, so I was going to hide you behind those boulders up there. The rocks. You can wait for me until I come out."

River stared at where Caleb was pointing and shook his head. "No. Go with you."

"It's not safe. That thing could grab you and take you away from me," Caleb explained, attempting to hide the fear creeping into his voice.

River's eyes gazed at the cave opening and he shook his head again, more determined this time. He scrunched his small face. "No. Go with you."

Caleb sighed. The boy was stubborn. He worried if he took River in and things got bad, he was risking the child's safety. "Riv, I don't want anything to happen to you, do you understand? I need you to be safe."

River nodded, then rubbed his nose as he peered at Caleb with his deep, dark eyes. "Go with you."

Caleb knew if he tried to leave River, the boy would follow him, anyway, like he did before through the woods. He considered his options, then acquiesced. "You need to stay right by me and if I tell you to run and hide, you need to do as I say. Do you understand me?"

His voice came out harsher than he intended but it seemed to get the message across. River's eyes grew wide and he bobbed his head. "Yes."

They finished off the crackers and guzzled some water from the creek. Caleb checked his weapons, then turned to River, handing him the smallest spear. "You need to carry this. If something comes at you, you point the sharp end toward it to keep it away. Just be careful not to point the sharp end to yourself. Okay?"

River clutched the spear in one hand, with the stuffed dog up under his other arm. He looked vulnerable, yet fierce, and Caleb felt proud of his tiny son. Caleb strapped the extra spear across his back with his belt and carried the largest one in his hand like a walking stick. This was it.

There was no going back.

Come hell or high water, they needed to face what was haunting them, chasing them. What possibly killed Shannon. He took River's hand in his as the boy adjusted his toy, so he didn't drop it. They headed up the hill toward the cave, not sure what they'd find. Caleb felt his insides quivering and prayed he'd find the strength to come face-to-face with the beast.

The mouth of the cave loomed in stillness. As Caleb paused to listen, he was greeted with silence. Maybe some air moving through the tunnels, creating a low howl. Even though they'd burned a fire close to the cave, the creature hadn't come for them at night like it did before. Caleb considered why.

Had it disappeared?

Or was it lying in wait to trap them inside?

"Hello?" Caleb yelled down into the tunnels, his own voice echoing back at him.

He waited a moment, then glanced at River. He cocked his head. "Let's go."

They slipped into the coolness of the cave when Caleb realized without his headlamp, they'd quickly be enveloped by the dark. He glanced around, searching for some source of light, but the cave was heavy in inky blackness. Caleb stood at the two tunnels as he thought about what to do. If his pack was still in the other tunnel, it had his headlamp in it. He removed the extra spear and squatted down, gesturing for River to climb on his back.

River dropped his spear and clutched Caleb's shoulders, as Caleb scooped him up onto his back. He reached down for the other two spears, however, with River on his back, he couldn't hold on to all three. He leaned the smaller two spears against the cave wall, grasping the largest one in his hand like a hiking stick. As they made their way blindly down the tunnel, he used the stick to try and find the pack on the ground. A couple of times, he thought he found it but it was just a large rock.

The creature could've grabbed the pack when the explosion went off. The explosion. It would account for so much debris on the ground. More than once, Caleb stumbled over pieces of cave wall on the ground. He knew they were getting close to where he'd set the C-4. His pack could even have gotten buried in the explosion.

As the light around them receded into pitch black, River's grip on Caleb's neck became tighter. The boy's breathing was erratic and Caleb could tell he was scared. Hell, so was Caleb. He slowed as they moved farther down and his foot hit something on the ground. Using the spear to stab at it, he realized it wasn't a rock. He swung River down and felt on the ground for the object. His hand brushed something cool and fabric.

His pack!

Caleb wanted to holler in relief but knew they needed to stay as quiet as possible. He fumbled through the pack until his fingers landed on a familiar shape. He pulled out the headlamp and clicked it on. The area illuminated, the light bouncing off the contours of the walls around them. As he rotated his head, Caleb could see around the area, chasing away the dark mystery of their surroundings.

Caleb glanced around and saw the explosion closed off the tunnel going any deeper into the earth. Which meant the creature wasn't down that way. One entrance was sealed off, leaving just the other tunnel. He peered at River and smiled. The boy seemed unsure and clutched his dog tightly in one hand, the other clinging to Caleb's jacket.

"It's okay. We have light, now," Caleb assured the child, fastening the headlamp on his own head. He picked up the pack, slinging it over his shoulder.

Something hard knocked him on the spine and he winced. He reached back behind him and felt the weight of the item in the pack. He slid the pack off his shoulder and slipped his hand inside. Relief washed over him when he felt the radio within the folds of the fabric.

Clicking on the radio, he switched it to the channel he and Tammy agreed to communicate on. "Tam, are you there?" he whispered, trying not to draw too much attention to them. He strained to listen for any sign of life coming from the black rectangle.

Static greeted him and he sighed. He'd try again once they were out of the cave. He shoved the radio into the pack and grasped River's hand. "Let's go back up. There's nothing down here."

They carefully inched their way out of the tunnel, the headlamp providing much-needed visibility. They got to the main cave room leading outside and Caleb peered down the other tunnel off the space. That was where the creature had a fire burning last time.

After going a few yards down that tunnel, Caleb decided it was best to turn around. It was dark, no fire was going, Everything was quiet, so the creature was either not there, or so deep in the tunnels, Caleb was afraid of getting lost if he went in too far to find it. They went back to the main cave and Caleb sat on a boulder, collecting his thoughts. They could wait it out. Surprise the creature when it either came in from outside or up from the depths of the cave.

After an hour, Caleb was tired of waiting and thought it best for him and River to head back to the campsite. They could see the cave from there and now with his pack, they had a little food and the radio. He could try Tammy again in a bit. She was sure to be worried. Caleb stood up and slipped the pack on. He collected the spears and cocked his head at River.

"You ready to go eat something?" he asked.

River's eyes gazed over to him, then locked in a frozen stare. He wasn't looking at Caleb, he was looking past him. The boy's mouth opened in a shocked circle and he raised his hand to point. Caleb whipped around to see what River was gesturing at when a large form rushed at him. Caleb raised the spear but there wasn't enough space for him to get it between him and the beast. One swipe of the creature's arm and the spear splintered against the cave wall. Caleb stepped back to try and put a barrier between the monster and River. He watched as the creature's large arm raised again, then swung at him.

Everything went black.

The Other Side

When the light cut through Caleb's closed eyelids, his head throbbed in pain. He shifted, trying to assess where he was and what was going on around him. Prying his eyes open, he glanced around and looked for River. He made out the walls of the cave and a flicker from a fire. He rolled over and peered toward the source of light, seeing River on the far side of the cave. He attempted jumping up to go to his son, but the room spun and he found himself flat on the ground, face-down.

Caleb pushed himself up on his knees and fumbled around for something to hold onto. His hands hit the cave wall but found no grip, slipping down toward the ground. On all fours, Caleb slowly pressed himself back onto his heels and crouched to let the spins recede. He felt a large knot on his head and remembered the creature taking a swing at him. Fuck. He'd managed again to let his guard down, and now they were paying the price.

Caleb stood up like an old man climbing out of bed and turned to face River. The boy was sitting on the other side of the fire, his eyes locked on Caleb. He didn't seem scared but his eyes didn't blink. Caleb moved around the fire to where River was and sat down next to him.

"Are you alright?" Caleb's voice croaked out.

River nodded and scooted close to Caleb. "Daddy ok?"

Caleb chuckled and shook his head, regretting it immediately as the room tilted. "Not really. Where is he?"

"He?"

Caleb thought about the creature and considered he didn't know if it was a he. It could be female, or both. Or neither. He sighed and pressed on the knot on his head. "The creature? Where did it go? How did we get in here?"

River looked confused. Caleb was asking too many questions of the boy all at once. River pointed toward the cave opening. "There."

Caleb squinted toward the opening and saw a groove in the dirt on the ground. Oh. He'd been dragged there. "Did it hurt you?"

"No." River moved the dog to his other arm and touched Caleb's arm. "Mad. Hurt Daddy."

The creature hit Caleb, that much he remembered. He'd tried to spear it, however, it was quicker and knocked Caleb out. Why did it drag Caleb in there? What did it want? Caleb scanned the area, then glanced down at himself. He took a beating but was still okay. Maybe they could sneak out while the creature was gone. Just as he built up the courage to move, a shadow fell over the opening. It was too late.

It had returned.

Caleb shifted River behind him. As much as he wanted to stand up to face the monster, the room spun too much for him to get his footing. He stared at the beast, who stared back from the only way out. As they eyed each other, Caleb was able to better see what the creature looked like. He could see why others called it the tree monster. Its body looked like it was carved from tree trunks. Every ounce of it was muscle and it moved effortlessly like it wasn't quite part of their world. Its eyes shone an orangish-red, set wide on its large skull. Not totally unhuman-like, but also not human-like. Its mouth was broad, turned down at the corners like it was always disapproving. It had large, pointy teeth, however, at least now didn't seem as threatening. Its nose sat flat on the face, barely more than flared nostrils.

What terrified Caleb the most was the creature's arms. They were long, ending in sharp talons. Like it could snap a person in half without even trying. Caleb thought about that. It could've easily killed him and River. It didn't. It gave Caleb a serious knock on the head, yet left him alive. This is why Caleb felt he needed to come back.

The creature kept its eyes on Caleb as it moved around the side of the fire toward them. Caleb felt his heart racing and did his best to shield River, knowing it was pointless. What he didn't expect was the creature to meet River's eyes and reach out its deadly-looking hand to him.

"Stay back!" Caleb yelled.

The creature let its eyes flick to Caleb, then back to River. A low growl came from its chest and Caleb felt his blood run cold. What could he do? He stood between the beast and River, knowing he was helpless. River stepped around him and wandered toward the beast. Caleb tried to stop him, but the creature pushed Caleb away and motioned to River. River went to it and took its hand. Caleb couldn't believe what the hell he was seeing.

"River, come back. Come to me."

River watched him but shook his head in response. "Daddy, listen."

Caleb paused and listened, expecting to hear something. The creature was making a series of clicks and grunts, but nothing that made any sense. River had his face turned up toward the creature, nodding. Caleb frowned, not comprehending what was happening. The creature must have put some sort of spell on River. Rage filled Caleb and he took a step at the monster. It snapped its head toward him and let out a sharp growl, stopping Caleb in his tracks. River stared at him and rubbed his nose.

"Daddy, listen."

"River, I don't hear anything. Come over here. I don't want it to hurt you," Caleb pleaded.

River shook his head. "No hurt. Listen."

Caleb was ready to lose his mind and was running out of hope. They were going to die there. At that moment, the creature came at Caleb and extended its arm. Caleb jerked back, almost falling, when he saw something dangling from the creature's hand. A necklace. Gold, with a charm. When he realized what it was, Caleb felt tears prick his eyes. The charm was a running horse. He knew that necklace. He'd *bought* that necklace. The night of prom, he'd fastened it around Shannon's neck and told her he'd love her forever. She loved horses and he loved her. Seeing the beast with it only confirmed his suspicions it had killed Shannon. The police never found the necklace and now he knew why. The fucking monster had killed her, then took the necklace as a prize.

All the years of pain and longing bubbled up in him. Before Caleb knew what he was doing, he launched himself at the creature. Ready to kill it with his bare hands. As he hit the creature's impossible body, he ricocheted off and hit the ground for a moment before getting up and going at the monster again. It grabbed him with one hand as it pushed River away. The boy cried out, fear breaking through his calmness.

"Daddy, stop! Listen!"

Caleb whipped around, trying to break free from the creature's grasp. "I won't listen to this monster, River. He killed Shannon!"

River frowned and stepped away, his eyes confused and scared. He'd seen Lien kill Trevor and understood what Caleb was saying. Caleb had told River about Shannon and showed him pictures, but Caleb wasn't sure River understood what was going on. He twisted and kicked, attempting to break the creature's grip. He met River's eyes.

"Run!"

River stood frozen, afraid to move. Caleb jerked free and ran toward the boy, hoping to grab him and flee from the cave. He almost made it to River when he was snatched back and felt himself being enfolded in the creature's arms. "Run!" he gasped as he lost the breath in him and quit fighting.

Expecting the creature to crush him to death, Caleb could only hope River would get away. But then what? The boy would be lost in the woods. Alone and vulnerable. Caleb quit fighting and mumbled, "Let the boy go and you can kill me. Please, just let him go."

At that, the creature dropped Caleb to the ground and stepped back. Caleb groaned and tried to get up, his legs like water. He barely got to his knees and glared up at the monster. It was watching River, its face contorted in sorrow. It made sounds at River, who whispered back.

"Leave my daddy alone."

Caleb crawled away, unable to stand. The creature didn't move but River ran to Caleb, wrapping his small arms around Caleb's neck. "Daddy, listen."

Caleb rolled onto his back and moaned. "Fine, fine, I'm listening."

The creature came near and leaned over Caleb, again making the clicks and grunts. Caleb waved his hand to show he didn't understand and clutched River to his side. "No comprendo, muchacho."

The creature continued making the sounds, coming even closer. Caleb closed his eyes, ready to meet his fate. Maybe he'd see his mother again. Maybe he'd get to hold Shannon again. The idea warmed him. What about Tammy and his father? How would they get through his death? What about River? Would he find his way home? He'd be an orphan.

Caleb forced his eyes open and met the creature's eyes. "What do you want?" he screamed.

The creature raised its arm, pointing one of its sharp claws at Caleb's forehead. It could impale Caleb with no effort whatsoever. River would have to witness another parent being murdered in front of him. Caleb felt the prick of the talon pierce his skin and tried to escape. The creature held him down with its other hand and leaned in so close, Caleb could feel heat radiating off its body onto him.

He quit fighting and resigned himself to his fate. There was no escape. He stared at the creature. "Don't hurt my son. Please. He's been through too much. He needs a family. Make sure he gets home."

The creature glanced at River, then back at Caleb as it continued making the sounds. Its talon was still pressed to Caleb's forehead, but it didn't push in any further. Instead, it spread out its claw, which completely covered Caleb's skull. It felt so hot, Caleb was sure his skin was burning off his head, praying for it to be over quickly.

As the heat increased, Caleb sensed another sensation. It was as if a flashlight was being shined from inside his head. Brighter than any light he'd ever seen. He closed his eyes and turned inward, focusing on the light. Behind the light, he heard a laugh. A delicate, beautiful laugh. Shannon's laugh.

The light faded into a smaller circle and he realized he was staring at the flashlight Shannon was holding the night she was murdered. She was laughing and flashing the light in his face. She tipped her head and smirked at him as she spoke.

"It's time to see the truth."

The Uncovering

C aleb followed Shannon as she headed up the hill to her house, the memory becoming reality. He wanted to change things but found his footsteps fell the same, his words came out no different. It was as if he was being forced to relive the memory with no way of changing it. He hoped somehow he was being led through the past to find the truth, to go back and stop things before Shannon was forced to take her last breath.

As they got to her street, Caleb said goodbye and turned, his current mind screaming for him to stop, to grab Shannon and run. At least to walk her all the way home, so she'd be safe. At the moment his feet headed for home, something happened.

A split of sorts.

He observed young Caleb head for home, while his current self stood in place. Shannon no longer saw him as she headed up the hill, her flashlight casting bobbing shadows on the trees as she went. Young Caleb watched her climb the road and flash her light at him once she got to the mailbox.

Current Caleb viewed both figures going their respective ways and wondered what to do next. His question was answered when he found himself transported to the top of the hill. He was seeing Shannon heading for her door when something in the trees caught her attention. She paused halfway down the driveway, focused on the woods by her house. That's when he heard it. It sounded like an injured animal. A kitten or small bird was crying out. Shannon moved toward the sound and Caleb yelled out to stop her. However, she couldn't hear him and continued into the tree line.

She stumbled through the woods, her flashlight swinging around to locate the source of the sound. Caleb couldn't follow on command but found himself placed in the woods to see what was going to happen unfold. Shannon walked deeper in, scanning the area for the injured animal. She stopped and twirled around with the flashlight, the area illuminating in segments.

That's when Caleb saw it. No, not it. *Who*. The figure of a person was standing behind a tree, watching Shannon. The figure was making the animal sound. Luring Shannon farther into the woods.

Caleb tried with all of his might to move, but it was as if he was a tree, rooted to the ground. The figure wasn't the creature. It was a man. Shannon didn't see him as she searched the ground for an animal that didn't exist. The figure stepped out from behind the tree. Shannon's flashlight hit the figure, lighting it up.

Trevor.

"Jesus, Trevor, you scared me. What are you doing out here?" Shannon asked, her words sounding casual, her inflection not so much.

Trevor chuckled and shrugged. "Out for a night hike. You live near here?"

Shannon frowned. It was a small town, everyone knew where everyone lived. Trevor was playing dumb, but why? "You know I do. Did you hear an injured animal?"

Trevor came closer, revealing a smirk on his face. Chills ran through Caleb. Knowing he couldn't help Shannon, he didn't want to see what happened next. Trevor put his hands to his mouth and made a noise that sounded like a kitten being hurt. Shannon took a step back, realizing it had been Trevor all along. Caleb could feel her breath pick up pace and sensed fear pouring out of her pores. Shannon glanced back toward her house.

"I need to get home. It's late. My parents are up waiting for me."

"No they aren't," Trevor replied, his voice dripping with condescension. "They went to bed an hour ago. Just you and me out here. Saw that asshole you're dating head for home. He could've at least escorted you to your door like a gentleman and not common trash."

Caleb felt guilt wash over him. He could've prevented all of this had he just walked Shannon to her door. Shannon snorted. "I'm a grown girl, Trevor. I don't need anyone holding my hand."

Trevor took another step in her direction. "Don't you? Out here all alone. I've been watching you. Waiting."

"Waiting for what?"

"Waiting for you to come to your senses and dump that hick piece of shit."

Shannon shone her flashlight in Trevor's eyes. "Fuck you, Trevor. Even if Caleb and I broke up, do you really think I'd want to date *you*?"

Trevor stormed out of the light and in a second knocked the flashlight out of her hand, grabbing her wrist. "Snob. You think you're too good for me?"

Shannon yanked her hand free and slapped him across the face. "Damn right, I am. Now, if you don't mind. I need to go home. I don't know what you are playing out, hiding in the woods by my house, but I *will* call the police. Go home."

Trevor put his hands in the air like he agreed and stepped back. Shannon inched away from Trevor, keeping her eyes on him the whole time. She searched the ground for her flashlight, but not seeing it, turned to leave. Trevor glared at her as she made her way back through the trees. Caleb saw his movement, however, Shannon didn't notice. Trevor scooped the flashlight off the ground and went at Shannon's retreating form. Caleb tried to call out, but neither of them could see or hear him. He was the ghost, now.

Trevor moved quicker toward Shannon and she tried to run when she realized he was coming after her. Trevor raised the flashlight and hit her as hard as he could on the skull. Shannon went ot her knees, clutching her head.

"Stop! Leave me alone," she murmured, trying to get to her feet.

Trevor pushed her down and pressed his body weight on her. Shannon was disoriented and attempted to get free, but between the knock on the head and Trevor lying on her, she wasn't able to move. Trevor began shoving her skirt up and tried to remove her underwear. Shannon blocked him, managing to get him off the top of her.

"Trevor, stop! What are you doing?"

"What do you think? You owe me this. I've been in love with you since we were in sixth grade," Trevor replied.

"No, you aren't. You don't even know me. Caleb is my boyfriend. You need to leave me alone."

"Or what?"

Shannon paused and Caleb could see from the expression on her face, she was thinking of a way to bargain with him. She tugged her skirt down and rubbed her head. "You'll go to jail."

Trevor laughed so loud and cruelly, Caleb wondered how no one heard him out there. Trevor got up and hovered over Shannon. "No, I won't. No one would believe you, anyway. Out here after dark. They'll say you were asking for it. I'm home sleeping in my in bed, right now. Just ask my parents. They'll confirm my story."

Shannon's eyes got wide as she realized he was right. Trevor always managed to escape punishment. She scooted back and tried to get to her feet. Trevor used his foot to push her back down. Shannon began to cry, which irritated Trevor and he rolled his eyes.

"Please. High and mighty Shannon. Stop blubbering and take what you deserve." Trevor unbuckled his pants and let them drop to the ground as he stepped out of them toward Shannon.

Shannon peered around for any sort of help. Seeing she was alone, she blurted out, "I'm pregnant!"

That stopped Trevor and the expression that crossed his face would've almost been comical had he not been intent on raping her. "What did you say?"

"I'm pregnant. It's Caleb's. Please, just let me go home, I won't tell anyone what you did."

Trevor squatted down to face her, his eyes dark and furious. "You whore. Now, you definitely deserve what I'm going to do to you."

Shannon took the opportunity to kick him as hard as she could between the legs, sending Trevor sprawling. As soon as she could, she scrambled to her feet and attempted to run. Trevor grabbed her ankle and yanked her feet out from under her. He got up and jumped on her, wrapping his fingers around her throat.

"You filthy bitch. I thought you were pure, waiting for marriage. You fucked that inbred garbage?"

"Get the hell off me," Shannon gasped as his fingers tightened around her throat.

Trevor grunted and squeezed even tighter. "Fuck you. You did this. We were supposed to be together. Now, I don't want you, knowing his dick was inside of you. You disgust me. You deserve to die."

Caleb watched helplessly as Trevor choked the breath out of Shannon. Trevor pulled a knife out of his waistband and began stabbing Shannon with such hatred, Caleb felt sick. His heart shattered all over again and he wondered what he'd done to earn such punishment. Trevor stood up, wiping the blade on his pants, then kicked Shannon in the stomach. She didn't move, her eyes open and glazed over. Trevor picked up the flashlight and shoved it into his back pocket. He peered around the area for any sign he'd been there. Deciding he was good, he strolled out of the woods without looking back.

Caleb stood staring at his dead, pregnant girlfriend and wondered why he was still there. He now knew the truth, but Trevor was dead and couldn't be held accountable for what he did to Shannon. He thought about Lien and realized she would've ended up dead had she not defended herself. And River. Trevor would have killed them and still gone on with his life. After all, not many people in their town cared about an Asian woman and her child.

Caleb heard noise coming through the woods, looking to see if Trevor was coming back. However, the shadow that approached was much larger than a human. As it approached, Caleb watched with shock. It was the creature. It paused a few feet away from Shannon and stared at her. It came closer, then bent down for a better view. It poked her with its sharp talon and peered around. Trevor was long gone and it couldn't see Caleb. It knelt and cradled Shannon gently in its arms, making the same grunts and clicks Caleb heard it make before.

"Listen, Daddy." River's words echoed in Caleb's ears.

The creature rocked gently, holding Shannon, then laid her back on the ground. A low, painful wail came from the creature as it knelt beside Shannon's body. It placed its large hand over Shannon's womb, then moved it over the same area on its body. It continued to cry softly and Caleb understood.

The creature was female and it was alone. Whatever family it had was gone. Whatever children it had were gone. It was like him, lost in the world. Caleb thought about River and realized the creature meant no harm, it was drawn to River as a child because it missed its own.

Her own.

The creature stayed with Shannon's body until Shannon's father came through the woods. It picked up her necklace off the ground where Trevor had thrown her down. As Shannon's father arrived, it rose and disappeared into the trees. From a distance, it observed as Shannon's father discovered his dead daughter and his soul ripped apart. At the moment Shannon's father cried out into the dark, the creature cried out as well, its soft pain hidden by the father's loud pain.

Caleb felt himself being pulled away from the scene. Away from the past and from Shannon. He sensed River on the other side and allowed that to be a beacon back to his son. Back to his life. When he came to, he was lying in the cave, River curled up beside him. He pried his eyes open and saw the creature kneeling beside him, its hand on his head. The creature removed its hand and stood up, moving away from Caleb and River. Caleb sat up and met her eyes, seeing the pain he'd not seen before. He was wrong. It wasn't the creature Shannon was warning him about.

"He's back."

It was Trevor.

Beyond the Stars

The creature kept its distance as Caleb put the pieces together. Trevor killed Shannon. They'd never found her flashlight that night. The police assumed the assailant had either taken it or it had gotten lost somewhere in the woods. Now, Caleb knew Trevor had taken it with him. Why? Some sort of sick prize for what he did? Had he also killed other women? Girls were always going missing, maybe Trevor was the cause of some of that. Or, maybe, he was stalking only Shannon.

Caleb gazed at River and gathered the boy in his arms. River clung tightly to his father and buried his face in Caleb's shirt. Caleb glanced at the creature, considering what he'd been shown. It made him come to the realization the creature wasn't after them. Sure, it swung at Caleb, but he'd attacked first. With the branch, the C-4, and the spear. In each situation, the creature was reacting to his actions, not the other way around.

It was defending itself.

Caleb thought about the toy they'd found along with the food and blankets. He met the creature's eyes and understood she was trying to help them. Again, he wondered how such a large creature made it into the house to gather the items. He thought about the flashlight and it was as if the creature could read his mind. It made a series of soft clicks and gestured for Caleb to come by the fire. Caleb waited, not sure if it was safe when River touched his arm.

"She wants to show us."

Caleb looked at his son with a frown on his face. River knew it was a female? He was communicating with it? Caleb nodded and rose, the cave spinning around him. Defending herself or not, the creature had done some damage to his head when she hit him. River clasped his hand and led him to the fire, pointing to a boulder.

"Sit, Daddy."

Caleb was happy to oblige and collapsed on the ground, falling on his back. He waited until his vision settled and sat up, face-to-face with the creature. She raised her long arms above the fire as the grunts and clicks from her chest became louder. River watched her intently, bobbing his head as if he understood what she was saying. Caleb braced himself against the rock and stared in amazement.

"River, do you know what she's saying?"

River met his eyes, his voice clear and sure. "She is sad. Stuck. No family... alone."

Caleb glanced at the creature, her eyes focused on the fire. She motioned to the flames and Caleb shifted his eyes there. Like a crystal ball, images began to form in the flickers of light. Bombs, destruction, children crying. Caleb shook his head, he didn't grasp what she was showing him. He looked at River for guidance.

"Her family came here. Long ago. To help." River paused as he listened to the sounds she was making. "Sick."

"Your family got sick?" Caleb asked. The creature met his eyes and all of a sudden, the clicks and grunts made more sense to him.

They'd come from another land, maybe another world. Caleb could only comprehend it was far off. They had skills and medicine they were bringing to an already sick Earth. They thought they'd be welcomed by the inhabitants. By humans. However, any sight of them caused chaos, anger, vengeance. They were hunted by humans, the youngest being slaughtered first. The older creatures, heartbroken and confused, fell ill. One by one they died, leaving her all alone.

The creature put her claws to her chest and made a sound that came out like, "Tur-ka."

Caleb repeated it, knitting his brow. "Turka? Is that your name? I'm Caleb, this is River."

"Tur-ka," she repeated.

Caleb glanced at River for confirmation and the boy nodded. "She is Turka."

Caleb stared back into the fire, as images of her family being killed and dying played out. He stroked his chin, thinking about what happened. If her family had been murdered, where were the bodies? The bones?

Turka waved her arm over the fire and another image popped up. It was of Turka collecting the bodies. Of her breaking into homes, garages, and warehouses. Wherever the bodies were taken after they were killed. She ripped off the roof of a garage, reaching in to gather the body of a small creature. She cradled it to her chest, the same painful moan Caleb heard coming from her outside the cave, now escaping her body. From the way she held the body and rocked it, Caleb understood it was her child. His heart broke with the realization.

"Your child? It died?"

Turka stared into the fire, not answering. Another image emerged. It was of Turka watching Caleb's house. Observing the children play, a sad expression on her face. Then the image shifted to Trevor and Lien on the day they moved in. Trevor was yelling at Lien about something and River was cowering behind her. Trevor reached around Lien and snatched River out from behind her. He shook the boy, then slapped him across the face. Lien was forcing herself between the boy and Trevor, begging Trevor to stop. Trevor glared at her with the same shit-eating expression he'd given Shannon the night he murdered her.

He got off on making others suffer.

Caleb dropped his eyes, not wanting to see anymore. It was too much. Turka made soft clicking sounds and Caleb raised his eyes. Now, in the flames were images of him. Talking to Lien outside, taking the leaf from River, playing with his niece and nephew. He didn't understand why she was showing him these images. The last was of Lien shoving River into his arms and telling him to hide the boy. To keep him safe. Caleb met Turka's eyes in question.

"Good," River said, then pointed at Caleb's chest.

Caleb peered down at his son, shaking his head. He didn't feel good. He felt like a failure. He'd failed Shannon, he'd failed Lien, too. He had nothing to offer anyone. "No, I'm not good."

Turka made a loud grunt, drawing Caleb's attention to her. She pointed at River. Caleb didn't understand. "What? You can't have him."

Turka responded with a series of clicks. River nodded. "You keep me safe."

"I do. You're everything to me, River. What does she want from us?"

"To listen, Daddy."

Caleb focused back on Turka and did his best to listen. As she made sounds, the fire responded, showing them images. This time, though, the images came with emotions. Turka was alone and she wanted to keep the children safe. She was drawn to Caleb because of his pure heart. She sensed his misery over losing Shannon and the baby. She wanted to comfort him. She showed him images of how he made a difference to his father, his sister, River, Lien, even Stephan and the kids. Caleb had been so buried in grief for so many years, he didn't accept his life was important.

A thought crossed his mind and he cocked his head. "Can you not go home? Do you have a ship or something?"

Turka paused, absorbing his words, then shook her head. She raised her arms above her head, then dropped them, her hands hitting the ground. Caleb was confused and shook his head. "Did it crash?"

Turka motioned toward the fire, an image forming. It showed the group of creatures in a circle with their arms raised. As they lowered their arms, a circle of light formed between them. As their hands moved to their sides, the light grew into a sphere, encompassing all of them. The light then vanished, taking the creatures with it.

Oh, their ship was made by them. Together. Turka was showing that by herself, she couldn't create it. She was stranded on Earth. Caleb could feel her pain and isolation, wondering what it would've been like after Shannon's death if he hadn't had his family. How alone he would've been. He didn't think he'd still be alive if it hadn't been for them loving and supporting him.

"I'm sorry, Turka." It was the only words he could think to say.

Turka fell silent, staring into the flames. In the fire, images of human cruelty and destruction streamed. Hurting each other, destroying the Earth, disregarding everything they'd been given. Caleb watched as one after another the images showed the darkness in humanity. Here he'd been chasing the creature when all around him humans were the real monsters.

He closed his eyes, feeling tears wet his lashes. It was easier to believe something inhuman out there was the danger, rather than accepting the threat was all around them. Caleb wanted nothing more than to go home and hug his father, see his sister, and play with his niece and nephew.

River climbed into his lap and wrapped his arms around Caleb's arms like a pretzel. Caleb had a second chance to be a father and needed to stop running. He couldn't bring Shannon or his baby back, but he could take care of River. He could be a good son and good brother to his family. He could start over and have a life. Shannon would always be part of him, the baby he believed was River.

He still wanted vengeance for Shannon's death. He wanted Trevor to pay. However, Trevor was dead and couldn't be held accountable. Caleb rubbed River's head when he knew the truth. To make Trevor pay, Caleb needed to find a way to get Lien out of prison. If Trevor killed Shannon, beat up girlfriends, and punched his wife and child, he'd probably done more than that. How could Caleb prove any of it?

The flashlight.

Caleb's heart began to race. If he could find the flashlight with Trevor's prints on it, it would at least be something to try and get the case reopened. If the flashlight even still existed. Trevor could have ditched it years ago. Something in Caleb told him Trevor *had* kept it. A sick memento. Trevor didn't seem like the type to cover his tracks too well. His ego would cause him to make mistakes. If the flashlight still existed, who knew what else they might find to incriminate Trevor?

Caleb stared at Turka, picturing the flashlight in his brain. The image of the flashlight appeared in the fire and Turka nodded with understanding. She rose and gestured for him to follow her out of the cave. Dizzy and disoriented, Caleb stood up, using the cave walls to balance himself. Turka was moving fast and he could hardly keep up. River pulled him along, so they didn't lose sight of Turka. The scared little boy Lien had shoved into his arms, was now a determined child on a mission.

Outside of the cave, Turka waited on the path for Caleb. As soon as he appeared, she moved down the trail, her steps focused and sure. Caleb staggered after her, River holding his hand for support. Turka knew exactly where she was going and Caleb trusted her to get them there safely. She wanted what he did. To help.

By the end of the first day, Caleb knew where they were on the trail and where they were going. Turka strode with purpose and checked repeatedly to make sure Caleb and River were still behind her. When River got tired, she picked him up and carried him on her shoulder. Caleb found a branch on the trail and used it to propel himself forward, the fresh air and hope giving him renewed purpose. Turka was leading the way Caleb wanted to go.

To the place calling to him in his bones, which had always been his sanctuary. Where all the answers were waiting for him to uncover. Where everything that mattered left in his life was waiting for him. The right direction.

They were heading home.

Home Again, Home Again

With Turka's help, they made it home in record time. Except, once they were in sight of the house, Turka paused and went in a different direction. Confused and exhausted, Caleb begrudgingly followed her. She went to Lien's house and stood in the tree line, staring out at the neighborhood. It was afternoon and it seemed she didn't want to come out of the trees into the broad daylight. Caleb understood her hesitancy. If anyone saw her, it would cause an uproar. Or worse.

She'd be hunted down and killed.

They stayed in the woods until the sun went down, despite Caleb wanting nothing more than a shower and his own bed. River was cranky and Caleb thought about at least taking him home. However, that would start too many inquiries. Where had they been? Why didn't he answer the radio?

What happened out there?

It hurt Caleb's head to even think about it. He wanted answers before he was asked questions.

Glancing over at Turka, Caleb saw River was tucked in her arms, sleeping. It broke Caleb's heart for Turka. She missed her own child desperately. He leaned against a tree and closed his eyes. He didn't know what she wanted in Lien's house but she was focused on it, so he didn't question.

A little while later, Turka's movements woke him up and he peered over. She was getting up, still holding River in her arms. Caleb rose and followed her as she headed to the house. It was dark and from what he could tell, sometime around midnight. Caleb shivered and glanced at his house, picturing his warm covers. He was surprised to see Stephan's truck outside the house, then realized he felt relieved. He was glad Stephan had hung around while he was gone.

They crept up to the house and Turka paused, her height reaching the top of the house. How did she ever get in there? Rounding the house answered Caleb's question as he saw the windows of the kitchen and River's bedroom had been broken out. Not just broken, torn from the walls. He laughed unexpectedly and Turka turned, her face twisted in confusion. Caleb went up to the kitchen window and peered in. It was destroyed inside. The table was turned over, the cabinet doors ripped off their hinges. He pictured Turka tearing the window out and reaching in for supplies.

She was taking care of them.

They went around to the garage and Turka placed her hand on the roof as if she was going to gouge a hole in it. Caleb raised his hand to stop her and slipped in through the unlocked garage door. It was dark in the space and he didn't know what he was looking for. Turka leaned down by a window and stared in at him. Caleb shrugged and clicked a workbench light on, hoping it didn't draw attention from any nosy neighbors.

Once the light was on, he peered around, assessing why he was there. Turka yanked the window out as if it were a sticker off a page. She set the window down and extended her long arm into the garage. Caleb watched in amazement as her claw extended halfway across the garage. She pointed to a row of boxes on shelves on the far wall. Caleb stumbled over and squinted at the dusty boxes. Most of them were labeled things like, "clothes", "yearbooks", "holiday". The one that caught his eye was one on the top shelf with the words, "Trevor memories". Memories? *Like pictures and stuff?* Caleb wondered.

He slid the box off the shelf and brought it over to the workbench to get a better look. The box was so taped up, Caleb wasn't sure he could get it open. He took his pocket knife out and slid it under the tape. Inside was another taped-up box that read "private". Whatever was in there, Trevor didn't want anyone seeing it. Caleb cut that box open and took out a bundle wrapped in tape and paper. No kid's toys and photo albums in there. It was bumpy and bulky, feeling like a bag of car parts. Caleb removed the tape and unfolded the paper, catching his breath.

Inside the paper was a plethora of random items, but the one that stopped him in his tracks was a flashlight. With blood and strands of blond hair stuck to it. Caleb recognized the flashlight right away and fell to his knees sobbing. The proof was there. Was it enough? He could hear clicking and looked up to see Turka gesturing for him to get up. There was work to be done.

Caleb forced himself to his feet, afraid to look at the flashlight. Instead, he focused his attention on the other items. A set of car keys that didn't go to Trevor's car. A wallet. What looked like a woman's bracelet with the initials KPL on it. A hardcover library book with what appeared very much like blood on it. A hair barrette with dark brown, curly hair caught up in the teeth. A pair of women's underwear. There were other items, but Caleb was afraid to touch any of it. What if it was evidence like the flashlight? Folding the paper back over the items, he fastened the tape as well as he could to secure the package.

He made his way back out of the garage to where Turka was waiting and came up to her, tears in his eyes. "Thank you, for showing me this. It won't bring Shannon back, but maybe it'll be enough to get Lien free."

River opened his eyes blearily and stared at Caleb. "Mama?"

"Yes, honey. Mama. Daddy is going to try and get Mama home. I can't promise you I can, but I'll try."

River nodded and clung on to Turka. Turka turned and set the boy down, heading back into the woods. Caleb froze, realizing she'd done what she'd come to do. Not expecting it, Caleb felt his heart hurt as she walked away.

"Turka, don't go. We need you."

She rotated and shook her head. She was right, it wasn't safe for her to be there. She'd been keeping an eye on them all this time to make sure they were safe, now they needed to find a way to do the same for her. Caleb touched his chest, where a medallion his mother gave him after Shannon's death hung. He pulled it off over his head and went over to her. It was too small to fit over her head, so he held it out. Turka touched it, tipping her head at him in question. Caleb fastened it around her arm. Turka stared at it and touched it again with her other hand, the medallion catching the moonlight.

"Thank you," Caleb whispered, fighting back tears. "Go to the caves. I'll come there again. I will help you any way I can. I promise."

Turka grunted and with a few clicks, spun and disappeared into the trees. Caleb gathered River up and headed home, grasping the package in his other hand. He tucked it in the woodbin before slipping inside the house. Immediately, the familiar smell overtook him and he let the tears flow freely down his face. His sanctuary. The house was dark and quiet. Caleb didn't want to disturb anyone, so he took River and they crept up to his room. As he was closing his door, Tammy's door opened and she peeked out, her eyes wide with surprise when she saw Caleb.

"You're home! Thank God. I was getting worried when you weren't answering the radio," she whispered.

Caleb, not wanting to get into it, shrugged. "Sorry, battery died. We're okay. I'm going to have River sleep in with me tonight, so we don't wake up the munchkins. Talk in the morning?"

"Of course. Get some sleep. I have a million questions to ask you. I'm glad you and River are home safe, Caleb. I really missed you."

"I missed you, too."

"I missed you, three," came a male voice from Tammy's room. Stephan. They'd obviously taken it to the next level.

"Hey, man. Thanks for keeping an eye on the homefront," Caleb responded.

"You know it. See you in the morning."

Caleb tucked River into bed and peered out the window to the backyard. It was dark, but the moonlight caught Turka standing in the trees, staring up at his window. Caleb raised his hand and smiled when she raised hers back to him. They were now family.

River was sound asleep, cuddling his now very dirty and ratty stuffed dog. Caleb thought he'd pass out immediately but found he was restless and got up. He thought about the package he'd found and wondered who the owners were of the other items. The way they were hidden with the flashlight, his gut told him Trevor *had* been after other women, as well. Stalking, confronting... murdering. Caleb rubbed his face with the horror of it all. In their midst lived a real monster. One that looked like them, but that's where the similarities ended.

Whatever existed in Trevor was evil.

Trevor was dead, Shannon was dead, whoever else Trevor went after was dead. Caleb couldn't go back and change the past. What he could do was try and save Lien. He could bring closure to the families of whomever those items belonged to. Caleb considered perhaps Trevor was sloppy and about to be discovered when he left for Vietnam. He'd been there a couple of years, probably to let things die down. Then he met Lien. Lien. Caleb tried to send her a message mentally that he was going to get her free.

Or at least try.

By morning, River was up and beyond excited to play with his cousins again. Caleb insisted River get a bath and clean clothes on first, then set him loose on the house. He could hear the three children running through the house and giggling. Slipping into the shower, he closed his eyes and leaned against the shower wall. Tammy was going to grill him, but he wanted to talk to Frank, the lawyer, first.

After the shower, he went back to his room and picked up the phone, dialing Frank's number. He was surprised to find his hands shaking with nerves as he waited for Frank to answer the phone.

Frank picked up after a few rings. "Hello?"

"Frank? It's Caleb. I need to talk to you. It's about Lien's case. Well, that and other things. I have some new evidence."

"Caleb, how are you? Not sure how much help I can be, but do you want to meet up? What kind of evidence?"

"I'll bring it with me. Trevor killed my girlfriend, Shannon, I have proof. I think he may have killed other women, as well. Lien was defending herself, he would've killed her otherwise," Caleb explained.

Frank whistled into the phone. "That must be some evidence. I don't doubt it, but let's not jump to conclusions. You want to meet at the diner?"

"Can we make it the river? I don't want to pull this stuff out in public. Can I trust you?"

"Of course, you can. I'm not a public defender because it's making me rich. I want to help people, to bring the truth out. How about in an hour? I need to eat something, first."

"An hour it is. Frank?"

"Yeah?" Frank responded.

"I need you to believe me... no matter what I tell you. It's crazy, but I need to tell someone the truth," Caleb replied.

"Okay? About what?"

"Turka."

A New Day

After he hung up with Frank, Caleb knew he needed to have a conversation with Tammy as soon as possible. To tell her everything. How much of it she'd believe was the question. He sighed and dressed, playing out the conversation in his head. He came up with responses to anything she might counter him with. Setting his resolve, Caleb made his way downstairs.

River and Drew were drawing at the table when Caleb came into the kitchen. He was relieved to see a pot of coffee was on and snagged a mug out of the cabinet. He hadn't had coffee in quite a while and the smell was intoxicating. He poured the rich, black liquid to the rim, breathing in the heady steam.

Tammy came in dressed for work and came up next to him. "You sleep okay? I bet you were glad to be back in your bed," she asked as she poured coffee into a travel mug.

"You know it. I was missing home."

239

"You could've come back sooner, you know?" Tammy chided, her face pinched in disapproval.

"No, I couldn't have. I had stuff I needed to do out there. Things to resolve."

Tammy eyed him, knowing more was coming. "Like?"

Caleb set his coffee cup down and grimaced. "Do you have time for this conversation? Looks like you are heading off to work."

"I am, but I have time. Hey, kids, the bus will be here in five minutes. Grab your lunches off the counter and make sure you have your homework."

Drew's eyes grew wide and he bolted out of the room, clearly in search of his homework. Sara came in from brushing her teeth and kissed her mother as she shoved her lunch into her backpack. River was sad the kids were leaving, so Caleb winked at him.

"Hey, we'll go to the park today, okay? Play on the swings? Then, they'll be home from school and you can hang out with them."

River nodded and went back to his drawing. Caleb turned to Tammy. "Remember what I told you that morning when I was leaving to go into the national forest?"

The bus horn honking distracted them and Tammy went to the kitchen door. "Drew, move it, boy! You're going to miss the bus! I don't have time to drive you to school."

Drew came barreling down the stairs with a stack of papers waving in his hand as he ran out the front door. They watched from the window as Sara and Drew scrambled onto the bus. The bus driver closed the door and drove off.

Tammy sighed, then faced Caleb. "The creature?"

Caleb ran his hand through his hair. "Yeah, I saw her. She showed me something. Answers to some questions."

Tammy frowned, not sure if he was pulling her leg or completely lost it. "Her?"

Caleb shrugged. "Turka is her name. She's uh... not of this world."

Stephan came in, freshly showered and shirtless, and plucked a coffee cup out of the sink, rinsing it before filling it with coffee. "Whose name?"

Caleb motioned to the table. "Let's sit. I have a lot to tell you. I know who killed Shannon."

Stephan's brows raised and he sat down next to River. "Hey, little dude. Glad to have you home again. You have fun hiking in the woods with your dad?"

River grinned, then went back to his drawing without answering. Caleb sat on his other side and Tammy sat across from them. Caleb glanced at River's drawing and the hair on his neck stood up as River drew their house. He focused back on Tammy.

"I know this all sounds batshit crazy, but I promise everything I'm about to tell you is the god's honest truth, okay? I need you to hear me out, at least."

Tammy sipped her coffee and met Stephan's eyes for a second before looking back at Caleb. "Okay?"

Caleb cleared his throat and began the tale. Of seeing the creature in the woods, of Shannon's warning. He fumbled through everything that happened to them out in the woods. About finding the cave entrance, confronting Turka, and discovering she wasn't what Caleb thought the creature was. He paused before he got to the part where he went into Lien's house, glancing between Tammy and Stephan. "So, have I lost you, yet?"

Stephan shook his head, his eyes unsure. "No, keep going. If nothing else, it's a hell of a story."

Tammy didn't respond.

Caleb went on to explain what Turka communicated to him about her family being killed and her being stuck there with no way home. Tammy snorted and shook her head in disbelief. River was watching their interaction and set his crayon down.

"Aunt Tammy, Turka sad. Misses baby and family."

Tammy's mouth dropped open at the many words River said. She set her coffee cup down and put her hand in the air in confusion. "When did this happen? When did he start talking again?"

"Out in the woods. Turka grabbed River and he called to me for help," Caleb explained. "Since then, he's been speaking again."

"She *took* him? I thought you said you were wrong and she wanted to help you. Why on Earth would she snatch a small child like that? She sounds mean, dangerous. She could've seriously hurt him!"

"I think she just missed her child and River made her happy. She didn't mean any harm, Tammy," Caleb responded cooly. He understood where she was coming from, but needed Tammy to hear him out.

"Really? Because I don't know of anyone who would steal a child out of the goodness of their heart, Caleb!" Her voice rose tensely. "What makes you think that? That she wasn't going to harm him?"

Caleb glanced at River, who was staring at them. "Because we're still here and not dead in the woods."

Tammy stood up and shoved her chair back. "I don't have time for this. This crazy story. What did you mean you know who killed Shannon? The monster?"

"She's not a monster, and no. Can you please sit down? I have more to tell you. I know this is upsetting, but it's important." Caleb gestured to the chair and pleaded at her with his eyes.

Tammy glared at Stephan, who put his hands up in confusion. She plopped down. "I need to leave in ten minutes, so make it quick."

Caleb went on to tell her the vision Turka showed him about Shannon's murder. He said how they followed her to Lien's house and she showed him where the box was in the garage of Trevor's "treasures". Caleb described what was in the box in detail.

Tammy's face went pale and she looked deflated. "Do you think he killed other women? I mean, if he actually killed Shannon," she asked.

"Yes, and he did. I'm about to go meet with Frank with the box of things. See if they can be tied to other murders. If nothing else, we have the flashlight with hopefully his prints and Shannon's blood on it," Caleb replied. Saying Shannon's blood choked him up and Tammy reached across the table, covering his hand with hers.

"I'm sorry, Caleb. I don't know what to make of all of this, but I can see you truly believe what you're telling me. Even if the box ties Trevor to the murders, he's dead, so how does that help anyone, now?"

Caleb nodded and watched River. "It would give those families answers. I'm also hoping it would allow them to reopen both Shannon's case and Lien's. Set Lien free and let Shannon finally rest."

"Let you finally rest," Stephan whispered from the end of the table.

"That too," Caleb agreed. "That too, man."

Tammy rose slowly and glanced at her watch. "I'm taking lunch at noon. Can you meet me after you talk to Frank? I need to go, but, Caleb, I believe you. As much as I can, anyway. Just give me some time to think about all this."

"I'll be there. Me and River."

Tammy leaned over and kissed Stephan on the lips. "Will you be here when I get home?"

"I should be. Why?" Stephan inquired.

"I think I'm going to need a stiff drink after all this and it's not good to drink alone."

Stephan laughed and squeezed her hand. "Then, I'll make sure I'm here. Do you want me to pick something up?"

Tammy glanced at Caleb and reconsidered her request, knowing the battle he'd had with alcohol. "Why don't we get some pizza and soda instead? Make it a family affair."

"You got it."

After Tammy left, Caleb checked the time and realized he needed to head out to meet with Frank. He helped River get on his shoes and peered at Stephan. "Do you believe me?"

Stephan shrugged. "I'm more likely to believe some out there shit than Tammy. I've seen and heard some weird things in my time. Besides, it's hard not to when your boy draws pictures like this one here."

Stephan held up the drawing and Caleb took a closer look. It was like the one River had drawn before of the house and creature. Except this time, Turka was standing by their house with a lost expression. No longer the scary beast, now a being without a family to call her own.

Caleb ran his fingers over the drawing and shook his head. "Damn."

Caleb's father came into the kitchen and seeing Caleb, embraced him. "Son, you're home. I missed you."

"I am Dad. We're okay. I missed you, too."

His father clapped him on the back with a grin and poured the last of the coffee into his cup, clicking off the coffee pot. He seemed more lucid than normal and Caleb frowned at Stephan in question.

"Your pop has been going to the senior center a few hours a day. I take him on the way to work. Tammy brings home once she gets off."

Caleb leaned against the counter and smiled. "You like that, Dad? Hanging out there?"

His father chuckled and gulped coffee. "I do and there's a cute lady down there who makes me mac and cheese just as I like."

Caleb laughed. "That right?"

Stephan got up and slipped his shirt on. "That's right. You ready to go, Pop? Don't want to leave her waiting."

Caleb was in awe at the change in his father. He seemed almost like he did before Caleb's mother died. He watched as Stephan helped his father to the door.

Stephan paused as the old man went out and gestured to Caleb. "He's in good hands. We had to do something with you gone. Your dad was slipping farther from reality, so Tammy arranged for him to get daily care when she worked at the senior center. After the home health nurse quit, she had to look into other options. This is covered by the state. Don't worry, the cute lady is like forty and married. She's just good to your father."

Caleb realized him taking care of his father when he himself was a raging alcoholic hadn't helped his father's mental state. His father was alone a lot and Caleb wasn't good company when he was around. Guilt washed over him for the shit son he'd been. "Thanks, Stephan. I really need you guys. I was a fucking mess."

"True, but you had every reason to be. You went through more than most people and still kept your sensitivity intact. I'm proud of you for taming that beast. We got this. You aren't alone anymore," Stephan replied and ducked out the door with a wave.

That's when it hit Caleb. He *had* been alone all those years after Shannon, then his mother, died. Isolated in his grief. He was wandering lost, part of his soul ripped from his body. Nothing more than a shell with a beating heart. Just like Turka. Now, he had family around and a son to raise. A purpose. Hopefully, he could get River's mother home safely to him. She could live with them. They could build from the ashes and create a family from what was left.

Caleb gathered River up and headed for the truck to meet with Frank. Once River was buckled in with his stuffed dog, Caleb grabbed the box from the woodbin and slipped it behind the seat for safekeeping. He hoped Frank would know what to do with the items in the box. Maybe he'd have connections in law enforcement to track down the owners of the belongings and find out why Trevor had them in his possession. Caleb knew in his heart why, but he needed the questions to finally have solid answers. It was the only way to move forward.

Caleb gazed over at River and smiled. Through all the tragedy, he was given the greatest gift. A child, a family, a reason to live. River kicked his small, sneakered feet and grinned back at Caleb like only a child could. Caleb felt all the love in the world fill his chest.

"I love you, River."

"Love you, Daddy."

Everything made sense, now. It was time to set things right. For Shannon, for River, for Lien, for himself.

For Turka.

Power of Belief

F rank was already at the river when Caleb arrived. Caleb slid his truck in next to Frank's car and waved at him as he unloaded River. Frank climbed out, appearing disheveled and tired. Caleb set River down and walked over.

"Hey, Frank! Man, you look rough."

Frank chuckled and made a half attempt at straightening his tie. "Late nights, long days."

"Working on a case?" Caleb asked.

"I wish. No, marital problems. Been sleeping at the office the last couple of weeks."

"Oh. I'm sorry. You working it out?"

"I sure hope so. Being a public defender is a lot of work with minimal pay. Takes its toll on a marriage," Frank explained, running his hand across the top of his head.

"I bet. Have you thought about going out on your own?" Caleb asked, grabbing the box out from behind the seat.

"Every day. It would help if I could win a big case."

Caleb shook the box. "I may have one for you."

Frank tipped his head and glanced at the worn cardboard box. "That it? You want to go over by the river? There's a picnic table and I brought some food for the ducks. Perhaps, River can feed the ducks while we talk."

Caleb nodded and waved his hand. "Lead the way."

They made their way to the table and Caleb set the box down. Frank pulled out a bag of dog kibble and handed it to River. "This is for the ducks. Dog food is better than bread. They may chase you but they're nice, just hungry. You want to feed them?"

River grinned and took the bag from Frank. He ran to where the ducks were. As soon as they saw the bag, they circled River, who giggled and threw out a handful of food. Frank sat at the table and drew the box toward him.

"So, you want to fill me in? What is this?"

Caleb sat across from him where he could watch River with the ducks, as well. "I'll start with the easy stuff. I believe my neighbor, Lien's husband, Trevor killed my girlfriend when we were all teens."

"Oh? Have you always felt that or is this something new?" Frank asked, drumming his fingers on the box.

"Something new. I'll need to backtrack, but this box contains items that were in Trevor's garage... including the flashlight my girlfriend was carrying the night she was murdered. The police never found it."

"Are you sure it was hers?"

"Yes. The flashlight was the one she had when I walked her to her street. It uh... damn, this is harder than I thought it would be. It has dried blood on it and what looks like strands of her hair. I'm hoping it has Trevor's prints on it, so we can tie her murder to him," Caleb explained.

"I'm sure it would allow Shannon's family to be at peace," Frank offered.

"Her father is dead and she was an only child, but I'm sure her mother would like to know. That's not all, though, Frank," Caleb said, pausing to think the best way to go on.

"What do you mean?"

"There's other things in the box. Things I think belong to other people Trevor may have hurt. May have killed."

Frank pulled open one of the flaps and gazed in, being careful not to touch the items. "Why do you think that this stuff belonged to other people and not just Trevor?"

Caleb shifted and glanced at River, who was sitting now and feeding the ducks from his hand. "Because Trevor always liked to knock his girlfriends around. Because he beat his wife and son. Because he disappeared after high school for years. Because Trevor was a piece of shit."

Frank chuckled dryly and cocked his head. "That he was. Lien told me how abusive he was. I just wish the courts would've listened. She doesn't belong in prison."

"No, she doesn't and I'm hoping this evidence can prove she needed to kill him to save her and River's life. I believe Trevor was a serial killer, and I'm asking for your help to prove it."

Frank peered back into the box and tipped it to move the items around for a better view. "I can see if we can get DNA and fingerprints run on these items. I have a buddy in a police department over in West Virginia. We might be able to connect the items to their owners if there are any cases still in the system. Do you want to tell me how you acquired these items?"

Caleb glanced at River, then shrugged. "You ready to hear some shit you might not believe?"

Frank laughed. "After all I've seen, there isn't much left I don't believe."

"Alright, so let me start from the beginning or the middle, I really don't know. Do you believe in like aliens, Bigfoot, things like that?"

"Like I said, there isn't much that surprises me or seems too out there. Just start wherever, I'll believe you," Frank assured him.

Caleb began from when he first saw Turka. He told Frank about his dream where Shannon warned him. *He's back.* The rest of the story poured out and as Frank said, he listened with understanding and never made Caleb feel like he was going off the rails. When Caleb got to the part about finding the box in Trevor's garage with Turka's help, Frank scribbled down some notes.

"Alright, so let me get this box of things to my buddy. I'm going to leave out the part about Turka because it won't help the case, however, I think we can at least get some info on the items and hopefully find Trevor's prints on at least some of them. I do think the flashlight is our strongest piece of evidence as it clearly has blood and hair on it. Since Trevor is dead, what are you wanting out of this?" Frank asked.

"I want Lien to be released from prison. To show not only was Trevor abusive, but that he was most likely a murderer. I know for a fact he was, but I want it to be proven," Caleb responded.

River, out of dog food, was coming back to the table, being chased by a flock of waddling ducks. As River ran faster, so did the ducks. Caleb got up and scooped River into his arms, confusing the ducks, who circled around him, quacking for more food.

Frank stood up and tucked the box under his arm. "Thank you, Caleb, for bringing this to me. I got into this field of work because I wanted to help people. I'm sure there are families out there who want answers and I think we may just be able to give them some. Unfortunately, we can't take away their pain, however, from what I've seen, sometimes even an answer brings some relief. I'll let you know as soon as I hear something back."

Caleb bounced River in his arms as the ducks gave up and went back to the water. "Thanks, Frank. For believing me, for being willing to take this on. Do you think it could get Lien set free?"

"I don't know, but I think we can build a good case to appeal. She deserves to be with her child. I could tell she has a gentle soul and would never have done what she did if she wasn't in fear for her and River's life."

River perked up at hearing his name and looked at Frank. "Mama?"

Frank reached over and tousled River's hair. "Yes, your mama. She loves you very much and misses you."

River chewed his fingers and appeared like he might cry. Caleb held him tightly and met Franks's eyes. "Have you spoken with her?"

"I have. She's holding on, but I can see the light going out in her. Her son is everything to her."

That, Caleb could understand. River had become everything to him. "If you see her, can you let her know she always has a place to come home to? She can live at my house, we'll make room. This way we can both have River."

"I sure will. You sure do love that boy, don't you?" Frank asked.

"More than anything in this world. He's my son."

River gazed up and patted Caleb gently on the cheek. "Daddy."

Frank watched the interaction and smiled at them. "Sometimes, through tragedy, we find what we've been waiting for. I'll give you a call as soon as I hear something."

Caleb waited until Frank was in the car, then carried River to the passenger side of the truck. He buckled River in and kissed him on the forehead. Frank was right. Now, Caleb couldn't imagine his life without River, but he came to him because of Shannon's murder. Because of Lien shooting Trevor. Caleb wanted to change the script. He wanted River in his life because Lien came home and they figured out a way to raise him together.

Checking the time, Caleb headed in the direction of the hospital to meet with Tammy. They were a little early, so Caleb took River to the park and let him swing until it was Tammy's lunch break. When he pulled into the parking lot, she was waiting outside and squeezed in next to River.

"You need a dad vehicle, now," she teased and handed River a cookie. "The cafeteria has the best chocolate chip cookies."

"You didn't bring me one, too?" Caleb teased, giving her a dramatic wink.

"You aren't four years old. Where do you want to go? I'm famished."

"How about the burger stand? It will be quick and they have those metal spring animals River can play on."

They parked at the burger place and ordered food. River ran over and climbed on the metal dog, or horse, it was hard to tell. Tammy watched him, then faced Caleb. She fiddled with a napkin and bit her lip.

"I've been thinking about what you told me this morning. About the creature."

"Turka."

"Sure, Turka. You need to understand how out there this all sounds to me. I worry you're losing your mind, however, you do seem more stable than you have in a long time. I need something more to prove this to really believe what you're telling me," Tammy said, a pained expression on her face. She obviously wanted to trust her brother but was having a tough time getting there.

Caleb frowned and shook his head. "Like what, Tammy? What would prove to you that I haven't lost my mind?"

"I want to meet her. I want to meet Turka."

At Peace

I t didn't take long for Frank to get answers on some of the items from the box. The blood on the flashlight was confirmed to be Shannon's, as was the hair. Trevor's prints were found on it, as well. Caleb hung up the phone after talking to Frank and stared out into the woods. Most of the other items did have Trevor's prints on them, but they were still trying to connect them to their owners, which Frank said could take a while longer. They were running prints and DNA through the database to see if any unsolved murders came up.

Caleb knew since Turka showed him that Trevor murdered Shannon, but hearing it made his knees feel weak. Caleb heard Tammy come in from work and throw her keys on the table. He tried to mask his face, but she stopped as soon as she saw him.

"Caleb? What happened?"

"Frank called. They matched the blood and hair on the flashlight to Shannon. Trevor's prints were all over it."

Tammy set her purse down gently and eyed him. "Caleb, I'm so sorry. I know it doesn't change anything, but does Frank think it will help Lien's case?"

Caleb shook his head. "He's not sure yet. He thinks it could, but only if they find the owners of the other items. If those prove to be what we think it is, then we'll have a solid case that Trevor wasn't just knocking his wife around, he was a sadistic murderer. A serial killer."

Tammy frowned. "Where's River?"

"He's playing out back with Sara. They're building a tunnel, or channel, or something like that. Basically, playing in the dirt."

"I need to run to the grocery store. Are you okay watching the kids?"

"I have been all afternoon, so they're good. Drew is in his room working on a project for school. A volcano for the science fair," Caleb replied.

Tammy picked her purse up, then sighed. "I'm sorry, I didn't mean to change the subject, this is just a lot to take in. I don't know what to say. I hope they let Lien out of prison."

Caleb understood where she was coming from. One thing their parents hadn't been good at was dealing with heavy emotions. He smiled and reached out to touch Tammy's hand. "It's okay. I don't know what to do with all these feelings inside me, either. I want answers, but with the answers comes more guilt."

"You have nothing to be guilty about, you didn't do this and you were only a kid when Trevor killed Shannon. We live in a small town where bad things don't happen. Or didn't. You couldn't have known that sick fucker would stalk her like he did. If you want to talk later once the kids go to bed, I'm here for you."

Caleb nodded and watched her leave, turning his attention back to the woods. He could hear Sara and River playing, their shrieks and giggles filling the air. He stepped outside and waved them in.

"Hey, you two, come get cleaned up. You can help me make dinner."

Both children ran for the porch, covered in mud and leaves. Caleb stopped them at the door and pointed upstairs. "Bathtime, now. Tammy will kill me if she sees the state of you. You're covered head to toe in dirt."

They ran past him to the bathroom, stripping as they went. Caleb followed behind, picking up their filthy clothes, then dropped them in the hamper. He snagged them each a clean outfit and put the clothes on the bathroom counter. Checking the water temperature, he faced the children.

"Put these on when you're done. Do you want me to stay in here with you?"

Sara gave him the look of someone much older. "Uncle Caleb, I can take a bath myself."

"I know you can, Sara. Do you want to help River wash his hair?"

Sara put her hand on her hip just like her mother and rolled her eyes. "Of course."

Caleb stopped by the children's bedroom and poked his head in at Drew. "Hey, your sister and River are getting cleaned up, can you keep an ear out?"

Drew looked up from his project and bobbed his head, still distracted by his work. "Yeah."

"Thanks, Drew. I'm going to step outside for a few minutes. Grandpa is watching television downstairs if you need him. I'll be right out back."

Drew didn't respond but nodded as he focused on shaping the sides of his volcano. Caleb chuckled and headed downstairs. He placed his hand on his father's shoulder.

"I'm going outside for a moment. Just out back, need some fresh air, okay? River and Sara are bathing and Drew is listening out for them. I'll be right back."

His father waved his hand in agreement and Caleb slipped outside. The air was cool and he shivered as he walked down the trail into the woods. As soon as he felt far enough away from the house, the emotions he'd been holding in bubbled up and he began to sob. Hearing that Trevor had killed Shannon was both a relief and heart-wrenching. Caleb went to his knees, his face pressed to the earth, and let the pain he'd been carrying for all those years ooze out of him.

He allowed himself to feel again.

By the time he was too exhausted to cry anymore, he heard Tammy's car pull in. He wiped his nose and sat up, staring at the back of the house. The only home he'd ever known. He rose and brushed off his clothes, attempting to make it appear he hadn't been crying in the woods. He wiped his eyes and took a deep breath, heading to the house.

A rustling caught his attention as he got up the hill near the driveway and he turned toward it. Turka was watching him from the trees, the expression on her face twisted in agony. She could feel his pain. Caleb met her eyes and sensed the tears welling up again. He froze, not sure what to do, when Turka made her way to him. Caleb felt like a little boy waking from a terrible nightmare and wanted to tell Turka his innermost secrets.

When she was yards away from him, Caleb ran to her, embracing her the best he could as he bawled into her thick skin. Turka leaned over, wrapping her arms around him like a mother, and drew him to her breast. Finally, finding comfort somewhere, Caleb let it all come out and clung onto Turka like a baby. She made soft clicks at him and cradled him gently while he broke down. For a moment, Caleb felt like a child in his mother's arms. Turka rocked from side to side and continued the soothing clicks until Caleb composed himself. He looked up at her.

"Thank you, Turka. For everything."

Turka stood to full height and touched Caleb's head softly. He felt a vibration pass between them. Caleb could hear the children inside running around and knew he needed to go in, so Tammy wasn't overwhelmed. He put his hand out to Turka and she rubbed one talon over it. One of the children yelled inside and Turka's attention shifted toward the sound. Her body tensed and she took a step in the direction of the house. Caleb stopped her.

"They're just playing. They're okay."

Turka paused and peered down at him, then back at the house. Her body relaxed and she turned to leave. Caleb wished she could come home with him, but not only would she not fit, she'd scare the hell out of everyone. He put his hand out again and this time she wrapped hers around his, dwarfing his hand in her clasp. Caleb walked with her into the woods for a bit, then it began to get dark. He needed to be able to find his way home. They stopped and Caleb stared up at Turka.

"I need to go home. My sister wants to meet you."

Turka cocked her head and made a few clicks. Then she stepped away, vanishing into the woods. Caleb watched her leave, his heart aching for her. Once, she had a family. Now, she was alone and trapped. Caleb went back up to the house and was surprised when he saw Tammy standing on the porch with her arms crossed and her eyes wide.

"Everything alright, Tammy? The kids okay?"

Tammy nodded, her attention elsewhere. "Yeah, Dad is teaching them poker. Where did you go?"

"Sorry. After the call from Frank, I needed to step away to deal with it. I was only in the woods behind the house. Dad said he'd listen out for the kids. Drew was up there while they bathed," Caleb fumbled over his words.

Should he not have left the kids without him?

Tammy waved her hand dismissively, then glanced over his shoulder into the forest. "They're fine. Semi-clean and the bathroom looks like a tornado went through it, but they're good. It's not that."

Caleb furrowed his brow. "Is there something else? You seem upset."

Tammy glared at him, her lips tight and thin. "Caleb, are you being honest with me? About everything?"

Caleb wracked his brain, trying to think of what he wouldn't have been honest about. If anything, he'd probably been too truthful about what happened. He shook his head and met Tammy's eyes. "I promise. You know what I know. What's going on, Tammy? Are you mad at me?"

Tammy's face softened as she looked at her little brother. "No, I'm not mad. I'm-"

Her voice trailed off and she appeared confused. Caleb waited but she didn't pick up where she left off. She just stared off into the woods with a disconnected look on her face. Then she whispered, "I thought I understood the world we live in. Everything about it. I figured you were reacting out of trauma and making it up about the monster."

"She's not a monster."

Tammy's eyes flicked to his as she nodded. "Right, the creature. Turta?"

"Turka."

"Turka. I love you Caleb, but honestly thought you were losing your mind. Stephan tried to convince me otherwise, however, I thought there was no way it was true."

"You believe me, now?" Caleb asked.

Tammy appeared as if she was fighting back tears and turned away, her voice above a whisper. "I do."

Caleb was relieved but he didn't know what brought the change in his sister. "Why now? What made you change your mind?"

"I saw her. I saw Turka."

Sweet Freedom

The morning started out raining, windy, and cold. Caleb woke up and glanced at the window as the wind blew small particles of leaves and branches against the glass. He smiled and swung his legs over the edge of his bed, ready for the day. Nothing could damper his spirits, now. It'd been a few months and many, many phone calls, but Lien was being released from prison. Frank kept up his end of the deal and with the assistance of some of his law enforcement friends, they were able to track down the owners of most of the items in the box. By tracking down, meant reopening unsolved murders of young women along the East Coast.

Five including Shannon.

Through fingerprinting and DNA, all but two of the items were identified and their owners traced back to the murders. In each case, either Trevor was connected as someone the women knew in passing, or his prints were found on the items along with the women's prints, hair, blood, or other

DNA. As Frank promised, he worked all of the cases with the local police departments until they could confirm Trevor was the most likely suspect.

A couple of the items were too old and didn't have substantial evidence on them. Even so, pictures of the items were sent to various police departments along the trail they suspected Trevor had taken. One with unsolved murders of young women, in the hopes those families could also be at peace. By connecting Trevor to five murders, Frank's request to revisit Lien's case was granted. After a short trial, it was determined she was acting in self-defense.

Caleb kept River out of the loop while the investigation was going on, as he didn't want to get his son's hopes up. He wanted to make sure Lien was being released before telling River she was coming home.

He'd bought new outfits for both of them and was going to surprise River with the news that morning before they headed to the prison to pick her up. Caleb also gathered what he could out of their old house that seemed like belonged to Lien and River. It wasn't much, but he had some clothes, tea, and any of the collectibles that were her's from the house. He placed them around his home so she'd feel welcome when she arrived.

Caleb got up and gathered River's outfit, heading to the children's room. River was sitting up in bed looking at a book when Caleb came in. Caleb put the clothes on the bed and sat down next to River.

"Big news today."

River tipped his head and smiled. "What, Daddy?"

"Mama is coming home."

River's eyes grew wide and he looked like Caleb was teasing him. "Really? My mama?"

"Your mama. She's coming to live here. Does that sound good?"

River nodded and jumped off the bed, hopping up and down. He rushed Caleb and threw his arms around his neck. "Mama is coming home!"

Caleb chuckled and handed River the clothes. "You want to get dressed? Do you need my help?"

River took the clothes, then shook his head. "No, I'm a big boy."

"I know you are. I'll leave you to it. We need to leave in about thirty minutes. Get dressed and eat some breakfast, then we'll go. Go brush your teeth and hair, okay?"

River bounced on one foot, nodding his head manically. He set the clothes down and bounded down the hall to the bathroom. Caleb got up and peered out the window at Lien's house.

Well, where Lien's house used to be. Now, a charred rubble of not much remained. Not long after Caleb went in and removed all Lien and River's items, the house went up in flames. The fire department rushed in, but they were too late. What was left was a steaming pile of what used to be a home. They chalked it up to bad wiring, but something in Caleb told him it had been intentional. By who, he wasn't sure, however, he had his suspicions.

The lot went up for sale and Stephan made an offer on it. He and Tammy made their relationship official and talked about moving into their own place together. Building a home. Stephan sold his small trailer in the country for the down payment and was working on clearing the rubble. He and Caleb agreed to start building once the land was cleared and Lien was home.

River came running back into the room, almost crashing into Caleb's legs. Caleb deftly sidestepped him and grabbed the boy to keep them both from falling.

"I know you're excited, but let's get dressed and eat, first. The sooner we do, the sooner we can leave."

River began removing his pajamas at record speed, then tried to get on his pants. Backwards. Caleb stopped him and turned the pants around, helping his son with the zipper. Once River was fully clothed, Caleb gently pushed him toward the door.

"Go eat and I'll meet you down there. I need to get dressed. Aunt Tammy is in the kitchen."

River bolted out the door and Caleb went in to dress. He glanced out his window to the woods but didn't see Turka. He hadn't seen her in a couple of weeks and was worried. Shaking it off, he finished dressing and went to the bathroom to get control of his unruly hair and brush his teeth. Once he was presentable, he headed downstairs to join River in the kitchen. Tammy turned and whistled.

"See, you clean up real nice, after all," she teased, shaking a spatula at him.

"Hush," Caleb replied as he snagged a muffin off the counter. "Drew and Sara go to school?"

"Yep, just caught the bus. Will you be back by the time the bus drops them off?"

"I hope so. It's about an hour each way, I think. Not sure if she'll be waiting and ready to go when I get there or if they'll drag it out for a while. I don't know how it all works. I guess I'll see once I get there."

"Alright, Stephan is picking up dinner on his way home from work. I have a couple of banners and balloons I was going to hang once you leave. Dad and I are going to the store after to make sure we're stocked up. Wait, so where is Lien going to sleep?"

Caleb shrugged. All the rooms were full. Tammy and Stephan in one, the kids in another. Dad had the master suite downstairs, and Caleb had the last available room. "I don't know. I have the cot Stephan used for now until we figure it out. We're packed in pretty tight."

"For the time being. If you two boys would get that house built next door already, Stephan, me, and my kids could move over there and free up a room."

Caleb laughed and shook his head. "Sure, let me just find my magic wand and get right to it."

Tammy clapped her hands together. "Chop chop."

River was done eating and was practically levitating off his seat. "Go now, Daddy?"

"Yeah, little man. We can go now."

Caleb collected their things and packed a lunch, not knowing how long it would take for Lien to be released. River kept running to the front door, then back to Caleb to see if he was ready. Once Caleb had their bags packed, he gave Tammy a kiss on the cheek and headed for the door. River sighed dramatically. Caleb grinned at him

"Alright, alright. We can go. Hold your horses."

River thought that was the funniest statement and tipped his head back, laughing. "Horses."

They loaded up and began the drive. River was content to stare out the window and Caleb played over in his head how the meet-up might go. He'd seen Lien a few times over the last couple of months, but this was different. She was coming home to a bunch of people she didn't know. He was worried it would be too much for her to adapt, however, she needed a place to stay. He didn't want River to leave his home, so hoped she'd agree to stay long-term and raise River with him. He feared she'd want to go back to Vietnam.

When they got to the prison, Lien was already waiting outside with a guard, holding a plastic bag of whatever belongings she'd had in there. She seemed so small and alone out there in front of the large, barbed-wire fence. River spied his mother and tried desperately to unbuckle himself. Caleb reached his hand out.

"Hold on, let me help you. Let's walk over together, okay? You can't be running across the parking lot."

River glanced at him, his eyes desperate. Caleb ruffled his hair and unclipped his seat belt. River waited until Caleb came around his side of the truck and took Caleb's extended hand to get out the door. Once they were within a few yards of Lien, Caleb let River's hand go and motioned for the boy to go to his mother.

Lien squatted with her arms extended as River launched himself into her outstretched arms. They both broke into tears as they clung on to one another. Even the guard wiped tears from his eyes for a moment. The guard met Caleb's eyes and nodded as he turned to go back through the gate. Caleb stood back and let the mother and son reconnect with each other.

Lien rose and smiled at Caleb. "Thank you. For taking care of River."

"Of course. He's my son now, too. I'd like us all to go home together."

Lien paused and frowned slightly. "Your home?"

Caleb nodded. "Our home."

Lien took River's hand and walked to the truck with Caleb. River sat between them and placed a hand on each of their laps. Caleb grinned down at his son, then over at Lien who was smiling, as well. She turned to stare out the window as the rain began to cease and the sun came out. She placed her hand against the glass and sighed. Caleb reached over and touched her other hand.

"I'm glad you're out of there. We've been waiting for you. We can all start over, alright?"

Lien tipped her head. "Alright."

The rest of the drive, they chatted about simple little things, getting used to each other's company. River's hands stayed on each of them, even when he began to doze off. His head fell against Caleb's arm, creating a warm glow between them. Caleb turned to Lien.

"Please don't take River away from me. I've grown to love him as my own son. I know we hardly know each other, however, I think we can find a way to live and raise him together."

Lien chewed her lip. "Where would I go?"

Caleb shook his head. "I don't know. Vietnam? I don't know how this all works, but are you allowed to stay here?"

"Oh. Maybe not. Not a citizen."

"What if we were to get married? On paper of course."

Lien stared at him, then looked back out the window without speaking. Caleb felt stupid for the suggestion and focused on the road. He didn't know how it all legally worked. Lien was here in the United States because she was married to Trevor before. A green card marriage of sorts.

Could she, and River, be sent away now that Trevor was dead?

Right before they arrived home, River opened his eyes and upon seeing his mother, began to cry. Not sad tears, but tears of relief. Of being with her, of finally not having a hole in his little heart. She patted his cheek and whispered something in Vietnamese to him. River nodded and wiped his eyes.

As they were unloading at the house, Caleb swore he saw movement in the trees. However, when he focused in, nothing was there. He paused and sent Turka a mental message, letting her know he hoped she was alright. A warm feeling washed over him and he could see her in his mind down by the creek. He wished her well and helped unbuckle River. Lien waited patiently for him and followed them inside.

Inside was a mad house. Drew and Sara were playing hide and seek, Dad was reading in the recliner, Tammy and Stephan were in the kitchen laying the food out on the table. Lien seemed unsure and stayed behind Caleb. He introduced her to everyone and took her bag to his room. Tammy had set up the cot in the corner for Lien with new blankets and pillows. Caleb smiled at the thoughtfulness and set Lien's belongings on the tidy cot.

As he stepped out of the room, he could hear his father talking with Lien. Telling her about when he was a boy and would go fishing at the pond. Caleb paused at the top of the stairs and listened as Lien responded about her village in Vietnam. How her father took her fishing.

Just as he was about to go down, something caught his eye in the kids' room and he went in to get a closer look. What he saw there let him know River was going to be okay.

On the boy's bed, sitting unattended was the ratty, stuffed, blue and white dog that had gone with River everywhere since the night his mother shoved him into Caleb's arms and begged them to run.

River knew he was safe.

It Runs Deep

O ver the next few months, a new sort of normal fell over the house. When they weren't at work, Caleb and Stephan built the house next door. Tammy's divorce from Bob was finalized and River was enrolled in school for the following fall. Summer came with a renewed sense of hope.

Lien and Caleb drew close, chatting from their respective beds after River went to sleep. What Caleb learned was how much he was drawn to Lien. She had a calm demeanor but laughed easily. Even at his stupid jokes. They became close friends and worked together as parents for River.

Turka wasn't seen very often, but every now and then, Caleb would catch her moving through the woods. Worse though, sometimes he could hear her painful wail deep in the forest. The cry of one who once loved and now was alone. He wanted to help her find her way home. Late one night, while he and Lien were talking in his room, he told Lien everything. Unlike the others, Lien listened in total belief. She nodded, her

271

attention rapt on his story. When Caleb was done, Lien rested her chin on her hand as she lay stomach down on her cot.

"Let's help her," she said.

"I don't know how. She came with a group of beings like her and she is the last one. It takes the group to create the portal or ship, whatever it is," Caleb explained.

"Oh. Does it have to be a group of them? Or can we be the group?" Lien inquired.

"I don't know. She showed me a group of them in a circle, creating a light. The light then absorbed them and took them where they needed to go."

"We could try."

"We could, but even if it worked, would it take us with her?" Caleb considered out loud.

"Ask her."

Caleb felt like slapping his forehead. He'd never thought about that. "Will you go with me? To find her?"

Lien tipped her head and smiled, which lit up her whole face. She brushed the hair off her face, meeting his eyes. Caleb had to admit, he was forming feelings for Lien. He pushed the thought away and lay back on his bed, his head resting back in his hands. "She really cares about River."

Lien didn't reply and when Caleb glanced over, he saw she'd fallen asleep. He got up and put a blanket over her. He slipped out of the room and could hear Tammy and Stephan talking softly in their room. They'd be moving into their home in the next few weeks. It wasn't done, but finished enough for them to complete the rest while they were living there. The house would seem so empty without them, but at least they were going to be living right next door.

Caleb went outside, sending a message to Turka in his mind. He felt her presence and could sense that she was getting more depressed being trapped there. He hoped they could find a way to get her back to her family. The ones wherever she was from. He left a rock on the railing of the porch and whispered, "Turka, we want to help you get back to your family. Please take this rock if you want our help... if there's a way we can get you home."

He headed back to bed, pausing at the kids' room. River was curled up under his blanket, breathing easy and soft without a care in the world. Caleb would do anything for the boy. He went over and placed his hand on River's head. River stirred and opened his eyes. He saw Caleb and smiled his mother's smile.

"Daddy."

"Go back to sleep, Riv. I love you."

River turned over and closed his eyes, murmuring, "Love you."

Caleb climbed into bed, careful not to disturb Lien. He rested with his eyes closed and thought about Turka. About Lien. Both mothers who'd suffered and had to fight for their young. Maybe Lien would be the key to setting Turka free from Earth. He closed his eyes and said a small prayer of thanks for his new family.

The next morning, Lien was already awake and packing things into a basket. Caleb met her in the kitchen and sat down at the table with a cup of coffee in hand. Lien wasn't a coffee drinker, so she had a cup of tea. She also had all of her loose-leaf teas out and was sorting them. She eyed Caleb when he came in and pointed at her teas.

"Tea is like magic. It helps break down walls," she said and slipped a large bag of loose tea into the basket. "I have an idea."

Caleb scratched his head and took a sip of coffee. "Yeah? What's that?"

"Tea circle. You said they were in a circle. We make a circle of tea, hold hands. Tea is protective. See?"

Caleb didn't totally, however, he did understand the tea would act as a barrier, both to create the light, but also to keep them safe. Lien was saying it had special properties, almost like the detonator for the C-4. By itself, it didn't do much, but adding it to the ceremony might give them the energy they needed.

Lien set the basket down and met Caleb's eyes. "We need mothers."

"Mothers? For the ceremony? Why?"

"Turka is mother. Need for guidance."

Caleb didn't know many mothers except Lien and Tammy. "I'll ask Tammy."

Lien went back to adding herbs and other items to the basket. Tammy came in dressed for work and watched Lien packing the basket.

"Going on a picnic?" she inquired.

Caleb chuckled. "Of sorts. We're going to try and find a way to get Turka home again. What time do you think you'll be off work?"

"Me? Around seven. Why?" Tammy asked, her voice unsure.

"Lien says we need mothers. You're the only other mother I know," Caleb answered.

Tammy glanced between them, then shrugged. "I guess. Is this safe?"

Caleb weighed the risk and avoided making eye contact. "I hope so. I think Turka would let us know if it wasn't. Oh! That reminds me."

He jumped up and went to the front porch. The rock was gone. In its place was a small flower. Caleb took this as a sign that Turka was open to their assistance. She'd helped him, now it was their turn to be there for her. He picked up the flower and went inside, twirling it between his thumb and forefinger. Tammy had her lunch bag and was heading for the front door when he came in. She saw the flower and paused, her brow knitted.

"What is that?"

"Turka telling me she wants our help," Caleb explained.

Tammy took her keys off the hook by the door and sighed. "Are you sure about this? It seems dangerous."

"I'm sure. I don't think Turka would allow us to be in any danger."

"Alright. I'll see you at seven. We're doing this tonight?" Tammy asked.

"We sure can try, at least," Caleb responded.

When he went back to the kitchen, Lien was making breakfast for Caleb's father, who had taken a shine to Lien. Often Caleb would find them with their heads bent together looking at photos, or sharing stories. His father was doing much better and lucid much of the time. The doctors couldn't explain it, but Caleb had his suspicions. Now that there were many people around and lots of conversations, his father was coming out of the depths of loneliness he'd been in since his wife died. Caleb had cared for him but wasn't enough company since he was always buried in his own mind.

Caleb checked in on River watching television. "Going to work, buddy. You okay?"

River waved him over and showed Caleb a picture he'd drawn. Caleb took the picture and frowned. How could he know? The picture was of the family standing in a circle holding hands, with Turka in a ball of light in the sky above them. Caleb set it down.

"Have you been talking to Turka?"

River nodded and pointed at the picture. "Take a trip."

Caleb kissed his son, then left for work. Take a trip. It was time for Turka to find her way home. She'd lost her family but gained his family. Like he lost Shannon but gained Lien and River.

~

Later that evening, when everyone was back home, they gathered around the table and went over the plan. They'd go into the woods with the basket of supplies. Hopefully, Turka would come to them and show them what to do. They discussed whether or not to bring the children. Caleb knew the more bodies they had, the more likely they were to create enough energy to make the transport. He also knew there was a risk and bringing the children might put them in harm's way.

Finally, Tammy slapped her hand on the table and got everyone's attention. "Look, I don't want my children to get hurt, or worse, taken with Turka to wherever she is from. I don't think it's fair to bring them. Can't we do it with just the four of us and Turka?"

Caleb shook his head. "I honestly don't know. All of this is a shot in the dark, to begin with. We can ask Dad to watch them and try without. Okay?"

Tammy nodded and got up. "No time like the present."

The group gathered their supplies and went to the living room where Dad was reading books to the children. He peered up at them, then sensing whatever was going on was important, set the book down. "Everything alright?"

"Yeah, Dad. Hey, uh... we need to head out for a bit. You okay with the kids?" Caleb asked.

His father gazed between the four adults and tipped his head. "I am. Are you in any trouble?"

"No, no trouble. Just something we need to do."

River eyed Caleb, then looked at his mother. He understood what was happening. "Want to go."

"No, River. You need to stay home with Grandpa, okay? We'll be back soon," Caleb replied.

River stared at him but didn't respond. Caleb knew the boy wanted to see Turka one last time, but he loved him too much to take the chance of him being hurt. River diverted his attention to Sara, who was flipping through a book. Caleb's father picked the book in his lap back up and began reading to distract the children as the four adults went outside.

The sun was beginning to set, so they moved quickly into the woods to get to a clearing before dark. Once they got to the clearing, Lien began to make a circle out of tea leaves. Caleb sent messages to Turka telepathically to let her know they were there and waiting. The forest remained silent.

About an hour after the sun went down, it seemed as if Turka wasn't coming. Caleb built a fire and wandered into the woods to see if he could find her. Seeing no sign of her, he used the fire to guide himself back to the group and came up on them sitting around the fire, sharing stories. Like a camping trip, but with heavier consequences. He sat down next to Lien and shook his head.

"I don't see her. I know she wants our assistance, but maybe she's scared or doesn't believe we can help her," Caleb said.

"Be patient," Lien replied, placing her hand over his.

The fire died down and Caleb felt discouraged. She wasn't coming. This was all for nothing. He stood up and grabbed a jug of water to put the fire out when movement in the woods got his attention. Lien had gotten up and wandered into the tree line. She was standing with her back to the group and her hand extended out into the dark.

When Lien turned to come back, something very large was shifting behind her. Lien moved into the circle but she wasn't alone.

Turka was holding her hand.

What Home Means

L ien led Turka to the fire. Tammy and Stephan's eyes were huge, staring at the enormous creature. Caleb went and embraced Turka, grateful she trusted them enough to come. She continued to hold Lien's hand and when Caleb stepped back, she embraced Lien the best she could. Tammy and Stephan stood silently, waiting for guidance on what to do next. Caleb gazed up at Turka.

"I know you miss your family. I brought mine to try and get you home. Lien made a circle of tea we can stand in."

Turka's eyes flitted to the circle and the fire and she made a series of grunts, this time Caleb understood. She was thanking them, however, she wasn't sure they had enough power to make it work.

Caleb led her to the circle, holding her talon in his hand. Lien joined her on the other side and Stephan and Tammy moved in. However, even with all of them extending their arms as much as they could, they still couldn't connect on the far side. Caleb suggested they move closer but no matter how they tried, they couldn't reach all the way around. He asked Turka if they needed the fire and she expressed they did. That was the source of light that needed to grow stronger to create the portal.

Caleb rubbed his head in frustration. "Damnit! We are so close."

Behind him came an unexpected voice. "Now, son, don't be cussing in front of the children."

Caleb whipped around to see his father standing with the three children. The children's eyes were fixed on Turka, though they didn't seem afraid. Tammy's mouth dropped open and she seemed upset.

"Dad! Why did you bring them out here? It's not safe!"

Her father shook his head. "Can't give me the credit. I put them to bed and when I went to check on them a bit later, River was missing. Drew, Sara, and I went to look for him. We found a trail of crackers in the woods and followed them until we came upon River. He was tracking you. Quite expertly, I might add."

Caleb stared at River, who showed no shame for his actions. "How did you find us?"

River pointed at Turka. "She called me."

Caleb realized Turka knew they needed the children's help. He turned to her. "Can you promise me the children won't be harmed?"

Turka made a few soft clicks and tipped her head to River. They'd be safe. Or at least that's what Caleb thought she was telling him. Tammy was angry and pushed her children away from the circle.

"No. They are *children* for fuck's sake. It's one thing for us to be out here, but I won't risk them."

Drew stepped forward. "Please, Mom. We want to help her get home to her family. She's sad. What if you weren't with us? Wouldn't you be sad?"

That took the steam out of Tammy and her shoulders dropped. She glanced at Turka. "Promise they can't get hurt."

River gazed up at his aunt. "She promises."

Tammy nodded and took Stephan's hand, then Drew's. Her father came into the circle, taking Drew's other hand and Sara's. Sara was able to reach around but seemed unsure about taking Turka's talon, so Caleb went over and stood between them and held River's hand as River held Sara's. Turka reached down and took Caleb's other hand. The circle now stretched all the way around the fire.

As their hands connected, Caleb felt a vibration passing between them. He could see the others felt it, as well. The vibration increased, causing their hands to heat up. Caleb considered they might not have thought about what would happen once the energy got to the level to create a portal. He peered at Turka. Her eyes were closed, her head tipped back, but she sensed his fear and mentally assured him they'd be alright.

The fire began to climb into the sky, not just from the wood it was burning. A loud whistling erupted, startling the humans. It was like when a top rotated at such high speed, it created a high-pitched sound. Caleb stared at Lien, who was watching River. Their eyes met for a second and he experienced something he hadn't felt since Shannon. A connection with another human beyond family or friendship.

A small smile played on her lips. She felt it, too.

As the whistle got louder, hurting their ears, light began to envelop all of them. Caleb could see the light start at the circle made by the tea leaves and come over them like a dome. Turka began to chant in clicks and grunts, almost melodic this time. As she did, the light turned a lavender blue, as bright as the sun. Caleb scanned the children's faces to see if they were alright. They were enthralled by what was happening but showed no sign of fear or discomfort.

About the time the whistling got too much to bear, it stopped and they were standing in a pool of light that was spinning around them. Caleb again worried it would try and take them with it when Turka reached into the center and pressed what seemed like a button. As she did, the light shifted to surround her and she dropped Lien and Caleb's hands as the light began to take her away. Caleb felt his heart breaking and let the tears flow.

"Turka, you always have a family here. Don't forget us," he begged through his tears.

Turka cocked her head at him, her eyes filled with love and gratitude. Caleb could feel their connection and her promise to remember them. The light turned her skin from gray to blue and she radiated with such intensity, Caleb had to drop his eyes. Afraid she'd disappear while he was looking away, he forced his eyes back onto her and watched as she began to fade from their world. All of a sudden, the light shot up into the sky from her, creating a beam. Turka began to rise in the beam, then the light went dark, taking Turka with it.

Caleb wiped the tears off his face and stared up at the stars. Lien walked over and embraced him, as River clung to his legs. Caleb leaned into his little family and felt Shannon with them. Turka had come to help, discovered Shannon dead, lost her family, then came to Caleb years later to help them both. Caleb would miss her forever.

The group stood silent, gazing at where they last saw the light. The children drew close to their parents. The sky was full of bright stars, however, Caleb could swear one was brighter than the others.

They waited until the fire died out and hiked back to the house. Caleb couldn't help but feel sad. He wanted Turka to go home, but he'd grown used to the idea of her watching over them in the woods. When they got to the house, Caleb stood on the driveway and gazed off into the trees. They seemed so empty, now. Lien joined him and took his hand.

"We all deserve to go home," she whispered.

Caleb turned to her. "Do you want to go home to Vietnam? I'd be heartbroken, but I don't want you trapped anywhere you don't want to be."

"No, this is home, now. With you and River. If you feel the same."

Caleb felt his heart in his throat. He felt the same. He wanted nothing more than to raise River with Lien and live in the house he'd always lived in. He met her eyes, a sad smile on his mouth. "I do."

Tammy took the children in. They were too amped to go back to bed, so she made everyone an ice cream sundae. They sat around the living room, eating ice cream and making small talk about what happened. The children took out crayons and drew pictures of the event. Seeing it made Caleb's heartache, but he knew it was for the best.

We all deserve to go home.

Lien's words echoed in his mind and he thought about Shannon, who was just trying to get home when Trevor took her life. He said a silent prayer for Shannon, feeling her release from the world. She'd set things right. As right as she could.

Caleb thought about the first time he saw Turka, how scared it made him feel. A monster in the woods. Except she wasn't the monster. Trevor was. A lot of humans were. They spent so much time worrying about imaginary evil beings, they often missed the ones living among them.

Caleb let his eyes drift to each member of his family and for the first time in a long time, he realized he was no longer alone in the world. Even missing Shannon had softened to a low twinge. River came over and climbed in his lap, resting his small head against Caleb's chest.

"Love you, Daddy."

Caleb kissed him. "I love you, River."

Tammy yawned and gathered her children. "I doubt they'll sleep, but I need to lie down. I'm planning on calling out of work tomorrow if we want to take the kids to do something fun as a family."

Caleb chuckled. "Sure. Not a walk in the woods, though."

Tammy touched his head and smiled. "Nah, let's stick to concrete and buildings."

Caleb picked up River and followed Tammy upstairs. They tucked the kids in and paused at the door. Tammy turned her face up to Caleb.

"Remember when Mom would tell us not to go too far into the woods because of the boogeyman?"

Caleb bobbed his head. "I do. Scared the crap out of me until I decided I kinda wanted to see the boogeyman."

Tammy snickered. "Yeah. Well, I guess in a twisted way, you did."

Caleb considered it, then shook his head. "I think it's more like all these stories we were told about angels and gods. I think we witnessed an angel."

"Maybe. Whatever Turka is, she brought peace to this family and for that I thank her. Do you think we'll ever see her again? That she'll come back?" Tammy asked.

"I don't know. I don't know if she *can* come back."

Tammy slipped out past him to meet Stephan in the hall. "Hopefully she can. She's family, now. Goodnight, Caleb. I love you."

"Love you, too, Tams," Caleb replied. He went to his bedroom. Lien was standing at the window, gazing out at the forest. She turned and smiled when he came in.

"The children go to sleep?" she asked.

"They're getting there. I can still hear them whispering to each other in the room. Might be a long night," Caleb answered.

Lien sat on the edge of Caleb's bed and patted the covers next to her. "Are you alright?"

Caleb sat down next to her. "Sad, but it was the right thing to do for her. Turka deserves to feel like I do with all of you here."

"She does. Still, okay to be sad."

Caleb smiled at Lien. "Thanks."

Lien got up and went to her cot. Caleb lay back on his bed, staring up at the ceiling. He'd spent so much of his life telling himself he didn't deserve to grieve. Turka taught him it was necessary to find happiness again, despite everything that happened.

He hoped she'd find the same.

As Caleb drifted off to sleep, he pictured Shannon in his mind. Laughing as they walked to her street. Not a care in the world. However, she'd had her secrets, as well. She'd been pregnant and not told him about it. Perhaps, she was scared, maybe she felt alone. He wished he'd known then, so he could've been there for her and the baby. He glanced over at Lien, who was now asleep. He could be there for her and River. They'd also suffered and lost so much, but together they could forge a new journey.

They could find joy again.

2002

River stepped off the bus, slinging his backpack over his shoulder. His cousin Sara got off behind him, saying goodbye to her friends on the back of the bus. She was in eighth grade, River in sixth. Drew would be home later as he took the high school bus. Sara smiled and said goodbye to River, then ran to her house next door. Uncle Stephan and Aunt Tammy greeted her at the door and waved at River, who raised his hand in response.

He paused at the porch and gazed out into the woods. He could feel something in the air today. Something different, yet familiar. He was about to turn and go in when a flash of light in the distance caught his attention. He squinted and grinned, knowing it was time. He went inside, throwing his backpack in a chair. His grandfather was napping in the recliner and opened his eyes.

"Hey there, River. How was school?"

"Hey, Grandpa. It was fine. Is my Dad around?"

"I don't think so. He's not home from work yet. Anything I can do for you?"

River shook his head. He wanted to tell his father first. "No, is Mom home?"

"No, she took your little sister to the park before it gets dark."

His little sister, Joy, was now five years old. His parents had gotten married not long after his mother was released from prison. River was the ring bearer. He begged for a sibling for years before Joy came along. When she was born, River didn't leave her side, except when he was at school.

After a little bit, River heard a car in the driveway and ran to see who it was. His mother was unloading Joy from the car. When Joy saw him, she ran full speed at his legs and adhered herself to them. His mother smiled.

"She missed you. Come help me with these bags."

River shuffled with Joy stuck to his legs to help his mother unload the groceries. Joy peeled herself loose to carry one. River stopped his mother as they walked to the porch. "I saw something out in the woods. A light."

Lien peered out and frowned. "When?"

"Like thirty minutes ago, maybe," he replied.

"Do you think it could be?" Lien asked.

"I think so."

As they got to the front door, Caleb's truck pulled in and River waited for his father. Lien went in to wrangle Joy, who was now plastered to her grandfather. River watched his father climb out of the truck.

Caleb grinned. "Hey, Riv. What are you doing out here? How was school today?"

"I was waiting for you. School was fine, got an A on my math test. Hey, Dad, I saw something out there," he answered, pointing above the trees.

As soon as he said it, Caleb's eyes flicked to the woods, then back to River. "You did?"

"Yeah, out in the forest. A flash of light."

Caleb appeared hopeful and put his hand on his son's shoulder. He knew. They could both feel it in their souls. Caleb threw his bag on the porch. The sun would be setting soon, but they still had some daylight to go. They'd be able to take the trail by the dimming light.

"You want to go see?" he asked, not as a question.

River nodded, having already packed a flashlight, water, and food for their trek. He couldn't wait anymore. "I'm ready. Dad, do you feel it in your bones? Could it be her? Turka?"

Caleb hugged River as hard as he could. He did.

"She's back."

Acknowledgments

Thank you to Eva Mout for allowing me to use her amazing piece for the cover. You can find her work at https://www.ursusart.studio/

Thank you to Justin Sexton, David Berberian, Jessica Nettles, Lizzy Johnston, Trevor Curtis, and Josette Thomas for taking the time to beta-read this novel.

Thank you to Stephan Silvey and Tammy Roberts for letting me use parts of them in the story and for being my friends for a very, very long time. Love you!

Thank you Octavia Butler for paving the way for the rest of us. I admire you and your work. You were a visionary.

Thank you to my readers, without you this is just voices in my head.

Books by the Author

Do Over
We Don't Matter
Prick of the Needle
Through the Surface
Trigger Point
Carrying the Dead
Catch the Earth
In Dreams, We Fly
Stitched Together
By the Dimming Light

Please visit my website for upcoming books, events, and news:

authorjulietrose.com